Serandica Pappas:
What a Name, What a Life

L.A. Layne

Eternal Fire Press

This first two parts of this book are memoirs. Part three is a work of fiction and the events described therein are imaginary and are not intended to refer to specific places or to living persons alive or dead.

ISBN: 0692131612
ISBN-13: 978-0692131619

Eternal Fire Press
Franklin, TN

This book is dedicated to Stephenie, my daughter, who encouraged me and helped me get it together.

CONTENTS

WHAT A LIFE 1

IN THE BEGINING 3

   PART I 7

      THE MONSTER 9

      ON THE FARM 19

      FARM LIFE 24

      MOVING AGAIN 28

      ON THE BUS 30

      A NEW BEGINNING 38

      ANOTHER BROTHER 44

      BACK TO SCHOOL 47

      FORT WORTH 52

      FRIENDS 56

      GOODBYE JUNIOR HIGH 60

      LEAVING HOME 65

      HEART TROUBLES 73

      NO GOING BACK 92

      JUST IN TIME 96

      SPRING AND SUMMER 116

      AN IMPORTANT DECISION 139

   PART II 151

      FEBRUARY NINETEEN FIFTY-SIX 153

      A PRETTY FLOWER 158

      JUNIOR 160

      A SHINING STAR 164

      GALVESTION 166

      A STRONG OAK 172

      A SPECIAL MESSENGER 175

NINETEEN SEVENTY-EIGHT...178

PART III...181

   WHAT NOW..183

   TOGETHER AGAIN 194

   LOVER'S LEGEND...201

THE SERANDICA PAPPAS SERIES

SERANDICA PAPPAS: WHAT A NAME, WHAT A LIFE

LIVING LEGENDS

GAMES OF THE GODS

WHAT A LIFE

East Texas in the late nineteen thirties was pretty much farm land and saw mills. My family originated in the deep piney woods of that area. Those days, filled with hard times, almost destroyed our parents will to keep going, but we children knew very little about it all. Kids were free to run and play and do their chores, whether we lived in the city or on a farm. I was fortunate to have lived both places. As I remember, I loved them both equally.

At a very early age, I learned the value of imagination. Movie theaters and silent movies had been around a while, but they were just beginning to broaden their horizons. Our town boasted two movie houses, each trying to outdo the other by showing the newest, most thrilling movies available at the time.

My sister who was seven years older than me, got a job during the summer at one of the movie theaters as a ticket seller and concession stand tender. She was only fourteen but smart and industrious at most things except helping our mother with the housework, which of course became my job. Age wasn't a factor in those days and children learned to get a job. Like I said, times were hard.

Every Saturday, if I had been a very good girl during the past week, I was allowed to go along with my boy cousin, who was my same age, to the movie theater where my sister worked. We were allowed to watch the movie and indulge in popcorn, soda and candy at concession time, which we did hungrily without knowing the price of our indulgence was being deducted from my sister's meager wages, which she resented.

Saturday afternoons became the best part of the week for me. Roy Rodgers and Dale Evans were our favorite western stars. Bambi made us cry but we watched it again and again. Superman was my hero, and Tarzan was my cousin's hero. We loved them all. Because of that exposure to make believe from movies, comic books, story books and play acting, we fancied ourselves as those characters and play acted imagined scenes starring ourselves as any of those characters we chose to be at the time.

Betty Grable was one of my favorite stars. My how she could dance. She had blond hair and long beautiful legs. I practiced dancing the way she danced in My Momma's high heeled shoes and stockings. I used My Momma's bath powder, face powder, lipstick, rouge and mascara. This I did with abandon and soon learned that My Momma's wrath was only assuaged by the use of a good keen switch on my behind and legs, which often left ugly blood blisters.

After such episodes only one person could make me feel better, my earliest childhood friend, Serandica Pappas. I don't know exactly when she came into my life. it seems as if she had just always been there, that my first recollection of her was the day I was born.

IN THE BEGINING

Although I've been told, and the records show, that I was born in a hospital, there is a scene, from I do not know where, that is etched indelibly in my mind. It has always seemed to me that this happened the day I was born. As long as I have remembered anything, this scene has been with me. It never changes, and it pops into my head when I am sad and alone. Only a couple of times has it happened when I have been with someone else. It has always happened when I need consoling. Each time after a bad incident in my life occurs, Serandica Pappas visits me.

The following is about the first time the scene happened. The one I think must have been the day I was born. Her visits always begin with this scene. It is always very vivid and real to me. Blackness surrounds me, except for a few feet in front of my eyes. I seem to be watching from somewhere, I do not know where, only it is dark there and the scene before my eyes is bright and colorful. I get an eerie feeling when it happens. There is a breeze blowing the few leaves that are left on the trees. Sometimes a gust blows a swirl of fallen leaves around the pine trees and cedars, their shades of dark and bright green bringing out the color in the autumn leaves wonderfully. The breeze also brings the smell of pine from the saw mills nearby. Wood smoke from chimneys fills the air. I can smell the scent of it.

A little girl sits on an upside-down washtub. Her hands clasped tightly together. She is short and a little chubby. maybe six or seven years old. Her hair is dark brown and curly. She has large dark brown eyes. The clothes she is wearing must be hand me downs for they fit her rather loosely.

She is wearing a pleated skirt and a buttoned sweater, over a blouse with a yellowed lace collar. The blouse is a print of blue flowers, the skirt and sweater are brown. Her feet barely touch the ground. She is kicking the tub with the heels of her black shoes. Her socks are green. She is looking at the

3

ground, almost sadly it seems.

In the background, there is a shanty of a house. Smoke spirals from the stack on the roof, indicating there is a wood stove burning inside. A nearby pile of freshly cut wood and chips are scattered about. The house is very small with weathered boards in hues of faded brown, gray and black. The house looks like it has never been painted. Beyond the woodpile, there is a large iron pot or caldron which was commonly used to heat water and other things such as cooking food in large amounts and washing clothes. Along the front and side of the yard there is a dilapidated picket fence which may have been whitewashed many years ago. It runs between where the little girl sits and the dirt road that leads somewhere. There is no gate, only an opening where a gate should be. There is no grass in the yard.

Suddenly the little girl looks up and toward the street. On the other side of the fence, a pretty, slender young lady is standing, looking at the little girl. The young woman has long golden hair curling at the ends. Her eyes are very green. Her dress is long made of satin and velvet. The overdress is sheer, it matches the shear scarf that she holds together with one hand. In the other hand she clutches a small brocaded valise made of the same material as the dress she wears.

The young woman is smiling at the child as she speaks, "Good morning child!" Her voice is light and cheerful. The little girl replies shyly, "Good morning." Then she tucks her head down and her lips form a pout. She looks timidly from the corners of her eyes thinking how pretty the young woman is.

At that moment the young woman speaks again, "Why are you sitting all alone in the yard so early on a cool morning?"

The little girl tucks her chin farther down into her sweater with her eyes still on the lady she replies, "My Momma said for me to sit right here until a little baby cries inside the house."

The young woman moves slowly into the yard, as if she doesn't want to frighten the little girl.

"May I sit by you and rest awhile?" she asks politely.

The child answers still timidly, "Yes Mam." Then she scoots over giving more room for the young woman to be seated.

They sit smiling at one another for a few seconds. The young lady holds the valise as if there might be something very valuable inside it. Suddenly the little girl brings a chubby hand up and coves her mouth. Then she points to the young woman's face and says, "I never saw anybody with eyes so green!" There is amusement in her voice.

The young woman smiles, showing beautiful white teeth. She says, "Well you have now!" Then she asked, "What is your name child?"

"Billie." the little girl says.

"Is that all of your name? Just Billie?"

Giggles erupt from Billie before she replies, "It's Billie Ruth!"

At that moment there is a strange sound from the house, then the faint crying of a baby. Billie jumps up from the tub and runs up the steps to the porch just as her dad opens the screen door. He hoists her into the air and asks, "Are you ready to see your new baby sister?"

Billie looks back to the tub. She is about to ask if the lady can come in and see the baby. There is nobody on the tub or in the yard.

Billie and her dad go into the room where her mother is propped up on pillows holding the baby who is still crying in a soft voice and squirming. The first thing Billie notices is the baby is wrapped in a blanket that has gold colored thread embroidered into flowers all over it. It makes her think of the pretty lady she had seen in the yard. She says, "Our baby has a blanket that matches Serandica Pappas's head scarf."

"Whose headscarf?" her mother asks, as Billie's dad lifts her onto the bed beside her mother and the baby.

"You can hold her for just a few seconds," her mother tells Billie, before she can answer about the scarf.

The baby quits crying and squirming and lays squinting up at Billie. Billie's eyes open wide and so does her mouth. She says excitedly, "Our baby has green eyes, just like the lady who was talking to me in the yard!"

Her mother laughs, "I think you must be imagining things, it is too soon to tell about the baby's eye color. Who did you say was in the yard?"

Billie's dad places the baby back in its mother's arms gently. Billie starts to tell her mother about the lady.

"Her name is Serandica Pappas! Isn't that a pretty name? Can we name our baby that?"

Her mother looks at her and says "That is a mighty big name for a tiny little baby. I don't know of anyone around here with a name like that. We had better stay with the name we have for her, Lois Ann."

"Come on Billie, let's go make some hot chocolate!" Billie's dad chimes in.

That might seem like a strange beginning to you but that is the way I remember it. In later years when I would try to talk to my sister Billie about it, she would just roll her eyes and say, "I don't know what you are talking about."

My parents would answer in almost the same way. My Momma would say one of two things.

"That little blond hussy was looking for your daddy," or "quit talking that stuff! Don't let me hear you talking about it around the kin folk. They will think you are crazy and we will have to send you to the insane asylum."

My father would always make some sort of joke about it, such as," That young lady better not let your mother catch her hanging around here."

In the years to come, there were four questions constantly in my mind about Serandica Pappas. Where did she come from? Why was she there? Where did she go? Who she was?

PART I

THE MONSTER

Some people believe that children cannot remember things until they are four years old. I beg to differ with them. This happened when I was two years old, growing toward three.

One morning my mom got me out of bed, gave breakfast to my sister and me, brushed our hair and helped us get dressed. When my sister, who was almost nine years old, asked her why we had to hurry she told us that our uncle Henry was going to buy a new truck and our Aunt Bertie had said if he could buy a new truck then she wanted money to go on a shopping spree. Uncle Henry gave her money for shopping and she had invited our mom, who was her sister, to go with her.

Momma told my sister Billie to go on to school, then she lifted me into her arms and set off walking fast toward the service station where my Daddy worked for my Uncle Henry. It was not very far from our house, so My Momma never put me down to walk. My little mind sensed that something exciting was going to happen that day. My Momma always made me walk when we brought my Daddy lunch.

Almost a block before we got to the station I saw my cousin, who was just a little younger than me, running to meet us with Aunt Bertie close behind him. My Momma stood me down on the side walk and told me not to run too fast or I would fall and skin my knees. As soon as we reached one another. we joined hands and started running again, toward the station.

My Daddy met us and swept us both up in his arms. He said, "You and Baby Glen are going to stay with me at the station today while your mothers go shopping. You two can play with the toys in the side room. No running about on the driveway. People won't be expecting two children to be running around out there and one or both of you might get run over by a car. Now that wouldn't be good would it?"

We both shook our heads no. When daddy sat us down on the floor. We headed straight for the box of toys that Aunt Bertie kept in the corner of the room for Baby Glen to play with when she came to help Uncle Henry do the book work. We never knew when our mothers left.

After a while we decided to ask Daddy if we could have some candy and soda pop. He said he would get it for us, but we would soon be needing to take a nap because we had gotten up early. We agreed, eager to get the soda and candy. I don't know when we fell asleep. We were playing one minute and asleep the next.

We must have slept for a long time because the next thing I remember was my Momma picking me up and telling me, in an excited voice, that Uncle Henry was going to give us a ride to our house in his new truck. I was rubbing my eyes as My Momma hurried out the front door.

My sleepy little eyes saw something with a giant red face and a shiny long round silver colored body. It was bigger than anything I had ever seen before. Its glowing eyes were round, yellow and bright. It was crawling slowly toward us on its big round black feet and it was growling, heaving and sighing. It was making a terrible noise!

The next thing I knew, my Momma was trying to put me into one of its big ears which was open, showing the inside of its head. She was handing me up to it! I was so scared I could not see. I was kicking, screaming and trying to reach back to get my arms around my Momma's neck. My Momma was trying to talk to me, but I was so terrified I could not hear what she was saying for my own screams drowned out her voice.

When I finally got my arms around my Momma's neck and opened my eyes my Aunt Bertie was standing behind My Momma holding Baby Glen in her arms and he was crying loudly too. I wondered why our Mommas were trying to stuff us into that monster's head. Then I felt something trying to pull me up, away from my Momma. For just a second, I lost my grasp on my Momma's neck and could feel myself being taken upward. I somehow wrenched away from it and fell back into my Momma' arms. She was shaking me and telling me to be quiet. Then I could hear her scolding me and telling me that I could have been hurt badly if she had not caught me. Then I started screaming for daddy to come and get me. His back was turned away from us and I could see him shaking. I reasoned in my child's way, that he was afraid too.

I started calling Serandica Pappas. Begging her to come and help me. While I was yelling for Serandica Pappas, I could not see again. The next thing I knew, my Momma was sitting inside the monster's head. My Aunt Bertie was holding me, but I didn't see Baby Glen anywhere, so I started screaming for Baby Glen. I would scream out his name and then for Serandica Pappas. Finally, I could hear my aunt telling me that Baby Glen was going to my house to play for a while but that didn't stop my screaming and clinging to her neck. She thrust me upward into my Momma's arms. Momma gave me a spanking and that made me scream more, for I did not know why she was spanking me. I heard a loud noise and turned to see that we were trapped inside the monster's head. It was taking us away from the gasoline station. Through my tears I could barely see my aunt and my daddy waving goodbye, and I was sure they were both shaking with fear.

When I turned back around the other way I saw Baby Glen sitting next to my Uncle Henry with his face buried in his arms. He was still crying too but not as loudly as me. The thing was taking us all away from the station. I turned back around, My Momma was trying as hard as she could to hold me still. I put my face against the glass we could see out the monster's ear and continued to scream for Serandica Pappas. The grape soda and candy gushed out of my throat. My Momma was yelling at me again.

Suddenly that monster stopped. Its ear flap opened and the next thing I knew was my Uncle Henry was standing on the ground, with Baby Glen beside him, still crying. My uncle was reaching up and My Momma was handing me down to him. He stood me on the ground beside Baby Glen and we got a bear hug on one another. My uncle helped my Momma get out, then he took one of my hands and one of Baby Glen's hands and starting walking away from that horrible monster. Baby Glen and I were walking as fast as our little legs would go to keep from falling down. I looked back once and saw My Momma trying to wipe throw up off of the monster with her tiny little hankie.

When we got to our house my uncle brought a big washtub into the yard and filled it with water. Momma socked Baby Glen and me both into it at once, clothes and all. My uncle stood with his hands on his side looking at us. He asked my Momma who I was calling to help me when I started throwing up. She told him that she did not know but that I had been saying that name since I had begun talking. Then she went into the house and brought a pail of water and some rags to Uncle Henry. We watched him hurry off down the street.

After my Momma had gotten us all cleaned up and we felt better, she asked Baby Glen why he had been crying. He said that he was crying because I was crying. When she asked me, I told her that I was so afraid of that giant monster that I could not help it. She made a big frown then she started laughing and I did not know why she was laughing about it. I sure didn't think it was a bit funny! Then she said that had been no monster, it was Uncle Henry's new truck.

Baby Glen and I had never seen a truck. We didn't really even know what a truck was. My Momma explained to us that it was a tank truck and uncle Henry would use it to bring gasoline from the refinery to his gasoline station and other stations in the surrounding area. She said Uncle Henry would be a rich man with all the money he was going to make. Baby Glen and I didn't know what rich was either, but we sure did wonder about it. We never heard the last of it either. Every time any of our family came around, the first thing they always asked me was if any more monsters had tried to get me. I would not answer them. I would run and hide....and talk to Serandica Pappas.

FUZZY

Times were extremely hard for our parents in the late nineteen thirties and early nineteen forties. There were wars and rumors of wars. Food shortages, gasoline shortages and people worried about what was going to happen next. In those days, parents tried to shelter their young children from anything that would make them anxious or fearful, if they possibly could. We children didn't know much about it all. Most of the time we were happily at play, at least those of us who didn't have to go to school all day.

Back then, if your birthday fell after Labor Day, you could not start to school until the next year. Only the children whose parents could afford to send them to private school went to kindergarten. Public school started with the First Grade, after the child had turned six years old. My birthday was in November. I didn't get to go to school until I was almost seven years old.

The summer before I was to start school, My Momma worried a lot about my stringy hair. My hair was long, blondish brown and thin. My sister Billie's hair was just the opposite. Her hair was dark brown, thick and curly. In our Momma's opinion, a girl or woman had to have curly, well-kept hair and it vexed my Momma that mine would not cooperate with her efforts to make it curl.

Sometimes, when I played with children other than my cousins, I felt out of place and lonely. My thinking was that nobody would like me because my hair was so ugly. After all, I was somewhat different looking with my stringy hair, freckles and green eyes. Most of the time, instead of trying to play with the other kids, I would slip away and hide from the others and think about Serandica Pappas. How pretty she was with her beautiful golden hair and her green eyes that were lovely to look at. Her skin was so nice and creamy white. She didn't even have one freckle. I loved spending time with her. She was usually smiling, unless I was crying, then she was sad too. When my Momma would ask where I had been I would tell her that I had been talking to Serandica Pappas and how I hoped that someday I would be pretty too. My Momma would always shake her head and go "tsk, tsk" and tell me that I was having daydreams.

One day I heard my Daddy tell one of my uncles that he hoped the conflict would soon be over, because he thought my Momma and all my aunts were going to have nervous breakdowns. I didn't know what conflict or nervous breakdown were but after listening to the men talk for a while, I was sure that I never wanted to have either one of them. It made me a little ashamed of myself because I was glad that my Momma was worried about something other than my hair. She had not mentioned it to me for weeks. I was tired of hearing her tell me not to worry, that she would think of something to do with it before I had to start to school.

Summer was almost over. I knew it would not be long until time for me to go to school. I started having more asthma attacks. Having them was no fun but my Momma said we would just have to put up with it because I had bronchial pneumonia when I was a baby. I did not know what either of the words meant but I was not happy that I had that when I was a baby, for it had caused me to miss many good times with others while having an asthma attack.

The doctor would come and give me an injection of adrenalin, he called it, and after a little while I would begin to feel better, but it sure was bad until then. I never knew what adrenalin was, but I was sure glad the doctor always had some of it. I did not like to see the big syringe with that long needle on it either, but after I was old enough to realize how much better I felt a little while after it was used, I did not cry so much when I saw it any more.

The big day finally came, and my Momma realized that she could not possibly let me go to school with such stringy, unkempt looking hair. She decided to put it in braids and send me on to school. At the last moment she couldn't find a bow to match what I was wearing. My sister was griping that we would be late, so I had to go with the two braids hanging loose. My hair was braided so tightly that the skin on my forehead and at the sides of my face felt like someone had stretched it and pined it back with my hair.

When I went to my classroom, sure enough, I was the only girl here in pig tails, as my boy cousins called them. I saw hands go over mouths and giggles erupting from the girls. Later at recess, when nobody asked me to play, I was so sad that I went to the corner of the playground, sat on the ground and talked to Serandica Pappas.

When recess was over, and we were back in our seats, a boy in the desk behind me, grabbed a braid in each hand and made a clicking sound with his tongue and said "giddy up horsey"

All the kids started laughing. I pulled my hair out of his hands and slapped him a good one right on the nose. He started crying and yelling that I made his nose bleed. I guess I did, because it was bleeding. The teacher came with tissues and dragged me to a seat next to her desk. She said that she would not tolerate such behavior. She told me I would find myself in the principal's office if such a thing ever happened again. I wanted to tell her what the boy had done but she kept smacking me on the hand with a ruler, which was almost as bad as my Mommas keen switch.

Right then I decided school was not for me. When the day was finally over, and I was at home again, I told Momma what had happened. She told me not to worry, it would not happen again because she had decided to get me a permanent wave. I didn't know what a permanent wave was, and I didn't care right then. All I knew was I didn't want to go back to school. My Momma snatched up her purse and told me to come with her. Obediently I followed her without asking why. Straight to the beauty parlor we went. I had gone there before with my Momma when she went to make an appointment for herself, but I really didn't know what an appointment meant. I reasoned that was why we were there. My Momma left me by the entrance and went to talk to one of the women, who were busy washing, cutting and rolling up women's hair. My Momma motioned for me to come to where she was, so I skipped back there and stood beside her, so she could tell me what she wanted. The woman she was talking to started messing with my hair. I heard her tell my Momma that she didn't know about giving me a perm, because she never had anyone ask her to put one in a child's hair. I was thinking to myself that a perm must be washing, cutting and rolling up hair and that looked like it would not be too bad. The next thing I knew, my Momma was lifting me up to sit on a board the woman had placed across the arms of a chair in front of a counter with a really big mirror behind it. Around my shoulders went a cape like the ladies in the other chairs had around them.

My Momma told me to stay there and be a good girl. She said she would come back for me after a while and out the door she went. I started getting nervous. I did not know why my Momma would leave me there with people I had never seen before. My chest was beginning to tighten up and I was afraid I might have an asthma attack. So, I started crying and told the woman I wanted my Momma. She told me to settle down, that my Momma was paying her money to make me pretty and she was going to roll up my hair and make me as pretty as Betty Grable. She rolled my hair very tightly and quickly then handed me a little towel and told me to use it to keep the solution she was going to put on the curlers out of my eyes. When I wanted to know how, she rolled up the towel, put it across my eyes and told me to hold it over them tightly. I didn't like having my eyes covered and liked it less when the stuff she called solution started running fast down my forehead and sides of my face. The smell of it was about to choke me. It was worse than the smell of a skunk. I had smelled skunk before.

Trying to get my mind off of that awful smell and the stuff running down my face and neck, I thought about the women in the other chairs. The last time I had looked at them, before the towel went over my eyes, I noticed their hair looked kind of blue, so I asked through the towel if my hair was going to be blue when it was finished. The hairdresser laughed and told me my hair would be the same color it was to start with. Then she announced it was time to go to the heat machine.

I thought she meant the hair dryers, so I hurried over and climbed into one of the chairs the hairdryers were attached to. The hairdresser did not come to where I was sitting. She walked to the back of the room and started looking and handling something that looked like a squid or octopus, with a lot of long skinny arms hanging down. I had seen sea creatures in a book my sister brought home one day. She showed me the pictures of creatures that live in the ocean and told me what they were, otherwise I would not have known what the thing looked like that the hair dresser was now dragging me toward. I was told to sit on the board, which she had brought with her from the other chair. Then she began poking cotton in my ears. Then she covered my ears with caps from the tops of milk bottles, which looked like little baking cups, handed me a folded-up newspaper and told me to fan myself if I started getting too warm. To my surprise and shock, she started fastening the curlers in my hair to that squid looking thing. I was horrified. What was she doing to me? It looked like what a villain in my cousin Baby Glen's comic books would do just before the hero came to help the victim. The hairdresser told me that the process would take a few minutes. She reminded me again to fan myself if I started getting too warm. Then she walked away to join the other hair-dressers at the front of the room. I watched them laughing and talking for a few minutes, until I was sure my hair was burning. I screamed as loud as I could to get the attention of the one who had attached me to the thing that was burning my hair. At the same time, I was thinking, I wouldn't have to worry about wearing my hair in braids again. I was sure my hair had already burned off and the thing was going to fry my head. All the women came running with newspapers and magazines and started fanning me. I was screaming for them to get the thing off my head. They just kept on fanning. The hairdresser leaned close and yelled that it would only be a few more minutes. I didn't care if I had any hair left. If it looked pretty or not. I just wanted out of there. I had not been so frightened since the truck monster!

It was a good thing I hadn't eaten anything since lunch or this little monster would have gotten throw-up all over it too. I kept crying out that I wanted my Momma. Finally, I was lifted from the chair and carried to the first chair again. I saw myself in the mirror with the curling rods still in my hair. My head felt like it was still burning, my face had very red spots all over it, and my throat was so dry I could not even swallow. I was told a little rinsing out would help, once the curling rods were out. The next thing I knew my head was over a huge basin and something was being poured over it. Some of that started getting in my eyes and I started screaming again. A towel was thrust into my hands and I was told to dry my eyes with it. Somebody plopped me back into the chair with a towel wrapped around my head. At that moment, I was sure my Momma was never coming back for me. She would not want a child whose hair had been burned off.

The towel was removed. I still had hair! The woman started combing it. My hair was much curlier than my sisters! She stopped to get something else she wanted to put on my hair. Out of the corner of my eye, I saw my Momma and sister coming in the door. I had never been so happy to see them in all my life. I was reaching for my Momma when the woman came back and rubbed whatever it was she had gotten, all in my hair, then she started combing again, very fast. When my feet touched the floor, I ran out the front door as fast as my feet and legs would go, my sister behind me.

We waited outside for our mother. She came out of the building all smiles. She told me that she thought my hair looked nice. She said she was proud of me and it did not matter that we had not eaten supper yet, we were going to get a double dip ice cream cone to celebrate. After what I had been through, that chocolate ice cream cone did not last long.

Things were not so good when we got home. My Daddy was upset because he did not know where we were. My Momma told him that he was only mad because supper wasn't ready when he got home. Then she told him about my bad day at school and what I said about not going back there. When my Daddy got a good look at my hair he did not like it one bit. He told my Momma that now my hair looked fuzzy.

I went to my Momma's room to look in her dresser mirror. It was the biggest mirror in the house. I was so worried about my hair that I forgot the switching I had gotten the last time I had gone into my parents' room and gotten into my Mommas make-up. All I could think about was looking like Betty Grable. My hair, although it was blondish, was not the white blond of the movie star's hair. I went to the bathroom, got my Mommas talcum powder, sprinkled it liberally in my hair. Then I took the hairbrush and brushed furiously at my new curls, adding more powder to it. Next came the eyebrow pencil for my eyebrows and mascara for my lashes. After using those two things, I took out the bright red lipstick and drew big puffy lips over my small narrow ones and thought to myself that maybe I did look like the movie star.

I tucked up my dress into the legs of my panties and started whirling about the room, jumping on and off the bed and chair, humming to myself what I was sure was a tune to dance to. Serandica Pappas showed up and watched me dance, she was smiling at me in approval. I was a happy child for a few minutes, until the door opened. My sister burst into the room, her mouth flew open wide, then she ran out of the room with her hand over her mouth. I knew she was going to tell on me, but I didn't care. I was happy, because I was almost as pretty as Serandica Pappas. Suddenly I heard someone say, "Oh my God!"

Then I saw my Momma, her hands over her mouth, my sister was behind my Momma laughing. My Daddy was there, and he was laughing too. I felt no shame. My mind was thinking that they could not believe how beautiful I was. My Momma was not laughing. She said, "Stop it, all of you, and I mean right now!"

She grabbed me by the shoulders and shook me very hard, asking me why I had put all that powder in my new hairdo. I told her that I wanted to be pretty like Betty Grable and Serandica Pappas. She said that I was a little girl and nothing I did would make me look like a grown woman. Then she scolded me about ruining my perm. She told me it had cost her twenty-five dollars of her grocery money for the month and now I had ruined it, and her money had been wasted.

My Daddy said that it was only powder and it should wash out easy enough. Momma told him that the beauty operator had told her not to wash my hair for a week. Then Daddy said that a good brushing would get most of the powder out. He took the brush and told me to come out into the backyard with him. We all headed for the back yard. When we opened the back door, there sat the cutest little puppy. He was solid white and had a lot of hair on him. It looked like he had just had a bath. His hair was a little curly. Daddy said that he had brought the puppy for us. Momma said no, because it would make me have asthma. My sister said it was a wonder all that powder hadn't made me have an attack. Then Daddy said, "If that permanent didn't make me have it, he didn't think the puppy would make me have it." Momma kept saying no.

We were playing with the puppy. It was chasing all around the yard with us. I heard Daddy tell Momma that the dog wouldn't be in the house, just in the yard and he thought it would be good for us to have him. Momma turned and went inside, slamming the door behind her. Daddy said the puppy would need to be named. My sister looked at me, then at the puppy, and said "We should call him Fuzzy!"

So, that was his name. It was mine too for a while until everybody got used to my hair.

ON THE FARM

My Aunt Trecie and Uncle Homer Grimes lived on a sandy land farm several miles from town. Aunt Trecie was another of my Mommas sisters. The couple had produced only one child, and she was almost grown and engaged to be married. Her parents were already missing their little girl. They knew it would be a while before they had grandchildren to spoil, so they invited the children of other family members out to the farm, sometimes for a weekend and even a whole week during the summer.

We children all loved going to visit them. Their farm was great place to go. There were huge trees with not just one but three tree swings. One with a wide flat board for a seat, the second from an old car tire and the third was a wide porch type swing. The farm house was built high off the ground with a long, covered porch across the front. Us kids loved playing under the porch. The sand was always cool under there in the summer. During the winter it was a warm place to play outdoors. The house was under pinned on three sides. The porch had underpinning at both ends. There was also a huge barn where we loved to play as well.

The shade of the tall pine trees, great oaks and china berry trees offered plenty of shade and that is where we mostly spent our time playing and eating the wonderful picnic lunches and sweet water melons our aunt and uncle provided in great abundance. Had we not run and played so much we might have gone home very chubby. We were sometimes put to work helping pick berries or other fruit. Some of the bigger kids helped with the animals. That farm was one place we knew there would always be plenty to eat, summer or winter. Aunt Trecie put up all kinds of fruits, vegetables and even soups and stew in canning jars. Sometimes we were allowed to help her or just watch how it was done. I learned to churn butter with my sisters help. I considered it fun, but my sister did not.

Back then, they had no indoor plumbing on the farm. We drank water from the well at the end of the porch near the kitchen. From the same well, water was drawn up and emptied into big washtubs for baths. There was an outhouse but most of the boys just went behind one of the big trees at the outer edge of the yard. Sometimes we girls would go behind the barn.

Imagine my surprise, and joy, when I found out, quite by accident, that my family would soon be moving to a farm near my Aunt Trecie and Uncle Homer. One night I was drying dishes after supper. I heard my parents talking on the back porch. They were sitting out on the back steps. The window over the kitchen sink was open, so I heard them clearly. Momma was telling Daddy how displeased she was that I hadn't been doing well in school. She said she could understand if I was retarded, but I was not. Then she told him that I was getting skinnier, the asthma attacks were coming more often, and I had been brought home from school twice in the last week with it. She said all my talking about that Serandica Pappas was the last thing she needed.

I seemed to freeze, unable to move on the chair I had been standing on, so I kept listening.

My Momma then said that she was afraid I was going to be held back because I wasn't trying. She said I was smart, but the teacher said I had not been applying what I knew in my classwork or home work. She ended by saying that she was at her wits end.

Daddy told her that he thought she was getting all worked up for nothing. He said that I was only in the first grade and needed more time to get used to school work. My Momma reminded him that I was already nearly seven. Even though I was skinny as a rail, I was already a lot bigger than most of the six-year-old children in my class. She said she would be ashamed of how big I would be compared to all the other first graders if I was held back.

My ears were burning. I didn't know if it was because I was ashamed that I had done so badly at school, or because my Momma said she would be ashamed if I was held in the same grade another year.

My Daddy said something about us moving to a farm. I leaned closer to the window so that I wouldn't miss a word. Momma told him that she had married him to get away from farm life. She asked him why he thought she would be interested in such a move. He told her, that his brother Johnny, had bought a place, not far from Homer and Trecie's farm. He said Johnny wanted him to work the farm. We could live out there because there was a large rock house and a good barn on the property. He went on to say that there were good water wells on the place and that Johnny was willing to buy a couple of cows, a couple of mules, and the equipment needed, as well as seed and plants to start the farm. He said after that was all paid for, the two of them would go halves on whatever the farm could produce. Both families would have plenty of fresh meat, eggs and vegetables, with maybe, some left to sell on market day. They figured the largest crops should be tomatoes and sweet potatoes because both grew well in east Texas soil, without special care.

I did not hear my Momma say anything for the longest time. Finally, she asked daddy what she was supposed to do when it was time for the baby to come. My eyes popped open at the same time my mouth did. I jumped down from the chair and ran to our room where my sister was already in her night gown, propped on pillows, reading. I jumped up on the bed and whispered in her ear that Momma was going to have a baby! My sister pushed me away and told me I was lying. I crossed my heart and hoped to die and told her to come to the kitchen and listen at the window.

We both tip toed back and climbed upon the chair, just in time to hear Daddy tell Momma that he would come from the field and check on her often during the day and for her to remember that her sister lived only a short distance down the road.

All was silent for a few minutes then Momma told Daddy that he was asking a lot of her for she had gotten used to living in town. Our daddy was not one to give up easily, he told Momma that we would be going to a different school and maybe that would be just what I needed to be inspired to try harder. He added that we could ride the bus to school. That would be something different that we might enjoy, instead of walking to school and back every day.

Momma went silent again, but Daddy kept right on. "Just say you will ride out there with me and look around this week end. Huh?"

Momma told him she would think about it. My sister and I ran back to our room and started talking about it. She could not believe Momma was having a baby! I could not wait to move to the farm!

I do not know how long it was before we fell asleep, but it seemed like we had just closed our eyes, when Momma called us for breakfast. Getting dressed, I began thinking maybe I had dreamed it all. I didn't have to wait long before I found out. As soon as we were seated at the table, my sister asked if we were going to have to move to the country. Momma said that it might be a good thing for us to do. I knew I would be happy living in the country, but my sister didn't seem to like the idea. Even though she loved visiting our Aunt Trecie, she was not sure about living there all the time and having all those chores to do every day.

It was actually pleasant for me walking to school that day. When time for recess came, I hurried to my favorite spot in the corner of the playground and told Serandica Pappas about it. Saturday afternoon, Uncle Johnny drove up and honked the horn. Daddy went outside, got into the car and they drove away. My heart sank. I ran with Fuzzy to the back yard and started crying. I was sure that Momma must have decided not to go look at the farm. Fuzzy licked my tears. Serandica Pappas came to comfort me and I spilled out my grief to Fuzzy and her. They seemed to understand how I felt. After a while I heard a car again. Fuzzy and I raced to the front yard to see who was there.

To my surprise it was daddy. He didn't even see Fuzzy and me. He hurried into the house and I followed. He told Momma to gather up some stuff for a picnic. Uncle Johnny was loaning us his car for the day, so we could all go out and look the farm over. Momma sounded angry. She said that she knew he wasn't going to shut up about it until she went out there.

In a few minutes we were on our way. Fuzzy was allowed to go with us. Momma said he could help watch out for snakes. There would probably be a lot of them. Daddy told her not to be trying to scare us. He said it was a nice place and he thought we would all like it.

Driving out into the country turned out to be fun after all. Momma tried to keep her thoughts to herself. Finally, she had to say that people could not live in the country without a car, and how funny she thought we would all look riding into town on the mules. We all had a good laugh picturing that.

Daddy told her that uncle Johnny was going to buy an old truck for the farm use. Before long we were near the Grimes' farm. Aunt Trecie and Uncle Homer were sitting in the shade resting after a long morning at the farmers market. They waved, Daddy honked the horn and we all waved back. Fuzzy had his head out the window and he barked. Daddy told us when we got around the curve, we should all look to the right, to see our place.

Just as he had said, there was a big rock house and a barn that looked bigger than the house. There was a rock fence around the house with big and little gates. A board fence which had been painted white surrounded the barn which was red, with very big white doors. Even my sister was on the edge of the seat. Her eyes were wide with excitement.

Before Daddy got the car completely stopped, Fuzzy jumped out the window and started running about in a frenzy. All of us, except Momma got out of the car as fast as we could. Billie and I started running toward the house, but Momma called out to us to wait until our Daddy went inside and checked things. There looked like plenty of good keen switches on the bushes in the yard, so we stopped and waited until Daddy came to the door and told us to come on in.

The big living room had a huge fire place. The kitchen was next. It was a long wide room. There was a big wooden table with benches at the side. There was a coal oil cook stove and a wide counter with cupboards above, they were painted white and had glass framed doors. Through the next door was another room, which my Daddy said was a dining room. Momma disagreed and said it was a small bedroom. Another door led into a long hall. There was a door into a large room. It had pretty wallpaper and a big closet. At the end of the hall was another large room with a door to the living room.

There were a lot of windows and a front and back porch. The front porch was low to the ground with only two steps up. The back porch was high off the ground with eight steps up to it. Underneath was the perfect place for a playhouse. When I said so, Billie said she thought that would be a good place for Serandica Pappas to live. I gave her a big shove and she just giggled instead of shoving me back, like she usually did.

Daddy said there was fifty acres of land and there was a creek running right through the middle of it. He said there was a big drip rock with a nice sized rock pool that we kids could wade in. Momma said she might enjoy sitting and soaking her feet awhile, so we all headed for the creek.

Daddy had gotten the picnic basket from the car and told Billie and me to go back and get the quilt and pillow for our mother to sit on. It seemed like a long way to the creek. The way we went was pasture for the cows. The long walk turned out to be worth it. Sure enough, there was a huge rock with a flat top and water ran over it into a very large pool, which was much lower than the creek running over the rock into it. Daddy said the previous owner had lined the bottom of the pool with enormous flat rocks that he figured had been cleared from the field that was now pasture.

Water from the pool drained into what looked like a wide deep ditch. Daddy told us the water was always cold because the creek was fed by a spring. Billie and I did not know what a spring was, so our parents explained it to us. We wanted to play in the water. Momma said it was probably too deep. Daddy took off his shoes and socks and stepped right in. He waded all around. He had rolled his pants legs up over his knees so as not to get them wet. The water never got over his knees. Billie and I giggled. We had never seen our daddy's bare legs.

Momma finally decided we could get in the water. It was cold! We waded around the way Daddy had done, holding up our skirts, so they wouldn't get wet. My sister decided we should tuck our skirts into our panties the way I had done when I tried to dance like Betty Grable. Momma tisk-tisked about it but let us leave them that way. Daddy was busy laying out the quilt and pillow nearby. Momma seemed to be enjoying soaking her feet in the water. How fun that day turned out to be. Within two weeks we were on the farm and I loved it. A few months later we had a new baby brother added to our family.

FARM LIFE

A year later at the farm, my sister and I thought we knew all there was to know about farm life. We were all happy as could be. When I wasn't doing chores, I was free to spend time in the play house I had made under the back porch. With Fuzzy and Serandica Pappas to keep me company it was my favorite place to be.

I had passed the first grade with no trouble at all. During the summer all our cousins, a few at a time, came to stay with us as well as with Aunt Trecie and Uncle Homer. All our relatives had come out at Easter and we had a big picnic and Easter egg hunt, down in the pasture by the drip rock. The cows and their calves had been penned up in the lot near the barn, so we had plenty of space to play games.

My uncles and older cousins even played a baseball game. My Uncle Homer Garrett, who was another one of Daddy's brothers, knew all about playing ball. He played on our town's team and they traveled around to other towns playing ball games for money. It was a lot of fun and exciting to watch them all play. Everything had been wonderful that year, except my asthma attacks had gotten worse.

Many a night my Daddy had walked to Aunt Trecie and Uncle Homer's to use their telephone to call for the doctor to come. He always came right away. I might have choked to death if he hadn't come to give me an injection. At least that is what I thought every time it happened. Momma griped at Daddy telling him it was that cigarette smoking he was doing that caused it. She said it almost choked her too.

I got into a lot of trouble that summer. It seemed like Mommas temper was quicker than it had ever been. One morning she gave me a big cooking pot and a fork and told me to go to the house garden and bring her back a pan full of new potatoes to go with the green beans she was cooking. I was proud that she had asked me, for the house garden was her pride and joy. She had never asked me to go in it for one single thing. She made it plain that she did not want me in her garden. Even though she didn't want it, helping in the garden was one job that had fallen to my sister Billie.

I went to the garden smiling because my Momma, trusted me to do something important to help her. I knew which plants the potatoes were. I set the pan on the ground and took out the fork. I did not know why she sent the fork, so I threw it back into the pan. I knew the potatoes would be under the ground for Aunt Trecie had told me once. I got both my hands around the plant, pulled as hard as I could, and almost fell into the next row of potatoes.

Looking at the bottom of the plant, I let out a sigh. There were only three tiny potatoes on the bottom of the plant. I shoved the whole thing into the pot and moved on to the next one. Good luck! That one had seven on it. Three of them pretty good sized. I counted on my fingers and decided I needed to get at least one more bunch. The next plant had four potatoes all a good size, so I pushed that plant into the pot and headed for the house, thinking how many potatoes each of us would have to eat with our green beans. I counted in my head the best I could, while walking slowly, trying not to stumble down with that big pot full of potatoes. The plants were hanging over the sides of the pot.

Two for little brother, two for Billie and two for me. That would leave four potatoes for Momma and four for Daddy. I agreed with myself that I had done a good job. I struggled up the back steps with that huge pot and its contents. At the back door I called for momma to come and open the screen door for me. When she got there, she yelled, "Oh my god! You have pulled up the whole plant."

I didn't know why she acted so surprised. She called out for my sister. She came in a hurry. When she saw the pan full of plants she started laughing. Momma turned on her and told her to get out to the garden and get her enough potatoes for dinner. I was trying to tell her how many were in the pot under the plants, but she gave me a big shove and told me to go with my sister so that I would not make the same mistake again.

Billie emptied the ones I had brought onto the back porch. When we were in the garden she got down on her knees with the fork and started scratching in the dirt under the plants. Before I knew it, we had almost half the pan filled. Each of us took a handle and headed back to the porch again.

Momma had filled a pail with water and told us to wash the potatoes. Billie told me that I had better wash them good or the switch might be next. I washed them so good the skin kept coming off. When we took them in to Momma, Billie laughed as she told momma about me washing off the skins of the potatoes. I didn't know why she was laughing because I was sure I would get the switch for ruining all those potatoes. Momma told me that the skins always came off when you washed the little new potatoes. My sister went back to our room and I went to the playhouse to tell Serandica Pappas about it all.

Daddy always came to the house for lunch. One day he had the sledge loaded down with baskets filled with big juicy tomatoes. He was going to unload them underneath a big shady tree in the front yard after he finished eating lunch. Uncle Homer Grimes would take them to the farmers market the next morning and sell them for Daddy.

Uncle Johnny still had not brought out a truck, so Uncle Homer offered to take them in to sell when he took his own to market. That particular day Daddy did something he usually didn't do. He had opened the big gate to the pasture and drove the sledge loaded with bushel baskets of big, tomatoes into the yard by the well. He gave the mules water in an old bucket, then poured water into a wash pan, which Momma had placed on an old table for that purpose. Momma never allowed anybody to eat at her table with dirty face and hands.

I was under the porch in my play house when Daddy went up the steps, he called down to me to not go near where he had tied the mules to Mommas clothes line. I called back and said I wouldn't.

After a few minutes I decided to get a few tomatoes and store them in my playhouse. Fuzzy and I went out to the sledge. I had seen Daddy drive the sledge. It was the way of moving everything heavy. It was only about five feet wide and eight feet long, made of boards. The flat frame made a good platform to set things on when they were too heavy to be lifted.

Fuzzy and I stood there looking at the thing loaded down with all those baskets of tomatoes. Fuzzy got on it and sat down by one of the baskets. The mules didn't move, they were busy swishing the flies away with their tails. Daddy had put feedbags on them and they were munching away at their lunch. I do not, to this day know what happened to me, but I remember smiling at Fuzzy and asking him if he wanted to go for a ride. I could have sworn he said he did, so like I had seen and heard Daddy do many times. I whistled as loud as I could and yelled at the top of my voice, 'Hey mules, giddy up!'

Before I knew what had happened the mules bolted forward! Fuzzy and I were thrown off the sledge along with the baskets of tomatoes! The mules were running as fast as they could go! The sledge was on its side! As they ran by the well, the sledge hit the well walls that were made out of rock like the house and knocked some of the rocks and the bucket into the well! The mules were scared, I guess, for they kept running.

I heard Daddy yelling and saw him running toward me! He grabbed me up and ran to the steps and put me down on the highest one he could reach from the ground. The mules had run all the way around the house and were headed toward the big gate and out to the pasture. Daddy followed them and closed the gate, then he came back toward me pulling off his belt. It was the first time I had ever seen Daddy that mad. He had never used his belt on me until then. Mommas keen switch hurt but that belt was a lot worse.

Momma came out, took me in her arms and told Daddy it was all his fault for bringing the mules into the yard. Not only could I have been killed or trampled, but the tomatoes were probably not fit to send to market and she hadn't had the courage to look at her flower beds in the front yard. When Daddy took his hands off his sides and started picking up the tomatoes, she told him that he had better get after fixing the well wall before one of us fell in the well. I was still crying so Momma made me go sit in a tub of water on the porch.

Luckily, I had nothing broken. The only thing that was hurt too bad to mend was my feelings because Daddy had used the belt on me. I knew I should have been punished, for what happened. I had disobeyed daddy and caused him a lot of trouble, but I did not understand why he had used the belt on me.

By the next summer I was skinny and pale, it seemed like everything was making me have asthma. The doctor told my parents that a lot of it was allergic reaction to all the sawmill dust in the area. He said the dog might be some of the problem, but the cigarette smoke was definitely bad for me. The musk, smut and mildew, along with the cedars and pine trees was also some of it, but he thought a lot of it was anxiety or nervousness. So far that summer I had not been allowed to play with my cousins much for Momma was afraid I would get too hot or too excited. No summer fun for me that year. I got weaker and skinnier by the day..

MOVING AGAIN

One night after the doctor had injected the adrenalin and I had calmed down, he told my parents the only thing that was going to help me was a higher, dryer climate. I did not know what that meant. My parents left the room with the doctor, so I didn't ask them. In the days that followed, I noticed a difference in Momma. She was quieter than I had ever known her to be. All day she hurried around here and there, packing things up in crates, moving certain things from one room to another, and placing items of all kinds into the little room by the kitchen. She gave most of the vegetables she had canned to Aunt Elsie, who was Uncle Johnny's wife.

One day, uncle Homer Grimes came and took away all the things Momma had placed in the little room. Things like my little brother's crib, high chair, potty chair, lamps, and fireplace tools. I even saw Daddy's fishing poles, tackle box and his tools. There were chairs that had belonged to my Grandmother Trotter, which Momma had said she would never part with. She told Uncle Homer to take whatever Aunt Trecie didn't want to keep for herself and sell it for whatever he could get for it all on market day.

I did not know what was going on until the next day. I was in my playhouse under the back porch. Daddy and Uncle Johnny came out and sat down on the porch. Before long I heard Daddy tell his brother that it was not what he wanted to do, it was something he had to do. He said, "If we don't take her out west, where it is higher and dryer, she could die."

When I realized it was me he was talking about, I sank to my knees and started weeping as quietly as I could. Soon Serandica Pappas was there. I could feel her arms around my shoulders. Fuzzy started licking the salty tears running down my face. In my mind, I pictured the things I had seen out west at the movie theater. Cowboys, Indians, train robbers, dance hall girls. People shooting, fighting, scalping and killing one another.

After my uncle had gone back into the house, I ran up the steps and sat down beside my daddy. He was smoking a cigarette. Momma had told me not to go near Daddy when he was smoking, but I had to find out something. I asked him if what I heard was true. When he said it was, I told him that I had rather stay on the farm and die, instead of going out west and us all maybe be murdered by gunslingers, robbers or Indians. Daddy just laughed, put his arm around me and told me I had seen too many movies.

He said, "The towns out west are just like our town. Movies are not real, they are just what somebody dreamed up and made a show about."

He told me not to worry, everything was going to be fine and we would probably all be healthier when we got out west.

The same week end, we had more relatives out at one time, from both sides of the family, than I had ever seen together. I noticed that each family was taking away something of ours when they left. Baby Glen came to me and told me not to worry, he would take very good care of Fuzzy for me. He gave me a big hug. In a few minutes I saw him putting Fuzzy into their car. They all drove away, Baby Glen waving and Fuzzy barking.

Out to the playhouse I went, crying again, telling Serandica Pappas that I didn't want to go out west. I only started feeling better when she said she would go with me. After a while Daddy called me in for supper and told my sister and me to help him keep our little brother, quiet as possible, because our mother had a sick headache and had to go to bed.

When the day came for us to leave, we had only large and small suitcases and bags, to carry with us. I didn't know how far it was out west or how we would get there. All I knew was Daddy told me that we would all be fine when we got out there, and that was enough for me.

Uncle Johnny came and took us to the bus station in town. Most of our relatives were there to see us off. We were given a few little keepsakes to remember them all with. In my mind, which meant we were never coming back. Boarding the big bus and seeing all the people already on it, I started thinking, they must all be having to move out west too. I wondered how many of them had asthma.

The bus pulled out of the station. We were on our way out west.

ON THE BUS

Out on the highway, the bus was moving very fast. Trees, houses and other vehicles seemed to be passing us. Looking out the window was beginning to make me dizzy. Now and then, I thought I felt something crawling on my shoulder. I kept looking at the place I had swiped at, until out of the corner of my eye, I saw a little dark brown hand inching it's was to the very spot where I had felt something.

Peeking around the back of the seat, I was surprised to see a little boy standing in front of the seat he was supposed to be sitting in. He opened his mouth in a big smile. He had the whitest teeth I had ever seen. He had on a red cap which he took off and put back on his head. Then he said he was going to Galveston. I asked him if that was out west. His replied that he didn't know but it was by a lot of water.

Then he said he was going to Cow town first, to get his granny, so she could go too. Just as I was about to say something else, Momma reached across the aisle and pinched me hard on my arm. She didn't have to say one word. I knew that pinch meant, "Stop what you are doing, right this minute." I asked my sister where Cow town was, she frowned and told me she didn't know and to be quiet.

We all sat in silence until my little brother woke up and started crying loudly. Daddy bounced him on his knee, but he kept reaching for Momma. She did not want to hold him right then, so Daddy started singing, 'Oh Susannah', and bouncing him on his knee again. To my surprise the little boy behind me started singing too. He knew every word. I wanted to sing but Momma was frowning, her mouth was drawn in a tight line. I knew it would be only a moment before she said something to Daddy, who continued singing. There it was, "My god Reagan! Shut up! That is giving me a headache!'

Daddy told little brother he would have to be satisfied to look out the window. He held him sideways on his lap facing the window. He started pointing at things he saw. Daddy was telling him what he was seeing in a very soft voice. The little boy in the seat behind me kept on singing loudly. Momma was still frowning. Suddenly she turned in her seat toward him and told the young lady, who must have been his mother, to quieten that kid down. I thought it sounded rude, but it worked. I heard him say, "Ouch!"

I figured his momma must have pinched him too.

Now and then the bus would stop. People were either getting on the bus or off, all along the way. The only bus I had ever been on before was the one we rode to school. Kids got on that bus in the morning and off in the afternoon, but this bus had old and young people on it. I wondered why so many people were getting on and off, so I asked my sister and she told me that some were going places and others had already been somewhere. I didn't understand that either, but she shushed at me, so I didn't keep on.

Everything got really quiet. The bus was gently rocking as it hurried along the highway. It made me feel sleepy. I must have gone fast asleep, because I was startled by a hand on my shoulder and a little voice saying, "You better wake up! We already to Cow town!"

The little boy who had been sitting behind me was standing in the aisle beside my seat. He told me he was getting off the bus now. I told him bye and waved as he and his momma went toward the front of the bus. The bus was stopped. I looked out the window and saw things I never even dreamed existed. Tall building reaching into the sky. Cars and buses everywhere. I kept looking all around, wondering where they kept all the cows if this was Cow town.

Just then the driver called out that we were in Fort Worth, and there would be an hour stop. Everybody started getting off of the bus. Daddy was telling Momma that we all should get off the bus and use the bathroom then get something to eat. Momma said she would be glad to get off and go to the bathroom, but she had made sandwiches of peanut butter and jelly for us all. After we had all gone to the bathroom, Daddy persuaded Momma to go into the bus restaurant for hamburgers. My sister had eaten one, but I never had. I had eaten a lot of peanut butter and jelly sandwiches, so I was really happy when Momma gave in.

While we were eating I told Daddy that the little boy had called this place Cow town, but I hadn't seen any cows yet. He laughed and told me that was what some people called it a long time ago, because the ranchers brought their cattle there to the stockyard. All I knew about ranchers was what I had seen in the movies. They were always driving the cattle somewhere, so I reasoned it must have been to Fort Worth.

The hamburger was so good. I ate the whole thing and drank a big glass of cherry cola. Momma said she would have to make us some homemade hamburgers when we got settled out west. I wanted to know how far, out west was. My sister told me that it was far away from east Texas. Then I wondered if out west was in Texas at all.

Daddy wanted pie, but Momma wanted to go back to the bus for she was afraid it would leave without us. Daddy told her that someone would tell us on the loud speaker when it was time to go back on the bus. Momma said she wasn't so sure of that, so back to the bus we went. The door was standing open and other people were getting back on. I guessed they were afraid the bus would leave without them too. The underside of the bus was open, and men were taking some bags off and putting other bags on. I wanted to watch them to make sure none of our bags were left there. Daddy laughed and told me not to worry about it. Our bags would get off the bus when we got where we were going.

Soon everybody was on the bus and the door shut. An elderly man came down the aisle and sat in the seat behind me. He smelled bad when he went by and my sister whispered that he must not have gotten to the bathroom in time. Momma leaned over as close as she could to Daddy, and said, "pee yew!" Daddy was shaking his head and tisk-tisking. A woman in the seat behind Momma, hurried toward the front of the bus. She was pointing back and telling the driver something. the bus stopped suddenly. The driver got up and came to our seats and told Momma that she should have changed our little brothers diaper while we were at the station. Momma opened her mouth wide, then told him she had done that, and her baby wasn't the one stinking. Then with her thumb she pointed toward the old man in the seat behind me.

The driver then went to speak to the old man. As he hurried back to the front of the bus, he announced that the bus would be returning to the station. We hadn't gone far, so it didn't take long to get back. Soon as the bus stopped the driver said for somebody to open a window or two, until we were on the road again.

When the old man got off the bus, Daddy got up and opened the window where the man had been sitting. He had already opened the one where he had been sitting and Momma had moved over by the window. The woman who had gone to the front of the bus came back toward her seat. Momma spoke in a very loud voice and said, "You, young lady, owe my baby an apology!"

The young woman said she was sorry for the mistake and got into her seat just as the driver got back on the bus, without the old man. We were back on the road as soon as all the windows were shut. It took a little while for the smell to be completely gone. Momma remarked that it was a wonder I hadn't had an asthma attack.

After a while my sister opened the bag she had brought on the bus. She took out a book to read. I asked her if she had some paper and a pencil. When she handed me two sheets of paper and a pencil and a book to lay the paper on, I thanked her and started drawing paper dolls and clothes for them. It didn't take long to draw up both sheets. When I asked her for more paper, Billie looked at what I had drawn. To my surprise she said the drawings were very good and told me to show them to Momma and Daddy. That made me proud because my sister was usually griping at me instead of giving me praise. Daddy told momma that he didn't know we had an artist in the family. Momma said she didn't know it either. Billie gave me more paper and some crayons and scissors without me even having to ask her. She told me to cut them out carefully and put them flat in the book I was using for a desk when I was done with them and that way, they would not get messed up. My drawing, coloring and cutting kept me busy for a very long time. My family finally thought I was good at something and I was happy.

The rest of the day was not as pleasant as the first part had been. In those days the speed limit on the highway was fifty-five miles an hour in the daytime and forty-miles an hour at night, which seemed pretty fast to me. The highways had only two lanes. One lane for going, and one for coming back. That all worked out until we got to what, Daddy said was "Ranger Hill." I did not know why it was called that, but it was the highest hill I had ever seen in my life. It seemed to me to go straight up into the air. Cars and trucks were barely moving. The bus slowed down until it seemed to just be crawling along.

The driver called out that it was going take a while to get to the top. He said everybody should try to relax, maybe read awhile or try and take a nap. There were some vehicles, especially big trucks, off to the side of the road with their hoods up. Some of them had smoke coming from the radiator. Daddy told us they had overheated because they were loaded with things they were hauling out west. The bus went slower and slower, until the driver pulled off the road and stopped. He told everybody to open the windows and stay seated while he checked the radiator. He said it would take a while for it to cool down enough for him to take the cap off and add some more water.

Momma said, "Oh my god Reagan! Get out and help the driver get the bus going again!" Daddy put up an argument, telling her that this was what probably happened every time the bus came up the hill. Momma told him it was too hot to have to sit there and I might have an asthma attack because there were so many cedar trees all around. Daddy got off the bus and went to talk to the driver. He came back and said with any luck, we would be in Abilene before dark.

My sister wanted to know if Abilene was where we were going to live. Daddy told her it was until he could work awhile and make enough money to go on farther west. Momma said it sounded like a God forsaken place to her. Then she told Daddy that she needed to use the bathroom, so he had better get back out and help that driver get the bus going as quick as possible. Daddy got up, handed Momma little brother and told her he would go see if he could find a cedar bush big enough for her to go behind. If looks could kill, the one Momma gave Daddy would have killed him. In a few minutes he came back and announced, loud enough for all the passengers to hear, that it would be only a few more minutes to wait. The driver had told him there was a truck stop cafe at the top of the hill, where everybody could get off the bus for a thirty-minute stop. My sister whispered that she hoped so for now she had to go to the bathroom. I hadn't thought about it until then and suddenly I needed to go too.

Sure enough, the bus got on its way again and there was the cafe just as the driver had said. The bathroom was small, so it took the whole thirty minutes for the passengers to go use the bathroom. I wanted a grape soda and my sister wanted an orange one. They were in a big tub of ice and looked so nice and cold. Momma said we must not have one, because the bus might not make another stop until we got to Abilene, adding that she hoped not anyway.

Back on the road the bus hummed along. No more hills like the one we were leaving behind us. Momma was sitting next to the window with her head turned away from us. I thought she was just looking out the window. Daddy was holding little brother on his shoulder and he had fallen asleep. Billie had taken out some more books from her bag. She was reading but I was only looking at pictures. Daddy was talking to Momma in a low voice. She turned to face him, and I could see that she had been crying. She laid her head on Daddy's other shoulder and dabbed at her eyes with her little hankie. I heard her say that she was sure it would be dark when we got there, and we had no place to stay. She was afraid we would have to spend the night sitting in the bus station. Daddy told her to quit worrying. He would see that we had a bed to sleep in when we got there. He said there was probably a hotel or boarding house where we could get a room until he found a job and a house for us.

I don't know what came over me, but I blurted out that I was sorry for causing us to have to go out west. Momma sat forward and told me that I couldn't help it because I had asthma. She told me that everything would be alright, that she was just tired, being on the bus for so long. Then she said it was Daddy's fault that we were having to go out west. Daddy looked shocked. He wrinkled up his face with a big frown and asked Momma why it was his fault. Momma said, "We had to come way out here because that blonde-haired hussy was chasing after you."

Then Daddy's face did look surprised. He told Momma he had no earthly idea what she was talking about. Billie stopped reading and started listening to our parents talking. Momma told Daddy that he knew very well what she was talking about. Then she poked her elbow into his ribs, making him jump enough that little brother woke up and started reaching for her. She took him on her lap and gave him a toy to play with.

She told Daddy that he ought to know who she was talking about because that woman had been hanging around ever since little sister was born. Then she poked him in his side again. He started smiling and shaking his head from side to side. Then they started talking about something else and Billie and I went back to our books, but I was still wondering about what they had just said. At that age I wasn't very quick to catch on to things and wondered about it a very long time afterward.

Momma said she felt sorry for the people who lived in the place we had just passed. Daddy asked why, and she said their peach orchard was dead because they had probably had no rain for a long time. Daddy said those were not peach trees, they were mesquite trees, and somebody had put something on them to kill them. Momma was horrified that anybody would want to kill a tree. I wondered about that too, thinking what if there were no shade trees out west, and why was somebody trying to kill trees?

It was very dark when the bus pulled into the station in Abilene. We had all fallen asleep and were surprised to see that we had arrived. Although I was glad, I was also anxious, not knowing what might happen next. When the bags were all unloaded Daddy told the rest of us to wait right there, while he went inside to get information on lodging. We all protested, telling him how badly we needed to find a place to use the bathroom. He heaved a great big sigh and told Momma to take us inside and find out about the facilities. While we got that business taken care of he would stay with our luggage until we returned.

That worked out very well for us. I don't suppose it crossed any of our minds that Daddy might have been in a hurry to use the bathroom too. All I knew was we felt a lot better coming out than we had going in. He then went inside. After a few minutes he came back to say there was a taxi cab coming to pick us up and take us to a tourist court for the night. I did not know anything about a tourist court, but I knew Abilene was not near as big as Cow town had been.

When I told my daddy, he said that Abilene had been a cattle town too. That had been a long time ago. Momma said she thought it might be a quiet town, because there weren't many cars on the street. The taxi drove up and whisked us away to the tourist court. It didn't take long for me to learn what a tourist court was. Momma said right away that we could not stay there. She said for one thing it was absolutely too small, but the worse part was that it smelled horrible. Daddy had already paid the taxi driver and it sped away before Momma made Daddy understand that she had no intentions of staying there. He said that we had no other choice. That was it.

There were two beds, but Momma would not lay down on either of them, she said she would sit on the luggage all night before she would lay on one of those beds. Daddy said if that was what she wanted to do, that he could not stop her, but he had to get some rest because he would be trying to find a house and a job the next day. Momma told him that he had better not think about leaving us there the next day, because she was leaving as soon as it was light enough to see. Daddy put our little brother on the bed with him, then he turned out the bedside lamp, which was the only light in the room.

We could hear Momma crying in the dark. My sister made a big flop when she turned over, and the bed we were on fell to the floor on her side. She rolled onto the floor. Momma screamed, "Oh my God!" and I started having an asthma attack from musky smell of the dust that flew up when the bed fell. The light came on and Daddy jumped out of bed. he was in only his undershorts, which looked funny to me, because I had never seen him without pants on.

Momma started yelling at him while he was helping us up from the floor. He was laughing about it and said for her not to worry he would fix it. When he asked Momma to hand him one of the pieces of luggage to put under the part he was holding up she jumped up and said she was not ruining the borrowed luggage by allowing him to use it to prop up a rattle trap bed in a run-down gyp joint. Furthermore, he had better find a doctor for me.

I guess he hadn't noticed in all the commotion. He turned, looked at me, grabbed his pants, put them on and raced out the door trying to put on his shirt. Momma didn't shut the door. She said a little night air might help. She dug out a wash cloth from one of the bags, ran water over it from the bathtub faucet, laid it on my throat and rushed over to pick up little brother.

By that time, daddy was back. He said the manager had called a doctor and he would be there as soon as he could drive across town. I was already gasping. It was hard to push the air out of my lungs in order to get some more in. Momma was back to yelling at Daddy, telling him that it looked like coming out west was not going to help me after all. Daddy yelled back, telling her that we had just gotten there, to quit making assumptions. He took his pack of cigarettes and went outside to smoke.

Momma told my sister to put more water on the washcloth she had put on my neck. She told me to wash my face with it. Then, carrying little brother with her she followed Daddy outside, still giving him a tongue lashing. I wondered if there were people in the little houses next to us, and what they would think about all the noise. Just then I saw car lights and sure enough, it was the doctor. I was thinking how glad I was that he came so fast.

He was an elderly man, a little bit on the heavy side, but he had a kind looking face and a big smile on it. He took out his stethoscope and listened to my lungs, said there was a lot of wheezing going on in there. He felt my pulse, took my temperature, putting the thermometer under my arm. Momma was trying to tell him that the doctor back home always gave me an injection of adrenalin. He just smiled and told her to get him a glass of water. He took a little bottle of pills from his bag. He took out a few little gray pills from the bottle, placed the cap back on the bottle and put the bottle back into his bag. He told me to put one of the pills in my mouth and take a big drink of the water. At first, I couldn't swallow the pill. He said it would be better to try again to swallow it, because it was very bitter and did not taste good crushed. Finally, I got the pill swallowed.

The doctor handed Momma the washcloth. He told us the pill would take a few minutes, but it would help me as quick as an injection. I hoped so, because nothing was helping right then. Momma started telling the doctor the reason why the attack had started, at least in her opinion. The doctor said that I was probably tired from the long trip and it would have probably happened where ever we had been. Daddy mentioned that he wished he had come ahead alone and found a place for us to stay at least. The doctor looked all around, rubbed his chin, and looked at all of us. Then he said that he might have a couple of extra rooms in his house, where we could stay a few days until Daddy could find a house for us.

Momma could not thank the man enough. The frown left her face and she smiled the biggest I had ever seen her smile in my life. Daddy said the favor would be much appreciated and he would be glad to pay for a better place to stay. The doctor just kept smiling. I tried to smile. I was already breathing easier. The doctor took out a little envelope, put the rest of the pills which he had been holding in his hand into it and gave it to Momma. He told her that she was only to give me one of them at a time with plenty of water. He wrote out a prescription for more them and gave it to Daddy telling him to get it filled in the morning.

Daddy wanted to know the address of the doctor's house so that he could give it to the taxi driver when it came for us. The doctor told him that a taxi wasn't necessary. His car was a big one and we and our bags could ride with him. He then went out to sit in the car until we got ready to go.

Momma told Daddy that she was sure God had sent that doctor to us and we should all start going to church as soon as we got settled in. She said in the meantime for us to be thankful for the help we had received on our first night in a strange, new part of the country. I thanked God all the way to that doctor's house, and it was a good thing too. His house looked like a palace compared to any I had ever seen.

We would all be safe and have a good night's sleep, and a new beginning, and I was happy.

A NEW BEGINNING

M_y family and I enjoyed the doctor's house for two whole weeks until Daddy found a job and a house for us. I had not been afflicted with anymore asthma attacks, the whole time we were at the home of the doctor and his wife. Momma told us not to think badly of the house we were moving into. She said that it would not be nice like Doctor and Mrs. Kirkpatrick's, but at least it would be ours. My sister and I wished we could stay at the doctor's house. We were afraid the house we were moving into might be like the tourist court we had gone to the night we first arrived. Soon enough we learned the house was not near as bad as the first place had been. It was not near as good as the doctor's house. Daddy said the wood frame structure had been one of many army barracks the army had left at Camp Barkley, where soldiers had been stationed during the war. The house was plain, with bare wood floors, which Momma said might be alright during the summer, but not in the winter. She had hopes of finding a much nicer place as soon as possible.

During that summer, we learned a lot about our new town. It was much bigger than the one we had come from in East Texas, but it wasn't near as big as Fort Worth. Every weekend we explored the area within eight to ten blocks of our house, each one of us took turns carrying little brother, when he got tired of walking.

Late one afternoon Daddy came driving up in a big, old car. It was two different colors, of brown and a pinkish color, which our Momma called, salmon. Daddy was all smiles, but Momma made a big face and told Daddy he knew she had been wanting a better house. Daddy said that he got the car for fifty dollars. Then Momma said the car wasn't much to look at but if it ran well, she guessed the price was not bad after all. Daddy said we should all go for a ride in it and find out how well it ran. He said that he had only driven it across town, but it ran like a new car. While we were driving around Momma asked him where he had found the car. He told her to take a guess. she wouldn't guess, so he told her the doctor had come by where he was working and asked him how we were all doing, then asked how he was getting to work. Daddy told him that he had been getting up early and walking to work, then catching a ride with one of the other workers back home.

He said the doctor told him that he admired a man so eager to take good care of his family, and he wanted to help him out by giving him the car he drove many years, before he bought the one he now owned. Daddy said he was not a man to take advantage of another person's generosity. He told the doctor that he wouldn't think of taking a car from him without payment. They agreed on fifty dollars and we now had transportation. Momma was even pleased and said the old thing sure did run quietly and was very comfortable to ride in.

We went more and farther away from the house. Our whole family loved going to Buffalo Gap, which was where a state park was located. Back then, there were not so many fences, and we could climb up what we thought were mountains, but later we learned they were only big hills, like Ranger Hill had been.

We had picnics, went fishing, and to the zoo where one of the big chimpanzees would smoke a cigarette! One day we were there, and somebody threw a cigarette into the cage. That chimp grabbed it up and started smoking it! People were laughing, but I was afraid he would burn himself with it. He might even get asthma! He took three puffs, one after the other, then threw it back out through the bars of the cage. If everyone hadn't been laughing so hard, they would have heard Momma say, "That monkey is probably smarter than the one that threw the cigarette in to him."

Summer in Abilene Texas was awfully hot that year, but Momma let us spray water on each other in the back yard. She didn't even complain when we got some on her. The house had a lot of windows and our parents bought a couple of circulating fans. We managed the heat better than we thought we might at the first of the summer.

The first time I felt it really bad, happened two days before school started. Our parents told Billie and me that we would be walking to school. We had been by the schools while out driving. Billie was going to get to skip a grade because the schools had only been going to the eleventh grade. Things had changed and for some reason students would go until the twelfth grade. I didn't understand it, but I didn't care, until I realized that Billie would be going to one school and I, another. We had always gone to the same school. Momma told me not to worry. She said that I was getting to be a big girl, who would be able to get to school and back alone, and anyway, in a couple of years, my little brother would be walking to school with me. She reminded me that his birthday was in July and he would just barely have turned six years old. I would know the way to school and be able to get him there and back home again.

That day was the first time, since we had left east Texas, that I had seen Serandica Pappas. To my delight, when I went outside to sit alone and think about everything she was there! She was smiling and as pretty as ever. I did not know how she got there. I was just extremely glad to see her. She told me not to worry about walking to school, that she would be walking with me. Of course, I had lots to tell her about our trip and what had been happening since we arrived. I told her that I had missed her terribly bad, but we had been so busy that I hadn't thought about when she would get there.

She told me that this was a new beginning. That I was going to meet a lot of new friends and I might not need her as much anymore. I told her I would always need her. Momma called me inside and when I went back, Serandica Pappas was not there. Billie came out and we started playing volley ball over the clothes line and I didn't worry much just then about anything except getting the ball back over to my sister.

It was the Labor Day week end. We would not start school until the day after Labor Day. For three days in a row Daddy walked the way I would take to school with me. He explained to me that Billie and I would have to walk to school and back because he was going to have to be at work too early in the morning to drive us to school. He would not be off the job until almost dark. He said it was a very big job and he had to be there. I must be very careful, and learn the way to go, so that I wouldn't get lost. I sure didn't want to get lost, so I paid special attention to everything he showed me that would help me remember the way. The day was really hot. By the time we got back to the house, I was wheezing and having an asthma attack.

The first day I walked slowly to school, taking time to look at the names of the streets and what the houses looked like on the little map my dad had made for me. He had taken time to write in the colors of roof tops, plants or trees in yards and many other helpful things like a corner house with the high fence which had a big barking dog in it. Serandica Pappas was true to her word, she was there every step of the way. When I finally saw the school building and started to run, Serandica Pappas was left on the corner a block from school.

I hurried in, located the office and presented a big envelope to the lady at the first desk. Momma had written a note and sent my report card from the school I had gone to in east Texas. Following her down two different, long, halls, I realized what a big school it was. Going into a school room late always brings stares from those already seated and beginning the days lesson. I was very embarrassed and apologized to the teacher for being late.

Even worse, I had to stand before the class, give my name and where I was from. Everybody laughed when the teacher told me to speak loudly so that those in the back of the room could hear. There was an empty seat toward the back of the second row. A girl with red hair was motioning and calling me to come sit by her. I wasted no time getting there and being seated. The red-haired girl said her name was Sofia and she would share her book with me until I got mine at recess. Sofia had a nice smile, so I thanked her.

My day at the new school began more easily than I had imagined it would have. When the bell rang for recess, the teacher told me to wait a few minutes before going to the playground. Sofia asked if she could stay and accompany me to the playground after I had gotten all the books to my desk. The teacher said she thought that was a nice thing to do. It did not take the two of us long to get the books and there covers to my desk. Hurrying down the hallway to the playground, I thought about how lucky I had been to meet a friend the very first day at a new school. Racing onto the playground some other girls came running to meet us. They all said their names and we all skipped off to play follow the leader. I had played that game before as well as London bridge is falling down, which it seemed, the bridge fell down a lot on me. Everybody was laughing and having fun, so I was too.

Lunch time was special, for it was done differently than in the school I had come from. This one was so much larger. The grades went to lunch two by two. First and second grade went to the cafeteria at eleven a.m. Third and fourth grade went at eleven thirty a.m., fifth and sixth ate at twelve noon. I was beginning to feel awfully hungry by the time my class went at eleven thirty. The long walk to school and exciting morning had taken away the cereal and milk from the early morning breakfast at home. The fish sticks, coleslaw, pinto beans and cookies, tasted better than anything I had eaten in the last few days. There was not one bite of anything on my plate left.

When the last bell rang for the day, I started pulling out all the books and covers from my desk, wondering how I was going to get them all home and back to school the next day. Once again, Sofia came to the rescue. She told me to take only a couple of books each day until I got them all home and covered, then take only the ones I had homework in. I felt silly for not thinking of it myself. Walking to the corner Sofia asked me where I lived. I told her, but then it popped into my head that Momma had told us strictly, not to invite friends to our house, until she had met their parents, and not to ask to go play at some body's house for the same reason. Quickly, after I had told her where I lived, I asked where she lived and was surprised when she replied that she lived just around the corner from me! Then she suggested we walk to school and back together. Nobody knows, except maybe Serandica Pappas, how glad I was to hear that. Sofia said it was her first year to walk to school alone too. She said she guessed that she had left a lot earlier than I had, but she would stop at my house the next morning and we could walk together. I asked her what time she would come so that I would be ready when she got there. Then she told me that she had seen us move in and had hoped I would want to become friends. So, friends we were and friends we remained until we finished the fourth grade and Sofia's family moved to another town.

Serandica Pappas and I spent a lot of time together out in the back yard the week they left. I really missed my friend Sofia. Serandica Pappas said I would make other friends. Then she said something I did not understand. She told me that she would be happy if I found a new friend. That she hoped it would be soon, for there was something she had to do. I told her I was happy with her as my friend and then asked what she had to do so important that she too might go away and leave me.

Her beautiful green eyes filled with glistening tears. All she said was, "I must find Justus.' I thought that meant her going away had something to do with finding justice for me, because of something I had, or had not done. When I asked her what for, she told me that Justus was her soul mate. She said his name was Justus Stephenoupolis. He was the only person she had ever loved. She had run away with him when she was very young. They had sailed to the Emerald Isle and it was there that they had become separated from one another in the water of an inlet from the ocean. She and Justus had gone into the water trying to hide from her Father who had come to try and find her. He had promised her in marriage to a very wealthy man. He was an old man and she loved her Justus. So, they had run away together but when the tide came in it washed them far out from the shore and they had gotten separated in the water. When she somehow got back to shore, a group of little people had told her that Justus thought she drowned and had gone off somewhere to mourn and never returned. Now, she said, since I was growing up, she must get on with her search for him, or she would go through eternity, trying to find him. Before I could ask any more questions, she was gone.

I called out to her until Momma opened the back door and told me to come into the house instantly. When I got inside she pinched my arm and told me that I was much too old now to keep up that nonsense about Serandica Pappas. She said it was getting on her nerves and she wanted it to stop, and she meant right then. I promised her that I would try not to bother her with it anymore. Then she told me that she was going to need my help more than she ever had. My sister Billie had gotten a job and could not be at home to help with things, so it was going to become my responsibility to look after my little brother, Ronnie, and help her with the laundry and meals. Then came something that shocked me into wanting to go back out and call for Serandica Pappas again. Momma said that she was going to have another baby and the doctor had told her that immediately afterward she would need a very, very, serious operation. The surgery would leave her unable to do very much for a couple of months. When I asked her when that would be happening, she said toward the first part of June.

I was frightened. When I started crying, she told me to quit that and get my mind on how she was telling me things were going to be. I looked at the long list of things Momma had written down for me to do when she went to the hospital. If I would do them without her having to tell me each time, it would help her tremendously, she told me. Most of the list was things I had already helped her with, but cooking meals? She told me not to worry that she was going to write down the way to prepare the food and all I would need to do is be careful while cooking it.

ANOTHER BROTHER

Just as Momma had said, on June seventh, during the night, Daddy woke us up, saying that he and Momma were about to be on their way to the hospital. Billie wanted to go with them, but Daddy told her it would be best for us to stay at the house. He said he would come back for us when Momma was safely tucked in at the hospital. We wanted to ask a dozen questions but there was no time. None of us could go back to sleep. Ronnie wanted to know if he was going to be the big brother now. We told him he would be, then he wanted to know if the baby was going to be another sister. We told him we did not know. Billie got a book and tried reading a story to us, but that didn't help. We all wondered what the baby's name would be and made up names for a boy or girl until we were tired of that. Finally, Billie said we might as well go to the kitchen and fix something to eat.

The pancakes, sausage and milk turned out to be very good, but then I started wheezing. Billie told me to drink some coffee that daddy had left in the coffee pot. That that was one of the things the doctor told us to try when I started wheezing if we didn't have any of the medicine. I drank the hot coffee slowly, she told me to prop up on the sofa and she would turn on some music. Then she turned the radio on low and we all lay around listening to music for a very long time. The wheezing got better, and I guess we all drifted off to sleep. The next thing we knew, Daddy was waking us up again. He said we had a new baby brother and the baby and Momma were doing fine. He said he hadn't had any sleep and wanted to rest a couple of hours then we could all get cleaned up and he would take us to see Momma and our new brother. Then, he lay down on the bed and was asleep before we got out of the room.

We finally got to see Momma and the baby late in the afternoon. None of us could hold the baby for he was being kept in the nursery until Momma was strong enough to have him with her. Daddy said she had already had the operation and was doing alright, but we must not stay too long until she was feeling much better. It made us sad to see her lying so still. Her skin was very pale, and her hair was a real mess. Billie brushed it the best she could with Momma laying almost flat on the bed. She told us she was going to have to stay in the hospital for several days, so we would all have to be good and take care of everything at home for her. Billie asked if she was going to have to quit her job to stay home and take care of Ronnie and me. Momma said that she figured I was old enough to watch my brother and keep things done at the house so that Billie could keep her job. That frightened me, because I had never done it before. I felt my chest getting tight. It made me think to ask Momma to tell me where my asthma medicine was in case I needed it. She told me to look in an old purse that was on the top shelf of her closet. Then she reminded me to only take one of the pills, and only when I really needed it. I promised to do that.

Leaving our mother there was hard for us to do. We knew we had to and rode all the way home in silence. Daddy left us at the door and went back to the hospital to stay with Momma until later that night. He said he wanted to stay all night and watch after her, but she and the nurses, insisted that she was doing well enough for him to go home. Momma had also told him to go on to work the next day, because there was nothing he could do at the hospital that would make her feel any better.

It was a very long week for Ronnie and me. The following Saturday Daddy came home to tell us to put clean sheets on the bed he had put up in the living room. He said that room was light and cheerful looking for Momma and the baby to come home to. Momma would have to be in bed a lot for a while longer and she wouldn't want to be stuck back in the tiny bedroom. We were surprised to see an ambulance backing up to our front door. Daddy told us to stay out of the way until it left. Billie was at work, so Ronnie and I stayed in the kitchen until we heard Momma ask about us. We rushed into the room with Daddy telling us to slow down. He said we must be very careful around Momma and the baby for several more days.

Sitting on the side of the bed we were allowed to hold our baby brother, Robert, for a few minutes. He was so light he felt like a doll in my arms. Over the next week he got heavier and heavier to me, for I was the one holding him the most. I rocked him, changed his diapers, and gave him his bottles regularly. I brought water for his bath, washed his cloth diapers, hung them on the clothes line out back, and when they were dry, brought them in and folded them. I made breakfast, lunch and supper, washed all the dishes, swept and mopped the floors. Ronnie carried out the trash, put away his toys and brought things back and forth to Momma. There was no time for bickering with one another. Momma might have been in bed most of the time, but there was plenty to be done and she kept us busy. Sometimes at night, she would call me in to rock little Robert, so that she could get some rest. The thing that surprised me most, was that I had not an asthma attack in several weeks, for which I was very happy!

Summer passed quickly. There had been so much keeping me busy, I hadn't looked at a calendar or thought about the date, all summer. Ronnie had his sixth birthday in July and I made my first birthday cake. Momma had written down the recipe, step by step, told me to be careful and not burn myself, the rest was up to me. It took all afternoon, but I got that cake made, stuck in six candles and served it to my brother proudly. It was chocolate inside with yellow powdered sugar frosting. The candles were the primary colors, which I had learned about in school. When they were lit, the cake looked really nice. It tasted good too. I was so proud of myself.

A couple of weeks later, was Daddy's birthday. When I asked Momma if I could make a cake for him, she told me it would be best to make cupcakes because it would take too many candles. Muffin making was about the same as cake making, only getting the right amount of batter into the muffin pan, had to be done very carefully. Daddy did not like chocolate, or frosting, so plain vanilla was what I made, and there was only enough left for him to take to work the next day. Billie even told me how good they were, and that really made my day.

Happiness was usually short lived for me. I never understood why. Sure enough, the week before school was to start, my parents told me that I was going to have to miss the first few weeks of classes. Momma still wasn't as strong as she had hoped to be and needed me at home to help with things awhile longer, until her health improved. Trying not to cry, I nodded my head that I understood and went into the bathroom and gave in to the hurt. Serandica Pappas came to console me, telling me that everything was going to be alright. She said that things would get better as soon as my Momma, got better, and once more left to search for her lost love Justus Stephanopoulos.

Wiping my eyes, I crept out into the back yard, trying to believe that things would get better. Gazing up at the starry sky I asked myself if I would ever have someone to love as much as Serandica Pappas loved Justus Stephanopoulos, then answered myself saying, "I hope so."

BACK TO SCHOOL

In mid-October, I went back to school. I had been walking Ronnie to school. An hour before time for him to get out of school, I went back to walk him home. Once in a while a former class mate would approach and ask when I was coming back to school. My answer was the same every time, "Soon, I hope."

Happy is the word for what I was that first day I went back to school, walking with my little brother of course. As usual, that happiness was short lived. I marched straight into the fifth-grade room where most of my class mates from the year before were going. I took the first empty desk I saw, which was the first desk on the third row, directly in front of the teacher's desk. When the roll was called, my name was not on it. I raised my hand to tell the teacher my name. When she looked up she came over to my desk and told me that I would need to go to the office before she could enroll me in class. I did not understand why I was being sent to the office, but obeyed, which I had known for a long time, was the best thing to do.

Suspicion that having missed so much school at the beginning of the year was the reason I had been sent to the office filled my mind and I had the answers ready. What I was not ready for was the first words out of the principle's mouth. He asked why one of my parents hadn't come in with me. After I explained he wanted to know where was a letter or note from them? Not knowing what else to say, I told him I had left it at home by mistake. He told me that his decision was for me to return to the fourth grade because I had missed absolutely too much and would not be able to catch up with the rest of my class in the fifth grade. Shock made me speechless for a couple of minutes, but when that principle got up and went to the door to call in the office lady to take me to the fourth-grade class room, I found my voice. I ran over to him, grabbed his shirt sleeve and commenced to tell him how hard I would work to catch up on everything I had missed and keep up with what was going on every day. I went into the fact that I was already a year older than some of my class mates and that keeping me back another year would embarrass me, and besides all that, it had not been my fault having to miss all that school. Before I could stop myself, I had told him all the things I had to do all summer. Rivers of tears were running down my face and I had no hankie to wipe them away.

The office lady came running in with a box of tissues. Finally, I got myself composed again. The office lady put an arm around my shoulders and whispered not to worry. Turning to the principle, who appeared to be in shock himself after all that, she asked on my behalf that he give me a chance in the fifth grade and added, "Then if she cannot get caught up, and stay up with the class you could still send her back to fourth grade."

She was a kind woman who had been with the school many years. He must have put a lot of stock in what she said because he shook his head in agreement and told me to go home for the rest of the day. He wrote a long note and told me to give it to my parents. He then told me to go to the fifth-grade class the next morning and do what I told him I could and would do, without fail. That was his final word on it. The office lady pushed me gently toward the door, whispering in my ear that she had faith in me. She said she knew I could do it because I wanted to so badly.

Walking home, I became nervous thinking of what Momma would say about it all. By the time I got there, I was needing the asthma medicine. While waiting for the pill to help me breathe easier my mind kept going over the note Momma was reading. It was in an unsealed envelope, so I had taken liberty and read it on the way home. It was telling my parents how fortunate they were to have such an independent child who could fend for herself when necessary. It went on to say that the road ahead of me was going to be long enough without my having to do the fourth grade over for no reason that I could help. His expectations were that I would do well, with the help of my parents and older sister. He said I had potential and they should very proud of me and help me in every way possible to achieve the goal I had set for myself. I did not know what potential was, but I figured it must be something good.

In the months to come I did do well and I did make my grades. School was a pleasure when I learned that I had something going for me. I became the class artist and poet. My class mates liked me. I learned to play softball and enjoyed that. My little brother Ronnie was good and minded me. He too had good grades. I was so happy. My sister Billie was happy too, not for me mind you, but for her own achievements. She graduated high school and went on to commercial college. She was engaged to be married. My baby brother Robert was growing like a weed. He was a little bit spoiled, but after all, he was the baby. Daddy had plenty of work. Having a regular paycheck coming in kept him from worrying about things so much. But Momma had changed since her operation. She was unhappy often it seemed. My guess was that she was feeling left behind. While we were all busy with school work and Daddy was busy with his job, she was home all alone with little Robert. She could drive but would not for fear of having a wreck. On the weekends Daddy would drive her around shopping for groceries and looking at houses. On Sundays they were both too tired for anything else because of doing so much on Saturdays. Eventually, Momma started letting Ronnie and me go to the church down the street from our house. Both of us loved going to Sunday school and church. Before long we sang in the children's choir and participated in the church programs. We learned about being in God's service. It made us proud.

Have I mentioned that happiness never lasted very long where I was concerned? That's right. You guessed it! Just when things couldn't get any better, Momma told us that she hated that "GOD FORSAKEN PLACE!"

In those exact words she told us and said she never wanted to leave her mother and sisters to come out west. She said she had made a big sacrifice leaving everything she loved, that she didn't even have any friends to comfort her. Finally, we found out what was upsetting her the most. My sister Billie would be moving to the state of Kentucky once she was married. Momma went on about how far away that was going to be and just when she needed us all the most. None of us, including Daddy, knew what to say to her anymore. Daddy tried to get her to go and see the nice doctor we had met our first night out west. She flatly refused. She told him that what she needed was to be around family and friends again.

I felt responsible for it all. If it had not been for me and that dreaded asthma, we would still be in east Texas and Momma would be happy. I was growing up, but still a child in a lot of ways and it broke my heart that Momma was so sad and unhappy. And it was all my fault.

If we hadn't come out west, Billie would have never met the man she was marrying. She would not be leaving Momma behind to go far away. In my child's mind, I wished we had stayed in east Texas, even if I had died there, it would have been better.

One day our mother got a letter from one of her friends whom she had known since her own childhood. In the letter her friend told her that she and her family were moving to Fort Worth and she was having a hard time getting her mind around moving to such a big city. She said there was not enough work in the town we had lived in, nor any of the surrounding towns. Her husband had found a good job, paying too much money for him to turn it down, so they would be moving to Fort Worth very soon and she would keep in touch.

That one letter did more for my Momma than anything any of us could have said. That night, before I fell asleep, I heard her asking Daddy if he would be willing to take a job in Fort Worth if he was offered one. He told her that he would do just about anything for his family and thought he had proved it already. Then he asked had she forgotten the reason they had come out west. She replied that now there was the medicine I could take for the asthma and besides, I didn't have it very often anymore.

Under my breath I begged for Serandica Pappas to come and comfort me, but she didn't come so I figured she must have found her long lost love and had already forgotten me, so I cried myself to sleep.

Nothing was ever the same anymore. Our parents quarreled constantly the result being that we children were pretty much on our own when it came to things at school. At home we played out doors most of the time so that we didn't have to hear the angry bickering of our parents. One Sunday, while sitting in the shade on the back steps, I overheard Daddy telling Momma that he was tired of it all. He told her to write to her friend and find out if she or her husband knew of a good paying job that he could go right to work at in Fort Worth. He said if he had a good job to go to that was all he would need. Next, we would need a place to live near enough to school for us to walk.

My chin would have fallen to the ground if it hadn't been attached to my jaws. I put my head on my knees and for the first time prayed to God, instead of calling for Serandica Pappas. I whispered my thoughts in the only way of praying I knew. Begging for God to hear my prayers and help us all. My love for west Texas had grown to the extent that I felt I could not live in a huge city like Fort Worth. My fear was that the people would be so much different than we were there. Having been almost asthma free lately my mind wondered if it might become worse again if we were to move back eastward that far. There was no voice, no answer that I was aware of from God. I didn't know that God worked in ways we didn't always understand. All I knew was that I was afraid, and I needed Serandica Pappas desperately.

Almost immediately, she was there! Smiling down at me. She sat down beside me, but she did not say a word. I poured out my heart to her, sobbing deeply while I whispered that I was afraid of moving to such a big place. How terrified of having to go to school there I was. Finally, she spoke, and whispered back to me that it took courage to live in different places, meet new people and learn new ways. She said our ancestors were probably afraid when they moved long distances away from what they had been used to all their lives. Then she told me that she had never been afraid when she was a child. Not even when she had run away with Justus Stephanopoulos. Many times, though, since that terrible night when they had been swept away from shore, she had been afraid many times. Wanting to know how she handled the fear, I asked what she did when she was afraid.

She was quiet, and I thought she was not going to tell me. After a while she answered, showing me a projected image of a strong, handsome figure, dressed in brilliant garments. There was light all around it. Light so bright it hurt my eyes. The figure did not move or speak. When I caught my breath, I asked Serandica Pappas who it was. She said it was her guardian angel and she wanted me to know that I had one just like it. She told me that no matter where I was, my guardian angel would always be near me. She said I would not be able to see the angel with my human eyes, only my spiritual eyes. I did not know what she meant, but I was sure she was telling the truth. Suddenly, they were both gone, and I sat wondering if my guardian angel looked anything like Serandica Pappas's. From that time forward, I made up my mind to go where ever I had to go and do whatever I had to do, just like Serandica Pappas, for I had a guardian angel of my very own to keep me safe.

FORT WORTH

Sixth grade had been a wonderful experience. It was the end of elementary school. Everyone in our class was looking forward to the next year. Something new was going to happen. Instead of staying in the same school until eighth grade, sixth grade through ninth grade would go to what they called Junior High. Oh, how great that sounded! It made us feel special.

The day school was out for the summer, I was as happy as a person could be. Ronnie and I were walking as fast as we could to get home and tell all our exciting news to Momma. Ronnie was as happy as I was. He had passed with top grades of the class. He too was eager for the next year to come because he would be eligible to run for class president, secretary or treasurer. Hurrying into the house, we let the screen door slam. Little Robert came out into the hall rubbing his eyes while running to meet us. I picked him up and gave him a big hug, then he reached for Ronnie saying, "us play." Just then Momma came out of the living room, where she had been listening to her radio program, hands on her sides, letting us know she had not appreciated our slamming the door and waking our little brother. We ignored the stance, both of us trying to tell our wonderful news at one time. She drew her lips tight and pointed toward the back door, yelling at us that she couldn't care less about what was going to happen at our schools in the fall. We were to take our little brother into the backyard and play with him until supper time. We knew better than to talk back, so we did what she said without another word.

Sitting around the table for supper, Ronnie and I tried once more to tell our good news. We had about as much luck as we had earlier. Before we could get started Momma told Daddy that she had the news she had been waiting for from her friend. Daddy put down his fork, pushed the chair away from the table, lit a cigarette and said, "Let's hear it."

Momma was bubbling over with joy. Her news was that we would be moving to Fort Worth, very soon. Our news didn't matter then.

On the highway, headed for Cow Town, the only good thing I could think about our going there was that Momma would be seeing her old friends. They were Daddy's friends too, but he didn't seem to have developed the closeness to them that Momma had. I remembered them very well. We had spent many a Sunday afternoon at their house and they had done the same with us. I hadn't thought much about them over the past few years. The last time we had seen them they had three boys. One of them was my sister Billie's age, the middle one a little older than me and a younger born around the same time as my brother Ronnie. We bigger kids had always played very well together. It was with them and my sister that I had learned to play table games, such as Monopoly and Chinese Checkers. Most of the time we all had to do the dishes after Sunday dinner. Thinking about them made me wonder how much they had grown.

I knew the oldest, like my sister, had gotten married. The one just older than me would now be in high school. My mind reasoned that my little brother Ronnie would be more likely to become good friends with the youngest boy, making me feel left out in a new place, a big place at that. I told myself not to worry, for I had a guardian angel to take care of me, and that was all that mattered. Then I started wondering if Serandica Pappas had found Justus Stephanopoulos.

I must have fallen asleep for the rest of the trip. Waking up, when the car stopped, I saw Daddy in a phone booth nearby. Momma had her window down calling out a phone number to him. After a bit Daddy seemed to be talking to someone but I couldn't hear what he was saying. Finally, he came to the car window and told Momma her friend wanted to talk to her. Momma got out of the car quicker than I had seen her move in a long time. She was smiling and happy, and that was what we all wanted to see, especially me. She even got back into the car smiling, telling Daddy that the whole family would be there tomorrow after church, to help unload things. Daddy asked if she had told her that we hadn't brought any furniture, or anything else which was very heavy. Momma replied quickly with, "For God's sake, why wouldn't she already know that? After all, she is the one who rented the place for us."

Daddy just shrugged and said the weather was clear and the tarp being fastened securely over everything, that it would probably be alright to wait to unload things until we had help. Once again Momma was way ahead of Daddy. She told him that we would do no such thing, there were things in that trailer we would need for the night. Then he fired back with, 'Why then, didn't you tell her that?'

Indignant, she replied that she wanted to see them all, was why. It was not far to the place we would be staying until we could find something more suitable, according to Momma. She told us this place was only for the summer and added that by the time school started in the fall we would be in a house near schools. Ronnie and I looked at one another, as if to say, "Here we go again."

It turned out that the place Momma's friend had rented for us was the same place that she and her family had lived in for a couple of months when they first arrived in Fort Worth. Daddy made a terrible face when he found out the small apartment was on the second floor of an old, turn of the century home. The wooden stair steps up the outside of the house were well built, but there were so many of them that it took Daddy, Ronnie and me a long while to get everything from the car and trailer up them. We were all too tired to eat anything that night. Momma promised a big meal tomorrow, as soon as she could find a grocery store and get food for the week. Again, Ronnie and I shared a knowing look, as if to say, "And guess who will be bringing all those groceries up that bunch of stairs."

Although I was tired, I started thinking about tomorrow. I wanted to look nice for our company. What did the girls in a big city wear? After all, I was going to be in Junior High next fall. Surely girls my age would be dressing differently than younger kids. Wasn't I almost a year older than most girls in the seventh grade? I would be a teen my next birthday. I didn't want to say thirteen, for everybody said that was an unlucky number. I sure didn't need any more bad luck.

We slept with the windows and doors open, to let in the cool south breeze, Daddy had told us. The screens were good, and they were latched securely. We slept much cooler that way. I woke when it was barely daylight. The smell of honeysuckle and roses filled the dewy morning air. I don't think I had ever smelled anything that nice, and never have since. Very quietly, not wanting to wake anybody up, I went into the bathroom, washed up and crept back out to find clean clothes, which were still packed in the suitcases. I found a pair of blue jeans and blouse. I had seen a girl dressed like that once in a movie.

With stealth, I found Momma's overnight case, which was where I had seen her put her makeup bag. Since that time long ago, playing as Betty Grable, I had not gotten into her makeup, until that morning. I hadn't had a keen switch or belt used on me for a very long time. Perhaps I forgot about the sting and hurt because of whatever was driving me to want to look good that day.

Back in the bathroom with door securely latched, I applied face powder, mascara and bright red lipstick. Admiring myself in the mirror, I hadn't heard the door knob when it was turned. What I did hear was Momma telling me to open that door and make it quick. Startled, I did as I was told. The look on Momma's face was one of pure horror. She pushed me back into the bathroom, grabbed a washcloth, wet it in soap and water and started scrubbing off the makeup which I had so carefully applied. I did not know why she didn't want me to look nice. After all, she used it didn't she? Of course, this is what I thought in my head, I knew not to say it aloud. Finally, she shoved me out the door and started running water in the bathtub.

Sorrowfully, I slipped out onto the little porch, sat down on the top step and breathed deeply, the wonderful morning air scented with honeysuckle and roses. It was light enough now that I could see the source of those wonderful smells. A tall fence around the house next door, was loaded with running roses and honey suckle vines. I crept quietly down the stairs and broke off enough to make a nice little bouquet. Upstairs I found an empty pint jar to put them in. I ran some water from the kitchen sink in them and waited patiently for Momma to come out of the bathroom. It was a peace offering, which I hoped would put the smile from yesterday back on her face. You have probably guessed by now that it did not happen. What did happen was this, I was told "There were more important things to be done than smearing makeup on my face and making silly flower bouquets, and for God's sake, keep that screen door latched. Little Robert might get out and fall to his death!"

All the commotion woke everybody else up and our day was off to a very bad start. I just kept hoping for it to get better. I kept right on thinking about my guardian angel, who I was sure was watching out for my well-being.

FRIENDS

Going to the grocery store was another unpleasant ordeal. Momma wanted to hurry and get back, make breakfast and get the apartment straightened up before our friends arrived. Thinking it was a good idea, I suggested my not going with them to the store, in order to start getting the place straightened up. Daddy thought it was a good idea, but Momma said flatly, no. Her reason was that she did not want our friends in the apartment until she thought it looked respectable enough to invite them in. She said if they showed up and nobody was there, and the door was locked, they would go away and come back later in the day, after things were in place properly. I didn't understand that reasoning, but I knew better than to question it. When we got to the grocery store I asked permission to stay in the car. Another no. That time I decided to ask why? Somebody had to look after little Robert while she and Daddy found the groceries for a whole week and that was going to be hard enough in a new store in which they had no idea where all the items were and would have to look for them. I was told to quit arguing and trying to get out of helping because she was in a hurry to get back and fix breakfast. Keeping on would have brought about consequences that I would not enjoy, so I obeyed without further question.

Getting the groceries up all those steps was a real effort. At one point, Ronnie sat down on one of the steps about halfway up and told Daddy he was getting out of breath. Daddy went on around him, picking up the bag Ronnie had been carrying as he went. I stopped to ask if he was going to be alright and he said he thought he would be if he could just stay there and rest awhile. We heard, "You kids hurry up and get in here!"

I told Ronnie to go ahead of me because he said he felt dizzy. Slowly we made our way into the house. Ronnie headed for the nearest bed and lay on it with his feet and legs hanging off the side. In the kitchen I told momma that Ronnie wasn't feeling well. She said he was probably hungry and for me to get the dishes unpacked and set the table.

When breakfast was ready she called Ronnie to come and eat. He looked more pale than usual. I asked if he was feeling better. He shook his head no. He ate slowly while the rest of us gobbled ours up quickly. Momma told him to stay at the table until he ate every bite of his food because he was feeling faint from hunger. I was told to wash the dishes and put away things still in crates on the floor. I could put them in the cabinet any way I liked, and Momma would arrange them the way she wanted later, when there was more time.

Ronnie had pushed away his plate and laid his head on the table. I felt his forehead and it didn't feel too warm, so I asked him if he was sick at his stomach. He told me that he was just really tired. I asked if he was going to eat the food left on his plate and he shook his head no. I scraped the food into the garbage, figuring with so much paper from the dish crate in the trash Momma wouldn't notice. Ronnie stayed at the table, head on one of his arms, until I had finished in the kitchen. Then he followed me into the living room, where Momma and Daddy were busy placing pictures in frames and putting knick-knacks on shelves. I asked what to do next and was told to put away my clothes in the closet and chest of drawers. Ronnie was to do the same with his own things. I got mine done and Ronnie had barely started on his. I helped him so that he could lie down and rest some more. I asked him if his head hurt. He said no, nothing hurt. He was just really, really, tired.

We heard lots of loud voices and footsteps on the stairs outside. Looking out a window, I was shocked to see our friends had arrived. At first Ronnie and I stayed in the room. We didn't want to go out and meet them. They all looked so different than I remembered. Two of the boys looked like grown men, another bigger than Ronnie and a little one about the same size as little Robert. I listened at the door while Ronnie stayed on the bed. He said he didn't feel like getting up and he hoped Momma and Daddy wouldn't make him. I waited in the room until Momma called out "You kids come on in here. Our friends are here."

Neither one of us made a move. After a few minutes, Momma came to drag us out, telling us it was rude and ill-mannered to act the way we were doing. I was still rubbing the sting out of the pinch she had given me on the way to the living room when I was approached by the whole family of people whom we had not seen in more than five years. Everybody was talking at one time and I didn't hear what any of them were saying. They all seemed much happier to see Ronnie and me than we were to see them. Ronnie stood quietly by the door on one side and I on the other. One of them said he believed the cat had got our tongues. Everybody laughed as if that was the funniest thing any of them had ever heard. I didn't know what it meant and didn't really care. I blurted out that Ronnie wasn't feeling well. Momma said he was just being bashful and would feel better once he had gotten used to them all. I wasn't too sure about that. Ronnie had always been a very friendly little boy. My notion was that my brother was sick, but Momma and Daddy were so carried away with our friends they didn't realize that he was really feeling bad.

The group returned to their seats, all smiling and happy, but Ronnie and I sat on the floor, where we had been standing. Momma was all atwitter, telling them all how good they looked. She said that living in the big city must be agreeing with them. They all talked and made jokes a while, then somebody suggested that a picnic at the park would be fun. That brought about a flurry of, "Yes, let's all go to Forest Park!'"

Daddy said that might be a good idea and asked Momma if they had gotten anything at the store good for a picnic. She said fried chicken would be good if the guys would go get a water melon and a tub of ice for ice cream, and we girls would all fry the chicken and make potato salad. That must have sounded good because they all ran out and down the stairs, slamming the screen door behind them. Daddy came back in and picked up little Robert and told Ronnie to come with them. Ronnie got up slowly and followed him down the steps. Momma laughed loudly and said now that she had gotten that bunch of men and boys out of the house we could get busy on the picnic food.

My job was to peel the potatoes and cut up onions. Wouldn't you just know, the onions made me cry and the little bit of mascara I had on my eyelashes started running. I didn't know it until Momma came over, gave me another pinch, in the same exact spot, and whispered in my ear, through clenched teeth, to get in that bathroom and get that mascara off, and she meant all of it! I didn't cry out from the pinch, but it was all I could do to keep from it. Once the bathroom door was latched, I had a real cry, a good one, asking myself was anything ever going to get better where I was concerned.

Serandica Pappas was there when I finally stopped crying enough to see her. She was sitting on the side of the bath tub, smiling as usual. She told me to be happy that things were going to get better very soon. Then she was gone. Washing my face and looking closely in the mirror, I finally got all the mascara off my eyelashes, but my eyes were red from the washing and crying. I did not go back into the kitchen. I crept out and sat on the top step, wishing I was back in Abilene.

Forrest Park turned out to be as wonderful as our friends had told us it would be. The picnic area was filled with people out enjoying the early summer weather. There were huge trees making wonderful shaded areas. The grass looked like lush green carpet. There were all kinds of picnic tables and places to cook food outdoors. The Trinity river ran through the park nearby. Some people were playing in the water and some were fishing. Later in the day, we were to find out the park also boasted a wonderful zoo, a carnival ride area and a miniature golf course. The two older boys seemed to know all about the place, for they had spent a lot of time there lately. Ronnie seemed to feel better. He and the boy his age had started running around all over the place, exploring the trees and the river bank. Daddy and the boys' father were making ice cream in the crank freezer. I had lost the dread which besieged me when our friends first arrived. I was actually enjoying myself. I was sure Momma was happy. She didn't quit smiling the whole day. The food was extra good. Daddy said food on a picnic had always tasted better than sitting around a table in the house had to him.

We learned what had been going on with our friends, and they heard about our time out west. The boy who was Ronnie's age was in school where Ronnie would be going. The middle one would graduate the next year and planned to move to Houston to pursue a career there. The oldest, the one my sister Billie's age, had been married, but it seemed that the marriage had not worked out and he and his wife of a few short months had gotten a divorce. I did not know what a divorce meant, and I really didn't care at the moment. Everybody was laughing, joking and having fun. Just as Serandica Pappas had predicted, everything had soon gotten better.

Just as the sun started to set, everybody said goodbye for the day, with promise to "See you next weekend." And so, it was, we all spent the summer happily. We learned a lot about big city life from our old friends. The re-acquaintance with them had made a huge impact on our lives. At a time when we needed friends they were always there.

I wrote a little poem about friends that summer. It came to me easy, so I just wrote it down. Over the years it would be published. The first time was in our school paper, when I was in the ninth grade. I thought you might like to read the poem I wrote as a teenager who had learned the meaning of friendship.

FRIENDS
Friends in happiness, Friends in sorrow,
They will be faithful today and tomorrow.
They will stand close beside you all along life's way.
In sickness they will comfort and watch and pray.
Some measure riches in houses and land,
I count my wealth in the clasp of a hand

GOODBYE JUNIOR HIGH

Middle school is what Junior high was eventually called. Instead of seventh, eighth, and ninth grade, it is sixth, seventh and eighth. At any rate, my first two years, in the one I started out at, Ernest Parker, almost took away any desire to go to school that was left in me.

'A bunch of juvenile delinquents,' is what Momma called the students who went to school there. I wasn't sure what a juvenile delinquent was, but I was certain it couldn't be anything good, by the way Momma said it. Whatever it meant I was also sure that I was not one.

One day, just as ninth grade started, I decided That I had enough of that school. I did not care for the nasty attitudes nor dirty words, the duck tails, black leather jackets, nor the switch blade knives, which boys and girls alike, carried and displayed openly. I wasn't afraid of anyone, they were just not my kind of people. Everybody talked about skipping school, evading the truant officer, and the best brand of cigarettes, which most of them smoked in the bathroom. When asked if I wanted a drag from one of their cigarettes, I would decline telling the person who offered, that asthmatics couldn't smoke. Usually I got a big shrug in return, and did not know if that meant, "What's an asthmatic?" "Who cares?" Or, "Whatever you say."

That day, I could not have cared less what one person in that school thought, one way or another. All I knew was I wouldn't be going there another day. Out the door I went to the bus stop. Mind you, kids in that school had school passes for the city buses. I never found out whether that was how big city schools operated or if the students were all so bad, a regular school bus wouldn't let them ride. I had my bus pass though and had learned how to use it. I presented the pass to the driver, asked for a transfer, which was needed to get on a different bus downtown, which took me in the direction that passed in front of where we lived.

The driver said, "Skipping school, are you?" then he laughed, so I didn't answer, went straight to the back of the bus and sat down, telling myself it wasn't any of his business. On the way downtown, my mind was making a plan. I would get off the bus at the point of transfer, and instead of getting

on to the bus which would take me home, I would walk on uptown and look around in some of the nice stores.

Walking along that big city street, in the middle of a school day was the most liberating thing, I had ever done in my life. For a while, I didn't think about school, home, or anything else. There were beautiful things in those stores and I was enjoying looking through new eyes, it seemed. Coming out of one of the stores, I saw a Drug store soda fountain sign at the next corner. I was feeling thirsty, but I didn't have any money. On the door was a sign which read "HELP WANTED" and in small print it said, "See soda fountain mgr."

I knew what a soda fountain was for Ronnie and I had been to the one near our house for ice cream cones. Knowing that everybody was given a glass of water to sip on while waiting for their order, I settled down on the first empty stool I saw. There weren't many people, just a few coffee drinkers. A man

wearing a white cap sat a glass of water in front of me asking, "Whaddya gonna have kid?" Fearing he would take away the glass of water if I didn't order, I took a long drink. Not really thinking about it, told him I came to find out about the job. His eyes narrowed, and he asked, "How old are you kid?

Without batting an eye, I lied and told him I sixteen. He looked at me hard for a few seconds and asked if I had ever worked anywhere before. Truthfully, I told him I had not. Then he wanted to know about school. I had heard some of the other kids in my class, talk about a high school thing which would allow a student to take classes in the morning and work in the afternoon, so again I lied, "I'm on the half day program."

He said, "Come on and I'll give you an application to fill out."

I grabbed the glass of water and followed him back to a seat at the far end of the long soda fountain counter. He brought the application and an ink pen, telling me to answer the questions he had put an "X" by, and walked away. I sat looking at the piece of paper, not really knowing what an application was. I proceeded to print my name and address. We had no telephone, which I thought might be a good thing. Clearly, I didn't want him to call and talk to Momma, who thought I was in school.

After a few more minutes, he came back, picked up the paper, looked at it, then at me and said, "How am I supposed to get in touch, if I decide to let you go to work here?"

At that point, I had had enough of this conversation too. I slid off the stool and told him I guessed I would have to check back, with no intention of doing that. Picking up my book bag, I walked slowly toward the front of the store. I heard, "Hey kid, wait a minute."

I turned, thinking maybe I had dropped something. He was motioning to me to come back. Wondering what he wanted, I started walking back. He came around the counter and said, "I am kind of in a bind and could sure use a good worker. You sure you want to work here?"

Taken by surprise, it was hard to think of an answer. For some reason, I told him that I could go to work right then, but he would have to show me what to do. Before I could say anything else, he called out to someone in the kitchen to come and show me to the dressing room. Wondering what I was getting myself into, I followed the friendly older girl through a swinging door, down a hall past another door with a sign, "LADIES RESTROOM" into a room which looked like the girl's locker room at school. There was a row of shelves which appeared to have folded clothing on them. The girl asked, "What size honey?"

It was my turn to question. I asked her why she wanted to know. She made a face and replied, "We have to wear uniforms here." pointing to her own.

She wore a white uniform, a green apron, and on her head a little peaked headband which was green and white stripped. She took a uniform off the shelf, handed it to me and told me to try it on for size. I had never dressed in front of a complete stranger and wasn't sure if I should do as she said. I just went right on with it, as if I knew what I was doing. I tried on two more before she decided the fit was right. She showed me my locker, gave me a little lock and key, telling me to put the key on a string and wear it around my neck so I wouldn't lose it. I stashed my clothes and book bag, then followed her back out.

The man came over and looked me up and down and told me that I had to wear stockings and white shoes and a hairnet. I didn't know what I was supposed to do about that, because I had none. Figuring he would say he didn't need my help after all. I stood shrugging. He told the girl to take me over to the other side of the store and get me fixed up, then told me the shoes and stockings would come out of my first pay check. Before I knew it, I had three pair of real silk hose, garters, hairnets, new shoes and a job.

He told me to go put my other shoes and extra stockings in my locker, put on a pair of the stockings with the new shoes and get back out there on the double to learn as much as I could before the lunch crowd started coming in. I hoped somebody knew what I was supposed to do. I sure didn't.

Six weeks passed, and I was still working at the soda fountain and lunch counter, smack dab in the middle of the big city. I had not gone back to school. Mornings, I got on the bus, got off at the transfer point and spent the morning browsing the stores, until eleven, then I would rush to work, slip into my work clothes and shoes and fly in to help with the lunch bunch. The place was always packed at lunch time. Workers from nearby stores and offices found the lunch counter a great place for a mid-day meal which was good and inexpensive. I ate two meals week days there myself. Free! My favorite thing was a grilled cheese sandwich and fountain cherry cola.

The manager asked me a few times when I was going to bring in my social security card so that I could be paid by check like the other employees. Back then, everybody didn't get a social security number as soon as they were born the way they do now. He had told me how to send for one, but the trouble was, it would be mailed to my address and Momma would, of course, want an explanation. My pay had been given to me, cash in an envelope. I rather liked it that way. I didn't have to worry about getting a check cashed.

I had spent very little of the money. Tips were good. Airmen from Carswell Airbase in the area were the best tippers. I traded the coins in for bills at the end of each day. I walked around for weeks, with all that money in my book bag.

I worked from eleven a.m. until five p.m. every week day. At the end of my shift, I changed into my other clothes, caught the bus back home and pretended to do homework. Knowing it wouldn't last forever the way it was, I decided to ask my parents if I could get a job after school and on weekends so that I could make money for some new school clothes. They talked it over and said I could try to find a job, but they didn't know who, in their right mind, would hire a kid who was only fourteen years old. I knew the way they said it they didn't expect me to find a job. I told them I had learned at school that kids wanting to work needed a social security card to get a job. Momma agreed that was what would have to be done and we sent off to get one for me.

I was so proud of myself I could hardly keep from smiling all the time. My boss had already told me that he would need me to work full-time when school was out in the spring. A full-time job would mean more money!

As usual, my bubble burst suddenly. One day I went home, and Momma was fit to be tied. A letter had come from the school and a truant officer would be coming by to find out why I had not been going to school. Silly me. Had I thought it through, I would have foreseen that happening. The job just came to me so easy, and I had been so happy with it. Momma went to pieces before Daddy got home from work. My poor little brothers were worried, not knowing what was about to happen.

Things went from bad to worse when I told Momma that I was never going back to that school and all the reasons why. She assured me that I would go back even if she had to drag me there. We were still at it when Daddy got home. Momma told him that I hadn't been to school for six weeks and had been "playing hooky!"

"The truant officer is coming to see why we have let it go on this long!" she screamed. Off came the belt. I was shoved into the bathroom; Daddy shut the door and raised his hand with the belt in it. I felt humiliated, knowing I had done wrong, but in my mind, the reason I did it was valid. I faced my Daddy and told him, without fear, if he whipped me with that belt, I would leave and never come back. He said, "We will see about that!"

It hurt my feelings as well as my body. When he had finished giving me the punishment with the belt, he told me that I might not have gotten as much if it hadn't been for my smart mouth. It opened again, and I couldn't stop it. while following him out of the bathroom, I told him through clenched teeth, that I was too old for him to be using a belt on, and I meant every word of what I had said. He whirled around and hit me square in the jaw with his fist. I stumbled across the room and said no more.

LEAVING HOME

Later, that night, when I was sure everyone was asleep, I went into the kitchen, for a glass of milk. There was a letter from my sister on the table. I took out the pages and read that she and her husband were back in Texas! They were going to live in Abilene for a while before coming on to Fort Worth. They had brought her husband's parents to live in Texas and were helping them get settled in, before it was time for the baby to be born! Then she had added, she hoped Momma and Daddy were happy they were going to be grandparents.

I wrote down the address and phone number she had included. I tried to eat a little something too but couldn't open my teeth enough to get anything into my mouth, so I went to bed, but I could not sleep. Very early the next morning, I slipped out of the house with only the clothes and shoes I had on and my book bag. I walked as far away from the house as I could before the city bus came along. The driver was the same one I had been riding into town with almost every morning. He wanted to know what I was doing out so early. I didn't answer, not because I didn't want to, it was because I couldn't; my mouth wouldn't open enough to talk. I took a seat and got out pen and paper, composing a lie to my boss.

I said I had a really bad tooth and it hurt terribly. I was going to the dentist and then to my sister's house because she was having a baby and needed me there to help her. I wrote that I didn't think I would be coming to work there any longer because my sister wanted me to come live with them. When I handed him the note and waited for him to read it. He took a good look at my swollen jaw. He said it looked like somebody had tried to get that tooth out the hard way. I didn't smile and neither did he. He told me that he had hoped I would stay on but understood that family came first. He also assured me that he would give me a good recommendation if I needed one, and If things didn't work out, I could come back to work there any time.

I walked to a shop down the street, bought a new skirt, top, underwear, and a pair of high heeled shoes, and my own bag of cosmetics. I then walked over to the bus station, which was only a couple of blocks away, went into the restroom, and changed into the new things I had purchased. I packed the clothes and shoes I had been wearing in the book bag, used the makeup and then stashed it in the bag too. Then I walked, as nicely as I could, in the tight skirt and high heeled shoes to the ticket counter, bought a one-way ticket to Abilene, got on the bus and was on my way.

I did not look back. I did not think about what my parents or little brothers would do, or think, once they realized I was gone. I just wanted my Daddy to remember what I had told him before he whipped me with the belt and hit me with his fist. I had not told them where I had been those six weeks of school I had missed. They didn't know I had any money and I figured I would never tell them either. As a matter of fact, I didn't intend to ever see my parents again if I could help it.

Most everybody on the bus seemed to be sleeping. I had deliberately stayed in the seat by the isle. The last thing I wanted was somebody sitting there chatting. In my mind, I was a mistreated young lady, who was making a break from the source of such treatment. Something caught my eye on the window side. Turning to see better what it was, I realized it was Serandica Pappas.

She was not smiling. In her eyes and tightened lips, I detected displeasure. She didn't move, just kept staring at me with an unpleasant look, which I had never seen on her face before. Using the most grown up voice I could I said, "Haven't found Justus yet?"

The look on her face stayed exactly the same. No answer. Trying again, I told her that I might be persuaded to help her look for him. That too got no response. Sitting quite a few more minutes, I heard her whisper in my ear, "You must go back."

Ready to argue that point, I whirled to face her, but she was gone. That incident got me started wondering where she went when she wasn't with me, or was she with me when I couldn't see her? Whispering toward the empty seat I asked if she was there. No reply. Well, I didn't care, she had assured me that I had a guardian angel watching over me and that was all I needed to know. I sat day dreaming about all the wonderful things I was going to do, now that I was a free woman. Yes, in my mind, I had become a woman the moment I had gone to work at that lunch counter.

It was late in the afternoon when the bus pulled into the station at Abilene. Rushing to the phone booth I dug in the book bag for the number I had copied from my sister's letter, dropped in a dime and waited for someone to answer. Nobody answered after a dozen rings. Outside again I stood thinking about whether I should call a taxi cab and go to the address which I had also copied from the letter or, just hang around the bus station awhile and try to call again. Looking this way and that up and down the familiar streets, I remembered that one of the girls I had made friends with at school, after Sofia had moved away, lived only three blocks from the bus station.

Quickly, I headed that way, thinking about my friend Betty and all the things we would have to talk about. High heeled shoes were the last thing I should have been wearing to walk in, but I was so proud to be wearing them I didn't notice the blister on the back of my heel. My jaw was better, and I could open my mouth.

I had planned on the way to my friend's house what I would tell them about why I had shown up at their door without notice. It was true that I didn't know their phone number, I thought as I raised my hand to knock on the door. Just then the door flew open and my friend's mother stood staring at me. I wasn't sure by her look if she remembered me or not, so I spoke up, reminding her who I was, then right in to why I was there.

It had gotten easy for me to lie lately and mixing truth with the lies made them seem not so bad. The story was that I had come to visit my sister, who had recently moved back to town from Kentucky, because she was going to have a baby and had asked for me to come and stay with her so that she would have someone to help her when it was time for the baby to be born.

By that time, Betty was at the door and glad to see me again. Her mother invited me in, then left the room so that Betty and I could visit awhile. We caught up on what had been going on with us over the past couple of years. I went as far as to tell Betty about the horrible junior high school I had gone to in Fort Worth and about the job I had at the lunch counter. She said she was just trying to get into high school before looking for a job. Of course, I did not tell her that I had been working instead of going to school.

After a while, I asked her if I could use their phone to call and see if my sister was home. Still, there was no answer and it was already dark outside. Betty's mother returned to ask if I would like to stay and eat supper with them. I told her I would and thanked her. She asked if I was sure my sister knew when to expect me. I replied that she might have forgotten, with all the trying to get her in-laws settled. Betty asked if I could spend the night with them if it was late when my sister answered the phone. Her mother said that would be fine and left us to ourselves again.

We sat on the front steps remembering the times we had ridden bicycles and roller skated up and down the block. We remembered the day we were allowed to go to the West Texas Fair alone on the city bus, how I had lost my spending money on one of the rides and Betty had shared her money with me and I, in return for that kindness, had drawn and painted a picture for her.

After supper was over and Betty and I had washed, dried and put away the dishes. I tried again to call my sister, but again no answer. Betty's mother said to keep on trying because my sister would worry if, perhaps, they had missed me at the bus station. I kept calling until after midnight. Finally, we went to bed. I would try again first thing in the morning. Betty dug out pajamas for me to sleep in, without question. When her mother came in to check on us, she asked if the rest of my things were at the bus station. I told her that my parents had sent them ahead a couple of days before I left. The more I lied, the better I got at it. She left the room without asking anymore questions. I left the number on the table by the phone so that I wouldn't have to dig it out of the bag again the next morning.

Early next morning I tried again to call. No answer. After breakfast Betty and I went for a walk. Walking uptown in Abilene was easy when you lived as close in as Betty and her family. We walked past the Windsor Hotel, past the post office, under the overpass and all the way to the big Thornton's department store a few blocks on the other side of the overpass.

It was a nice day. The wind was a little brisk, but that was nothing unusual for Abilene. We spent the rest of the morning exploring the store. It was the only one of its kind in town. Betty and I talked about the times our parents had taken us to the lovely old store to see the Christmas decorations displayed in all the front windows. The store covered the whole block. It boasted a bargain basement, a mezzanine and third floor. The escalator to and from all three levels was the first in town.

Before we started back to Betty's house, we went into the little cafeteria. It was my treat since I was the one with the money this time. We ate and talked some more about that day, long ago it seemed, when I had lost my money on one of the fair rides and Betty had shared her money with me. I was the happiest that afternoon, walking back across town to Betty's house than I had been in a very long time. We stopped a few minutes in front of the Paramount theater reading the playbills. We had decided to ask Betty's parents if we could go back later to watch a movie.

We were hurrying along at a pretty good pace, laughing and happy as could be. When we turned the corner onto Betty's street, I stopped in my tracks. Betty turned back to find out why I had stopped so suddenly. My heart seemed to be in my throat for a few seconds, my eyes felt glazed over. I took a deep breath and rubbed my eyes on the sleeve of my blouse, hoping I hadn't seen my Daddy's car by the curb in front of Betty's house. She asked what the matter was. I knew I was caught but could not tell her the truth. I wanted to turn and run away, but I knew it was too late, someone was walking toward us. It was my sister Billie, her husband Paul, and J.C., the oldest of the boys of our East Texas friends. I had not moved another step toward them. I told Betty who they were before they reached us and added that I wondered how they knew I was there.

Billie spoke first and told us that Betty's mom had found their number where I left it, on the bedside table, and had kept calling until she got them. They had spent the night at her in-law's new place and gotten home after eating breakfast with them. She said she had called J.C.'s parents to find out what was going on since our parents had no phone. J.C. And Paul stood quietly, letting Billie do all the talking. She said that J.C. had rushed right over to our parents' house with the news because our mother had already called from a pay phone to ask if I had come to their house.

Betty's eyes were full of question marks, but she didn't say a word. I thought to myself how I could defend the action I had taken. The lies wouldn't do any more. I had to tell the truth.

In a short version of what had happened I blurted out, what I felt was the truth. Billie gave me a hug, told me not to worry, everything would be alright, and we all started walking toward the house again. I kept saying over and over, that I was not going back to Fort Worth with my parents.

My parents had come into the yard and stood waiting for us; hands on hips Daddy took a few steps forward. Billie stepped between us and told him that it might be a good idea for them to all go to lunch and leave me to explain myself to Betty's parents. Daddy said he didn't think that would be a good idea, he sure wasn't going to give me the opportunity to take off again. J.C. stepped forward and said he would stay and keep an eye on me while they went to grab a bite to eat. That seemed to be acceptable to Daddy so off they went.

Right away I started apologizing to Betty and her parents. Betty's dad said it was sometimes hard for children and their parents to understand one another's' feelings. Betty and her mom looked as if they agreed. They asked J.C. and me if we wanted to come in and discuss things. Before I could answer, J.C. said it might be a good idea if we stayed out on the front steps. He thanked them for watching out for me and they went inside. I slumped down on the doorstep and J.C. sat down beside me. I was embarrassed that he and his family knew what had happened, but it didn't keep me from talking to him about it all.

He and two of his brothers had escorted Ronnie and me all over Fort Worth for almost two years. During that time, we had all become the best of friends. He asked why I hadn't come to him and his family for help when I needed it. The only answer I could give him was that I was ashamed of myself and hadn't wanted to face anybody I knew.

That was not the truth, I did not feel ashamed of myself. I was actually proud of myself. He told me that he wanted me to know that he and his family would always be there for me, no matter what, and to always call on them if I had a problem and they would help me work it out. Feeling it was time to remind him that I wasn't going back to Fort Worth with my parents, I opened my mouth to speak and Serandica Pappas showed up, standing behind him. She smiled and told me that I had to go back. She pointed to J.C. and said, "Go."

I did not say what I had planned to, instead I told him that I appreciated his concern, but I could not possibly live with my parents again. He asked me if I trusted him to help me with things. I was silent a few minutes, so he spoke up again. He said there was only two ways to go at it, the hard way or the easy way. Without giving me time to say anything, he went on to tell me that I could go back with them and give him a chance to try to help me or, I could run away again, and my parents would bring law enforcement into it and make me stay with them. He said that I should not consider running away again, because that would prove me to be just like some of the kids in that junior high that I hated so much.

I kept trying to speak but he went right on with what he wanted to say. He told me when Daddy stopped at the curb, I was to walk out beside him, get in the car and keep my mouth shut. He said if I had to give an answer to be sure it was a polite and respectable one.

At that point it was beginning to sound as if I was the one who had done all the bad, and I was not going to let it rest. I got up, stood in front of him and told him in no uncertain terms that I would not be respectful to my parents if they didn't have any respect for me. The next words out of his mouth were, that I should lower my voice. I turned away thinking "Who are you to be telling me what I should do and what I should not do?"

Feeling the anger boiling up within myself, I turned on him and asked what gave him the right to be bossing me around. He smiled and told me that he was older than I was for one thing, and another was that he somehow felt my pain and wanted to help me, if I would let him. I looked him in the eyes and felt something which I did not understand. My heart was telling me he meant what he said. My mind was telling me not to trust anybody.

Then he stood up, stretched and said they should be back at any moment, and I should do as he had said so we could get back and get the whole situation under control. I knew that would mean going back to school. Knowing how much I had already missed, I wasn't sure I could cope with it if I didn't make my grades. It seemed like a lose-lose situation for me. His back was turned to me when Serandica Pappas popped up between us. She moved close to my face and whispered, "Go, he is your Justus."

Confused, I whispered back, "How can he get justice for me?"

She put her finger to her lips and shook her head, then she said again,

"He is your Justus."

All I thought at the moment was, she must be saying he was my guardian angel. Just then the car came to a stop at the curb. I stood perfectly still, feeling stuck to the side walk. Daddy started to get out of the car, but J.C. called out that I would be there as soon as I got my bag. He walked back for the bag that Betty was handing me, took my hand in his and said, "Let's go."

With my hand in his, I felt no urge to pull away, so I walked beside him to the car. He opened the door and I slid into the backseat beside my two little brothers who began to hug me and tell me how glad they were that I was going with them. My parents didn't speak a word to me. J.C. got into the seat beside me and once more we were on our way to cow town.

It was late when we got to the house in Fort Worth. J.C.'s car was parked in the driveway. When he got out to move it so that Daddy could park in the driveway, I was right on his heels. My little brothers were both asleep, so he helped Daddy carry them into the house. I stayed in his car.

My mind was made up, I was not going in that house alone to face my parents. When he came back out he told me that they said it was alright for me to go with him to get something to eat. He was going to pick up takeout food for everybody at the burger joint a few blocks away. While we waited for the food we sipped on big frosty mugs of root beer. He said it tasted particularly good because he hadn't eaten anything since breakfast. That made me feel sorry for him, but he just laughed and told me it was worth it all to have me back where I belonged.

Thinking I wasn't so sure of that, I reached for the book bag to get some money out to help pay for the food. Figuring it was the least I could do. When I peeled off a twenty-dollar bill, he shook his head and asked me where I had been going all those days when I didn't go to school and where I had gotten all that money. I told him. Then he laughed and told me I wasn't such a bad kid after all. I told him I wasn't a kid and I would appreciate it if he didn't refer to me as one.

I pulled out the high heels and the skirt from the bag and told him that was the way I intended to dress from then on. He frowned and said that while I might think myself a grown woman, I had a whole lot of growing up to do. Then he smiled again and told me that I might be growing up, but I wasn't nearly grown up enough to wear such things. I reminded him that he wasn't the boss of me.

The food came and back to my parents' house we went. Again, I refused to go inside. The two of us sat on the front porch and ate our hamburgers, fries and more root beer. The moon was big and high in the sky. It was a beautiful night, for which I was glad, not wanting to go inside.

Finally, he asked if I would go in to bed if he slept in his car. When I said no, he said, "Okay. What if I sleep on the sofa?"

We then had to go find a payphone, so he could call and let his parents know that we were back, and all was well, so far. He told them he would be home when he was sure I was out of harm's way. The house was completely dark when we got back. He went straight for the sofa. Propping his head on one end and feet on the other and told me to go to bed, he would see me in the morning. I made him promise that he would be there, or I would take the money I had left and leave and none of them would find me next time. He squeezed my hand tightly and said "Now you know you don't want to do that. Go on in there and get in bed. I told you I would be here in the morning and I will."

My bed did not feel right to me anymore. I tossed and turned and could not get comfortable until I saw Serandica Pappas at the foot of the bed. There was a golden glow around her. She looked so happy. I asked if she had found Justus. She nodded then pointed toward the living room with her right hand and put the other one over her heart and said, "My Justus, your Justus."

I wanted to ask her to explain what she was telling me, but she was already gone before I could speak. I fell asleep feeling that my guardian angel was on the living room sofa, keeping me safe.

HEART TROUBLES

Upon waking the next morning, which was Monday, and finding the house empty, except for me, I almost panicked. Daddy's car was not in the drive way and J.C.'s car was nowhere in sight. After a few minutes I decided that Daddy had gone to work and Ronnie to school, but where was Momma and my little brother, and where was my guardian angel, who had promised to be there?

I sat on the back porch, thinking things through for a long time. It was ten a.m. and I had never been allowed to sleep so late. I heard a car door slam, so I ran out of the back yard and around to the front of the house, to be sure of who was there.

I was sure I was not going to let my dad use the belt on me anymore and wanted to make sure it wasn't him. It was J. C. helping Momma and both my little brothers out of the car. I hurried over, but stood silent, waiting for someone to tell me what was going on. Momma rushed the two little boys into the house without a word. When she had shut the door, J.C. told me to come with him.

I didn't ask why or where or anything else, I just hopped right into his car and away we went. He spoke first. He told me that we were going to his parents' house, where we could both get cleaned up, since neither of us had a bath in the last three days. I told him that all the clothes I had with me were the ones I had on and those in my book bag, which was still in his car. He told me not to worry about it that his mother would find something at their house for me to put on while she washed and dried the clothes I was wearing. That sounded alright to me.

I asked him where he had been with Momma and my brothers. He told me that Momma had ask him to give her a ride to the doctor's office. I asked if she was sick and he said, "No, it's Ronnie."

That disturbed me, and I asked what was wrong with my brother. He told me that I should talk to my mom about it. I wanted to know if it was anything serious. He said he thought it was, and I should talk to my mother about it. I asked why he hadn't someone told me before we left the house. He replied that he and I had important business to attend to. At first, I couldn't think of anything being more important than my little brother being sick, then my mind flashed back to the night before, and I figured that was what he meant.

His mother greeted me as she always had. She didn't scold me or tease me. J.C. asked if she thought they could round me up something to wear while my clothes were being washed and dried. She said she was sure she could and hurried off to find the clothes.

He said that his mother and youngest brother were the only ones at home and that his mom wanted to go stay with my mother the rest of the day, while he and I took care of the business of my getting back into school. Again, I reminded him that I was not going back to the same school. He told me that he hadn't forgotten and had a plan.

His mother came back with some clothes of the younger boys and told me to use anything that I wanted to of them while my clothes were in the washer. She also told J.C. to go ahead and get cleaned up and she would start my clothes. When he left the room, she told that she was sorry she wouldn't be there to help me get ready for the meeting, but she thought it was better for her to go spend the day with my mother. Then she said that while I got cleaned up, J.C. would take her and her youngest to our apartment. She explained that I should not to be afraid alone in their house, it was a good neighborhood and the doors and windows were locked. I didn't understand it all but, went along with it as it seemed at the moment I had no other choice, and I did not like that one bit.

When J.C. came back into the living room, his mother told me to go ahead and get cleaned up and J.C. would be back for me in a little while. She instructed me to hang my clothes on the line to dry once they were done washing and to iron them if I needed. She showed me the ironing board on the screened in porch and said that the iron is still out.

I watched them leave and thought about leaving again myself. I still had around a hundred dollars in my book bag. I could put on my new things, just as I had when I left for Abilene. I could call a taxi cab and be at the bus station and gone before anybody knew it. My mind rushed over my options and the only place I could go was to East Texas, where all my aunts, uncles and cousins lived, but that was where I had been when we had to leave because my asthma was so bad. The only thing left for me to do at the moment was wait and see what J.C.'s plan amounted to. Meantime, maybe I could think of somewhere I could go if things didn't work out in my favor.

While I was taking a bath, I wondered what was wrong with my little brother. Then I wondered what the meeting J.C.'s mother had mentioned would be about other than my getting back in school. I had put way too much shampoo in my hair and was having trouble getting it all out, but I knew I had to get it done and be ready to go when J.C. returned. I finally got it done and put it up in a pony tail, then I went out back to the clothes line, got my own clothes, brought them in, ironed them and still had time to spare.

Again, something inside me told me to call a cab and be on my way but, Serandica Pappas showed up shaking her head and giving me that stern look of hers, which I wasn't too fond of. She didn't say a word and I knew she wanted me to do what J.C. said for me to do. I left her in the living room and went into the bathroom, picked up my wet towels and took them to the laundry room along with the clothes which had been lent to me. She followed me with that look until A key turned in the lock on the front door. When J.C. entered the room, she was gone in a flash.

J.C. asked if I was finished getting read. In response, I picked up my book bag and followed him out. He opened the car door and reached for the bag to put it in the trunk of the car. He held it up, frowning and said, "There's no books in there, right?"

I shook my head and once again we were on the road somewhere. On the way he told me he was taking his vacation early in order to help me get my life straightened, out and that he would be very disappointed if I did anything silly, like running off again. The car was on the freeway. I didn't ask where we were going. At the moment I didn't really care. He turned on the radio and we didn't talk. After a while he turned right at a small grocery store and headed down a dirt road. There was a Y in the road where he went to the right. The car slid to a stop under a huge oak tree, in front of a neat looking old house with a porch across the front and a porch swing, which was swaying gently in the breeze. There were no other cars that I could see. I asked what the place was, and he replied that it might just be my new home.

As usual, I didn't know what he meant so I just followed him to the door. He knocked a couple of times, then we were greeted by an elderly gentleman who led us into a room he called "the parlor," where a trim little elderly lady sat with another younger woman on the sofa. They both got up when we entered the room. The younger woman looked as if she might be Momma's age. I was introduced to her by J.C., who said she was a social worker that attended the same church his family did, and he had taken liberty of discussing my situation with her. The older couple were her parents and at various times they took on some of the children their daughter felt were worth trying to help.

She spoke freely in front of her parents about what J.C. had told her about my circumstances. I wondered if I was going to be allowed to say anything on my own behalf. It turned out that she already knew everything I would have told her, so I sat with my head down and my mouth shut.

Finally, she got up and said she wanted to show us around the house. She went through the living room and opened a door to a small but nicely made up bedroom with a lovely pink comforter and ruffled pink curtains over wide windows on the front and side. It was a light, bright room. She told me if she was able to work with my parents and get their permission, the room would be mine to use for the duration. I wondered what she meant by that, but thought, it might be better to keep my mouth shut.

When the tour of the house ended she told me she would be at my parents address around seven p.m. and added that I looked like the kind of girl who would appreciate the help I was being offered. J.C. assured her that I would be there. I thanked her, and we got in his car. He asked me if I would like to visit the school I would attend if everything worked out. My heart told me to ignore his question, but my mind told me to be calm. Don't rock the boat. I nodded, and we were off in the direction of the highway. I asked what town it was, and he said it really wasn't a town, it was a little community, with its own school.

When we reached the highway instead of turning left, which would have taken us back into the greater Fort Worth area, he stopped looked both ways and sped across the highway into a big parking lot. There were quite a few cars, so he drove around until he found a parking place. He got out came around to my side of the car, opened the door and told me to get out and we would look around the campus.

Until that moment I had not noticed the two buildings which sat farther back from the highway. There was a U.S. flag fluttering in the breeze, so I assumed those buildings were the school. A bell rung loudly, and kids started pouring out of both buildings. Some were getting into cars out front, others into cars on the parking lot, most speeding away as if they were going to a fire or something.

I noticed that the kids from the one-story building were much younger than the ones coming from the older looking three-story building. While we were walking around I also noticed there was a football field with bleachers behind the older looking building. I asked why there were little children and big kids all at the same place. He told me that the newer looking one-story building was for kids up to the eighth grade and the older three-story was for kids from the ninth to twelfth grades. There was no "Junior High."

We walked around the whole campus looked inside the gymnasium then we went back to the car. He asked me if I was hungry. I was so we drove back toward Fort Worth stopping at the first burger joint and stuffing ourselves with cheese fries and malted shakes. Carhops on roller skates brought out trays of food and placed them carefully at the car windows. I admired their skating ability, wishing I could skate that well.

While we were eating, J.C. told me about his plan. He said, if things worked out, he would bring my things to the place we had just been, help me get enrolled in school there and help me with my homework every evening when he got off work. That sounded good. I wanted to know how the social worker knew so much about me. He told me that his mother had asked my mother if there was anything she could do to help, before they left to go to Abilene to bring me home.

He said my parents had told his parents that they would appreciate any help they could get which concerned me and getting me back in school. His parents were friends with the lady who was the social worker. She not only went to the same church, she lived only a short distance from them. His parents had asked her help on my behalf. She had suggested a short period of separation sometimes was all it took to get teens and their parents back on the same track. I wanted to know if she knew my side of the story. He said there would be plenty of time for that because the woman would be paying me visits as well as getting feedback from her parents on my behavior.

He told me he thought it would be smart of me to decide if that was what I wanted to do before our meeting with my parents that evening. I wanted to know how soon I could move into the old couple's house! Anything would be better than having to live with my parents again. He said as far as he knew, I could go there as soon as my parents signed whatever papers they needed to sign. I told him that I thought it was a good plan but wouldn't hold my breath. He laughed and asked if I had another one so well executed. I didn't know what he meant so I just smiled. He chucked my chin and we were on our way into town again.

One thing was tugging at my mind. I had some money left but I was sure it wouldn't last too long, so I asked if he thought it would be a good idea for me to go back to work. He said, "Weekends only."

J.C. suggested taking me by to see if the offer for me to work at the soda fountain again was still good. He told me to explain that I would be living outside of town, and weekends, until school was out for the summer, would be all I could handle because that school did not offer a half day program. If the offer for full time work during the summer was still open to me to take it, if I was sure that was what I wanted to do. I knew that was what I wanted to do but how was I going to get back and forth to work? Once more, J.C. was way ahead of me. He would be taking me to work, picking me back up after work and bringing me home. Then he added, "That's what friends do, they help one another."

My boss was happy as he could be that I was coming back to work, and the other workers seemed to like me and were glad I was still going to be coming back as well. The last word from my boss as I was leaving was, "Be sure and get that social security number in here."

It was settled as far as I was concerned, and I couldn't keep from smiling. We picked up J.C.'s mom and little brother and took them back to their house so that his mother could get supper ready. She asked J.C. if he was going to be there for supper. He said no, his plan was to stick with me until I was settled in my new situation. We waved bye to them and were off again.

J.C. said, "I'm getting a little tired of this car. What do you say to a round of miniature golf or two before we go for the meeting with your parents?"

I told him I had never played the game before and told me not to worry, he was a miniature golf pro. I didn't know what being a "pro" meant but he was laughing so I figured it was something good. By the time we left to go to the meeting with my parents and the social worker, I knew all there was to know about miniature golf and never forgot how much I enjoyed learning about it, or how relaxed I was, when we faced my parents that evening.

We sat in the car until the social worker got there. My family had finished their dinner and sat around the cleared table playing a game of Chinese checkers. I had never known my parents to play any game other than dominoes. Ronnie and Robert seemed to be enjoying it very much. Daddy said, in an almost too pleasant voice, "Come in. Come in and sit down."

Then Daddy told the boys to take the game into their room and play until the grownups were done visiting. Nervously, I sat down and made sure I stayed between J.C. and the social worker. Before any formal conversation began, Momma said she had something really important to say to me and she wanted to tell me before anything else was brought up.

You could have knocked me over with a feather when she said that my little brother Ronnie was going to have major surgery. Without waiting for me to get a grip on myself and ask any questions, she went on to tell me that she thought it was awfully selfish of me to be only thinking of what I wanted, when my little brother was facing such an ordeal, and when she and daddy were so desperately in need of my help.

I could not be silent a minute longer. I wanted to know what kind of surgery he was going to have and when he would be having it. She fired back with, "It's his heart. They are going to have to go in and repair it, and it will be as soon as we find out if we can get any help with paying the hospital bill."

I asked what would happen if he didn't have the surgery and she yelled at me, "He could die!"

Part of me wanted to ask forgiveness for the trouble I had caused them and tell them that I would stay home and do anything they wanted me to do until my little brother was well again. Instead, a voice that didn't really sound like my own came out of my mouth with. "I am truly sorry that Ronnie has to have a horrible operation, and I will do all I can to help when the time comes, but I cannot live with you and Daddy anymore. I love you with all my heart, and I always will, but I will have to do what I can to help with things from somewhere else. I will not take a chance on being whipped with a belt or hit with a fist again, not from Daddy or anyone else."

The pleasant look on Daddy's face changed to one of anger. Momma drew her lips into a fine line. The social worker told me to go and pack whatever I wanted to take with me and she would discuss the separation and what was involved where all of us were concerned.

I got up from the table and started walking slowly to my room. J.C. got up to follow and then I heard a chair being scooted across the floor and turned to see Daddy in J.C.'s face. He said, "Boy, did you have anything to do with all this?"

Calmly but firmly J.C. said, "First, don't call me boy, and second, yes I did."

They stood glaring at one another. The social worker banged on the table with a heavy glass someone had been drinking iced tea from. Her voice was calm when she asked Momma if she had solicited her friend, J.C.'s mother, to help with our situation. Momma explained that she had asked for help because I had threatened to run away again. When Daddy sat back down in his chair, staring now at Momma, the social worker got out some papers and a pen from her briefcase, laid them on the table and began to tell my parents what she proposed.

I went on into my room and started gathering up everything I felt I couldn't leave behind. I was sure the move was going to be a permanent one. When I had finished, I went into the room where my little brothers sat in the floor playing the game of checkers. I sat down with them and told them that I would not be living at home anymore, but I would try to come and see them. Ronnie asked me if I would come when he went to the hospital. I gave him a long assuring hug and told him that nobody had better try to keep me away.

He asked me if I knew he might get to meet a famous movie star when his surgery was finished. I told him how wonderful that would be. Little Robert was just at the mischievous age. When I tried to give him a hug he pointed his finger at me and said, "If you run off again, I am going to get the 'tater masher and mash you like a baked 'tater."

Ronnie started laughing and so did I. Then Ronnie said, "Maybe if we could move back to West Texas, my heart would get better, like your asthma did."

I told him that would be a good idea, maybe he should talk to Momma and Daddy about it later. I gave them another hug and I told them I would be going but hoped to see them really soon. We all blew kisses until I was out of sight up the hallway and tears began to pour from my eyes. I had to stop in at the bathroom and clean up my face.

Before I knew what was happening I was whisked away to my new home and spent most of the evening there unpacking. The elderly lady, Mrs. Jones, came into the room, gave me a key to the front door of the house and sked if there was anything I needed that I didn't bring with me. I told her that I thought I had everything. She turned to J.C. and told him not to make a habit of being in my room. He replied that he had known me since I was in diapers. She said, "Just mind your manners young man."

J.C. asked me if I was going to be alright staying there alone the first few nights. He offered to sleep in his car, which was parked only a few feet away if I wanted him to. I told him that I wasn't one bit scared. Then I asked him how far he thought it was to the school. He said it wasn't over a mile but for me to sit tight the next morning and he would be there to help me get enrolled in school and show me around that community.

I watched him drive away into the night until I couldn't see the car lights any more, then I closed the door and locked it and went into my new room to lay down on what happened to be the most comfortable bed I had ever been on. I must have fallen asleep with the light on and without turning down the covers, but it was the best night's sleep ever, and I awoke a happy young lady.

In the months ahead, my grades at school soared, due to the fact that J.C. had kept his word. He had been there every day to help me in any way I needed him to. After work he came straight to my house, until dinner time.

My little brother came through the heart surgery and recovered enough by Valentine's Day to present a huge heart shaped box of candy to Miss Lucile Ball. The American Heart Association had helped pay for his surgery. In his little suit and tie, and the biggest smile I had ever seen on a little boy, he greeted Miss Ball at the airport. The American Heart Associate was her charity and she was in town for a meeting. Their picture was in the paper and he was a happy little boy and I was happy for him being so brave.

During that year, J.C. And I became inseparable. When school was out for the summer I worked full-time. The only thing that kept us apart was our work. He would leave the house in the country and go to his parents' house after midnight. By eight a.m., he was back at my house again.

We ate our meals together. We confided everything to one another. He was my hero. His strength, his knowledge, his easy way with me, had me on cloud nine. My self-esteem soared, and I was the happiest girl in the world.

Things kept getting better. One weekend I didn't have to work. Two whole days off! J.C. suggested that we go out to Benbrook Lake. He said the spillway was over flowing because there had been more rain than normal, and people drove their cars onto the concreted area behind the dam and washed them. He also said he might give me a driving lesson if I helped him clean the car. I had been wanting to learn to drive so it was a deal.

I hurried into my room and slipped into a pair of cut offs and a backless halter top, grabbed a pair of tennis shoes and hurried out to the car where he was waiting patiently. We stopped for carry-out burgers and root beer, then drove to the lake chatting happily, enjoying our food and soda on the way. There were whole families out there washing their cars. I could see that the water was only a little over ankle deep, so it didn't scare me when J.C. drove his little blue Plymouth into the water until it touched the bumpers.

I hadn't put on my shoes, so I watched as J. C. opened the car door and started to remove his boots. He stopped suddenly and said, "These things are not coming off. Come around here and help me."

I had seen girls helping pull off a cowboy's boots in some of the western movies, so it didn't surprise me when he asked my help. I waded in the water around to his side of the car. He stuck out his leg and I pulled the boot from his foot easily enough. He took it and threw it into the back seat along with the sock and put his unshod foot into the water. There was a big smile on his face when he lifted the other foot up to me. Just as the boot was slipping from his foot he stretched his leg forward rather quickly, sending me stumbling backward into the shallow water. He jumped up grabbed the boot before it went into the water, threw it and the other sock into the back seat and held out a hand to help me up. He said, "We should have brought a camera. That would have been a good one for your school year book."

My face was red with anger. I didn't think it was a bit funny and told him so. He said, "A little water never hurt anybody." then walked around to the back of the car and brought out a couple of pails and some old rags.

Pouting was something I was good at, so that's what I did the whole time we were washing the car. Finally, the opportunity I had been waiting on came. He was squatting, scrubbing furiously on a wheel. His back was turned to me. I was working on the back bumper a couple of feet behind him. I dipped my pail in the water until it was almost full then turned, taking one step and emptied it all on top of his head. He stood slowly turned to face me. His look let me know it was time to run. I sloshed around the car trying to put distance between us, but I was too slow. He grabbed me whirled me around, so I could see that he was smiling, then he threw me down into the water and drug me around until my clothes were completely saturated. I was begging him to stop, which he finally did. He picked me up and set me on the car fender, handed me a dry rag to wipe the water from my eyes then took his comb out of his hip pocket and started combing his hair.

He was grinning when he said, "If you want to pick on somebody, you better do it to somebody your own size."

Not to be out done, I said, "Maybe you should do the same."

He really laughed, then and said, "You are absolutely right and, so am I."

We stretched out on the car hood to let our clothes dry and talked about things we remembered happening when we were little kids. We had been singing with the car radio, both of us terribly off key, when it got so bad we couldn't stand to hear ourselves, he said, "Come on. We are dry enough. Let's go."

When he drove out of the water he turned onto the road in the direction which led around the side of the lake instead of the one back to the highway. A little way down the road he stopped the car, got his boots and socks and my shoes, handed me mine and said, "Put 'em on. You can't drive barefoot."

I wanted to know why I couldn't drive barefooted. He said, "It's against the law."

I hurriedly got into my shoes. When he had gotten his boots on and straightened his pants legs just so, he came around to the passenger side and told me to slide over behind the wheel. I sat stiffly awaiting his command to start the engine. Instead, I had to listen to a long lecture of do'-s and don'ts, ending with, "Do exactly as I tell you or this will also be your last driving lesson from me."

I said, "You don't have to be so mean all the time." He drew down his chin and gave me the bad eye.

"I am not trying to be mean to you, but you had better remember what I just told you." he said.

When I didn't answer he took a deep breath, let it out and said, "Now you can turn on the key."

I could barely see over the steering wheel. He said, "Uh-oh, I forgot to adjust the seat for you."

It had to be done. I could not reach the brake and clutch even sitting on the edge of the seat and stretching my legs. I was proud of myself for turning the key off without having to be told. No comment. He came around, helped me get the seat right then told me to adjust the rear-view mirror and the driver side mirror making sure I could see clearly what was behind and beside the car.

Driving turned out to be more of a chore than I had imagined. After much lurching forward, screeching brakes and running off the narrow road, I finally got the gear shifting, starting and stopping and keeping the car on the road done right. I was driving! For the first time in my life! After an hour of it J.C. said, "Enough for one day."

I stopped the car. We switched places and headed for town. "How about a round of miniature golf and supper before we go back to the house?" he said. Nothing could have pleased me more.

My summer had been as good as it gets. I was feeling a little down with school starting in less than a week. Thursday was registration and homeroom assignments. Friday was assembly and "meet the teachers" day. I was moping around in my room on Sunday morning trying to decide if I should spend some of the money I had been hoarding for some new school clothes.

My work schedule had already been changed to weekends only with every third weekend off. I was already missing my weekends with J.C. and that hadn't even started yet. Mrs. Jones came to my door and said she and Papa were about to leave for church. They would be late coming home because it was dinner and song night at church. She told me to be sure and lock the front door if I left the house.

After a while I got dressed and went out to sit on the porch swing. It was a beautiful morning, not too hot. The roses were blooming. Blue and white morning glories were still open, the vines wrapping themselves artfully climbing the porch posts. It was peaceful and quiet and lovely. Wondering what could possibly be nicer I lay back in the swing and rocked myself by pushing at the boards with my feet.

J.C. didn't usually come out until after lunch, so it surprised me when his car stopped at the gate. I didn't get up from the swing and run to meet him the way I had always done. What could have brought him out so early?

He was smiling as he stepped up on the porch, skipping the three steps completely. He was tall, and his legs were long and strong. I had seen him do the same thing before, but something seemed different in his manner. He sat down beside me in the swing, stretched his legs and crossed his booted feet at the ankles and spread his arms across the back of the swing. He took a deep breath of the morning air, let it out, then said, "Nice morning."

I wanted to know what brought him out so early. He said he had been thinking about school starting and figured we should go in and get the things I was going to need. The department stores were going to open early and close late. Most of them were closed on Sunday but all of them opened the last Sunday before school started so that everybody could do their last-minute shopping. Noticing that he was in his jeans and not his Sunday best and feeling a little lazy I said, "If casual is good, I'm ready to go."

He said, "Casual is great. We can grab some breakfast. I don't know about you, but I haven't had mine yet."

I told him I hadn't eaten either and went inside to get my purse. I dug out the money I had been saving then turned to find him standing in the doorway of my room. He was just standing there looking at me, but there was something different in the way he was looking at me. I said, "What?

Should I change into something else?"

He shook his head no, then said "You are perfect, just the way you are."

A little chill ran through me. I shrugged it off and stuffed the money into my handbag then said, "I am ready if you are."

He didn't move out of the doorway, so I asked, "Am I forgetting something?"

He shook his head no and stepped back enough for me to squeeze through the door but not enough to keep my body from coming in contact with his as I passed. I felt that chill and kind of a tingle again. Something was different. Not knowing what it was, I fumbled for the door key which had gone to the bottom of my handbag. He was standing very close behind me. I could feel the heat radiating from his body. He reached around my shoulders, took the purse from my hands and held it open using both hands. He said, "Here, I will hold it. You dig for the key."

For a few seconds I actually couldn't see, but I kept digging hoping he wouldn't notice how nervous the closeness of his body to mine was making me. The key somehow turned up in my hand. We stepped out on the porch. I locked the door and noticed he was still standing close. He usually went to the car and had started it by the time I got the door locked. When we started down the steps he placed his hand around my upper arm as if he was afraid I might trip on the steps. He opened the car door for me and when I was seated he closed it. I was perplexed. There was something going on with him which was different.

We ate our late breakfast then drove downtown to one of the department stores. He said I could probably find everything I needed there without us having to drive all over town. He left me trying on clothes and told me he would be back in an hour. There were some things marked down which made my money go farther. My shopping bag was getting heavy. I had bought a pair of penny loafers and a pair of dress shoes with two-inch wedged heels, three blouses, two skirts, one full, the other tight fitting and new panties and bras.

The new bras were 'B' instead of 'A' cup size. The dressing room mirror revealed a curvier body than I had been used to having. I didn't care what anyone thought about my wearing tight skirts. I was beginning to have curves and I wanted to show them off.

When J.C. came back empty handed, I was surprised that he hadn't bought anything and told him so. He said he wasn't the one going back to school. When I said he was the lucky one, he launched into a lecture about the necessity of a good education, which lasted until we got near the Forest Park area. We had to stop there and play a few rounds of miniature golf. I couldn't seem to make par on a couple of holes, the same ones I always failed to make par on. He always made par on them and decided to show me how it was done. You had to tap the ball in a manner which made it hit the side board in just the right place sending it straight into the hole.

In order to show me how to hold and swing the club properly, he had to stand behind me, placing his hands over mine causing our bodies to move together when tapping the ball. Our faces were even very close together. His cologne smelled good. His hands over mine were warm and sure. Before long, with his help, the ball started sinking into the hole every time. When he moved away and told me to try it myself, I missed it again and again. He showed me how it was done over and over. I think we were both probably enjoying the body contact more than we should have been doing.

After two games he asked if I would like to go on a picnic. One of his co-workers had bought a lake house. They had used it all summer, but they had children. With school starting they would not be using it much. J.C, they had said, was welcome to go out there for rest and relaxation anytime he wanted. He said the guy sympathized with his living at home with his parents not knowing how good he actually had it there.

I was not about to pass up a picnic on such a beautiful day. We bought lunch meat, bread, chips, cookies, soda and ice for the chest which he always kept in the trunk of his car. When we finally found the place, it was nice. The house wasn't a big one, but it was clean and roomy inside. We found a table cloth and went down by the lake for our picnic.

He asked if I wanted to take a dip in the lake before we ate. I pointed at myself and looked at him as if there was no way I could get into the water in a skirt and blouse. He laughed and asked if I had never heard of skinny dipping. My mouth flew open wide. He said, "Fine, I am going in." and he pulled off his boots and socks and took off his top shirt, then lay back on his elbow smiling.

I said, "Well, don't let me stop you."

He said, "Nah, wouldn't be any fun all by myself."

I didn't want to seem childish, so I said, "Maybe some other time," and started making sandwiches.

I caught him looking at me several times in the way he had earlier. I tried to ignore it, but it was so intense at one point, I had to ask, "Why are you looking at me that way?"

He said, "You're changing. You are growing up rather nicely. I like looking at you."

What could I say to that? I shrugged, which was my usual way of letting something go when I had no answer. He asked if his looking at me bothered me or made me feel uncomfortable. I lied and told him it didn't bother me at all.

It was dusk when we left the lake. Neither of us wanted to go but we had eaten all the food and soda, while lounging around all afternoon talking about all the good times we had as children and what good times we had been having together over the past couple of years. Then we moved on to how people should make plans for the future. He said we had to look at the big picture while deciding what we wanted out of life. I didn't understand exactly what he meant but I always enjoyed listening to him talk. It was late when he took me home. It had been such a wonderful day I wished it could have lasted forever.

The lights were all out in the Joneses house. I tiptoed very quietly into my room setting the shopping bag on the bed. When I turned around. J.C. was standing so close behind me that it startled me. I whispered, "You are not supposed to be in my room."

He put his mouth close to my ear and said, "I know."

He placed a couple of fingers under my chin tilting it upward and kissed me gently. Then he gathered me into his arms lifting me off my feet and kissed me on the mouth, and I liked it. I didn't try to pull away from him, so he kissed me again and I kissed him back, liking it even better. Still whispering close to my ear, he said, "You know you are my little sweetheart, don't you?"

My arms went around his neck and I whispered back, "I do now."

He kissed me again then let my body slide slowly back to the floor. We walked back out onto the porch, which took some effort on my part. I was week in the knees from the excitement I had just experienced. I didn't want him to go. He said if he didn't go then he wouldn't go at all. He squeezed my hand tightly and told me to go in to bed, we would have many more happy days together. He waited on the porch until the lock clicked shut then went to his car and drove away, leaving me wondering about it all.

Over the next few months I was happier than I had ever thought a person could be. Some days I felt like Cinderella must have, after her prince found her. Nothing else mattered to me as much as being with him. He was always there. I knew he felt the same way about me. For my birthday he gave me a beautiful little round music box. He said it was an antique. It had been made in Germany. It was pale green porcelain and ivory, trimmed in fourteen caret gold. There was a mirror inside the lid and a thin gold plated, shallow place for face powder, which could be lifted out revealing a compartment for storing tiny objects like rings, ear rings, necklaces or bracelets. It played "Let Me Call You Sweetheart" softly and beautifully. I knew I would cherish it always.

By Thanksgiving we were discussing getting married someday. He said it would have to be awhile because we couldn't get a license without my parents' signatures. We both knew that wasn't going to happen. They were already mad because I did not come home for Thanksgiving.

When the Joneses found out I wasn't going home, they graciously invited J.C. and me to share dinner with them. Their daughter was spending the day with her husband's family. Christmas would be the same. They rotated between their parents' houses in that manner every year.

To my surprise, J.C. agreed to be there. His mother must have hit the ceiling when he told her because he was back in the country with me before noon saying he didn't intend to be tied to his mother's apron strings the rest of his life. The Joneses were not going to have dinner until evening. Their church was having something earlier in the day they wanted to attend. We asked if there was anything we could get or do to help with dinner. Mr. Jones spoke right up, "Mother has stuffed a turkey in there big enough to feed the whole community. I sure would appreciate it if you could put it in the oven for us in a couple of hours."

That he said looking at J.C., who assured him he would tend to it. I could set the table, being sure to use the good plates, glasses and silverware. A few more instructions and we were left to ourselves. We went out to sit on the front porch. It wasn't cold enough for even a wrap. It was nice just sitting there together. He said, "A penny for your thoughts,"

I teased back with, "My thoughts are worth much more than that."

He kissed me lightly then said, "Will that do for a down payment?"

"Actually, I was wondering how long it will be until we get married."

He held his eyes on mine and asked, "Do you really think you are ready for marriage?"

Without removing my eyes from his I said, "You know I am. I would follow you to the end of the earth and never ask why we were going there."

His eyes were still glued to mine. He said, "We can talk about it when you finish high school."

My mouth flew open and the words came tumbling out with force. "What? That is almost three years!"

I got up and walked a few steps away. Tears burned my eyes. I couldn't hold them back. He came to me and wrapped his arms around me holding me tightly. He said, "This was supposed to have been a happy day. I'm sorry if I've upset you."

He brought out his handkerchief and dabbed at my teary eyes, but I couldn't stop them from gushing more. He sat down in the chair by the door and pulled me onto his lap. His voice was low and comforting. He said, "Marriage is something I want you to be very sure about before we go there. I don't plan to go through another divorce. Ever. When you and I make our vows, it's going to be forever. I want you now, body and soul, but I want you to be absolutely sure. I want you to have your high school experience with the freedom you deserve. I am prepared to wait until you have finished college. If you decide you want to go I will help you every step of the way. You are still too young to know what you want for sure, and I am not going to hinder you from finding out. We cannot just jump into marriage without really thinking it through. I learned that the hard way. You deserve the best of everything and I want to help you get it, but we have to wait on the getting married part."

The tears had slowed to a trickle. The whole front of his shirt was wet where my head had rested against his chest. He lifted my chin and kissed me ever so gently again then said, "Let's keep going the way we are until spring before we talk about it anymore. Right now, we better get in there and put that turkey in the oven."

We were engaged! My ring was white gold with a tiny diamond which sparkled in the light and reminded me of the Christmas star. He had also bought a set of gold wedding bands. They were beautiful and meaningful. I wanted to get married right away but he was adamant on waiting until I finished high school. We had never discussed the fact that J.C. had been married. It had never even crossed my mind.

The only thing I knew about it was that he and a girl he had gone to school with had gotten married right after they graduated from high school. They weren't right for one another, so they got divorced. That was the end of the matter as far as I was concerned. I was his one and only now and it was going to stay that way forever. Maybe we weren't married in the church yet, but we had spoken our vows before God and the whole universe out on the lake earlier in the summer. Vows of forever. Someday we would do the usual ceremony, but the vows we made out on the lake, were the ones that counted the most to us.

One Sunday morning after the Joneses had left for church, I was getting dressed. J.C. and I had plans for the afternoon He had spent the night at home and was going to attend church with his family before coming out to the country. I was standing by the window, brushing my hair when Daddy's car stopped out front. Momma got out hurriedly and rushed up the walk. Her knock was not a normal one. It was more of an urgent pounding.

I wanted to pretend there was no one at home until she went away, and probably should have. When she was persistent with it, I thought maybe something had happened to one of our family members, so I opened the door. She said, "Well, It's about time. What are you up to in there?"

She pushed her way past me into the house then walked around peeking into my room, down the hall and into the parlor. I asked why she had come out. She walked over and sat down on the sofa and told me to come sit by her. She said she had something important to talk to me about and a picture for me to see.

Still apprehensive, I sat down taking a deep breath and letting it out. She didn't waste any time getting to the point. Digging around in her purse she said, "I have come specially to show you this picture of J.C. and his little son."

She shoved a picture into my hand. I tried to look at it, but my eyes wouldn't focus at the moment. Her words were repeating themselves in my head. "J.C. And his little son" kept reverberating. She had launched into a lecture about him being too old for me if he was hanging around out there as much as his mother had said.

"He needs to be at home taking care of his own child instead of doing whatever he is doing out here with you." She said.

Staring at the picture in shock I wondered why he had never mentioned the child to me. When I recovered enough to walk, I went into my room and shut the door behind me. Momma followed me telling me that I was wrong if I was doing anything to keep him away from his child. She ranted on and on about his taking advantage of my innocence if anything was going on between us. If so she and Daddy would fix him good even if it meant the loss of friendship between them and his parents.

"If that is the case you had better be very careful. You might be the next mother of one of his kid," she yelled through the door.

I had heard all I could stand. In order to shut her up I said that I would talk to him about it when he came out again. I would try to make him see that he needed to spend some time with his child. That was enough to satisfy her. She left as quickly as she had come, having accomplished her mission.

By the time he arrived I had worked myself into a frenzy, fit to be tied. I had honestly tried to push it out of my mind right after Momma left but it kept coming back. Her words echoed more loudly each time, "J.C. and his little son."

I met him on the porch, took his hand and walked over to the porch swing, and waited for him to sit down. I didn't sit close beside him as I usually did. After a few seconds of silence between us he asked how my day had been going. Instead of answering I burst into uncontrollable tears. He pulled me over close to him, hugging me tightly for a few minutes. He gave me his handkerchief and sat waiting for me to tell him why I was so upset. I couldn't look at him.

Finally, he pushed my head against his shoulder and held it there. He said, "Didn't we agree that you and I can talk about anything and everything. You can tell me anything. You know that"

I answered him while still sobbing hard, "I thought that was supposed to work both ways."

When he didn't say anything, I wiped at my tears until I could see his face. He was frowning, which was something he seldom did. He was usually happy and upbeat. His eyes were questioning mine without a word being spoken. When I didn't say anything he asked, "What is it you think I need to tell you?"

I blurted out, "I didn't know you had a child!"

The tears started flowing profusely again. His frown deepened. He said, "I don't have a child."

The hurt in me became anger so quickly I couldn't help myself. I had seen the picture with my own two eyes and read the words on back of it.

"Our first grandson. Maybe a girl next time." Now he had lied about it. The one person I thought would always tell me the truth had just lied to me. I ran into the house shut the door and locked it. He kept talking to me from the porch, but I couldn't hear what he was saying and at the moment I didn't want to hear it. After a while he left, and I went into my room wondering why every good thing in my life always managed to get messed up.

Over the next couple of weeks, I stubbornly refused to take his phone calls. He hadn't been back, knowing it wouldn't do any good to try and talk to me face to face. I quit my job and stayed in my room either crying or fuming. Serandica Pappas tried to console me by telling me everything was going to be alright. I thought it was strange because at one point she said, "We have to trust Justus."

I shrugged wondering what she thought Justus could do, but she disappeared before I could ask her. Mrs. Jones tried to help all she could too. She was always asking me to go to the garden and help her pick black eyed peas and okra, or tomatoes or some other veggie she really needed help with. Didn't I want to come to church with her and Papa? Would I like to help make homemade ice cream? My favorite, Tutti Frutti! I appreciated their caring and tried to act happy around them, but they could see through it. I couldn't eat, I couldn't sleep, I didn't want to get up mornings. I was a total mess.

Finally, I told my reflection in the bathroom mirror, while brushing my teeth, that I had been wrong to confront J.C. about the child the way I had. The next time he called I would apologize and promise to never mention it to him again. Ever.

Two months later my bubble burst completely when he came to me one evening and told me that he had joined the army. He would be away until I finished high school. It was not something he wanted to do, but something he had to do in order to secure a good place for us in the big picture, his favorite thing to call the future.

He said I was too young to know for sure what I wanted out of life and he was going to give me the opportunity to decide for myself. He had me off to a good start and if I would stay on track, I could go to college and become anything I wanted to become. My heart was broken. My little brother's heart had been repaired and he was doing great, but my heart's damage could never be repaired. My spirit suffered the anguish. Had it not been for Serandica Pappas, I might have sunk too low to ever find my way back to the land of the living. She was there, telling me constantly, to never give up, for we would someday find Justus together and everything would be wonderful again.

During those dark winter days when I had to drag myself out of bed and go to school, her presence was all that kept me going. When I cried, she cried. I could feel her arms around me, her soft voice telling me to be patient, for in time, things would get better. Other times she would repeat over and over, "Oh Justus, where are you?"

When that happened, I felt sorrier for her than for myself. Working at the lunch counter in Fort Worth was no longer an option. J.C. had offered to leave me his car for school and work, but I declined the offer. As a matter of fact, I declined even a polite conversation with him the last time he came out before leaving. I pulled the engagement ring from my finger and thrust it into his shirt pocket. He said, "Sweetheart, don't do this. Don't throw away what we have together because you are mad at me. I don't want to leave you, but I have no choice, I have to do this.'"

For the last time, I ran inside and locked the door. He raised his voice so that I would be sure to hear him, "Okay, if that's the way you want it, but you've got my soul whether you want it or not. You are mine. Don't you ever forget that."

In the lonely days to come, I regretted what I had done very much. But it was done, there was no way to change it.

NO GOING BACK

Ginger, the social worker, sat in the big easy chair in the living room. I had been studying hard, getting ready for midterm exams. My books were scattered all over the floor. She said she was glad to see me out of the bedroom for a change. Trying to keep my eyes on the algebra, which was way over my head, I nodded, indicating that I heard what she said, but it was all a blur, so I put the book down and leaned back against the sofa.

Opening a folder from her briefcase and sitting with her pen ready to take down whatever information she needed, she looked over at me smiling. I didn't feel like smiling back but managed a polite look in return.

She asked if I had invited any friends over to visit. I shook my head no. When she asked why not, I said I had no friends. "You know that is not true." She said it as if I had a lot of friends, which I clearly did not have. J.C. Had been enough for me. I hadn't even entertained the idea of having anyone over when he was there.

Her mother came in with a tray of steaming hot chocolate and a big bowl of popped corn. I got up and took the tray from her and set it on the coffee table. Then I sat down on the sofa while she poured the creamy liquid into big brightly colored mugs and passed them around, then she sat beside me on the sofa. We all took sips of the warm, delicious chocolate and expressed our gratitude for such wonderful refreshment.

My taste buds were still savoring the sweetness of the cocoa when Ginger said that she thought it might be time for me to have a visit from my parents. She said my mother and sister were very upset when I had chosen not to spend Christmas at home with my family. I felt the resentment rising within. Shaking my head negatively, let her know that I was not ready.

She went on, "Your mother, and mine, tell me that you have been refusing any calls from your family members and friends, except for your little brothers."

I nodded. There was a long silence while we all sipped at our chocolate. Finally, her mother said she was going to her room to get ready for bed. We said good night and sat in front of the warm fireplace enjoying our drinks and popcorn. She asked me when I thought I might be ready for a visit either to or from my parents. I told her truthfully that I did not want to see my parents, but I would love to see my two little brothers. Then she told me that after my sixteenth birthday, I could no longer live with her parents, because that was the age they had agreed upon before I came to live with them. During the year, she told me, I must prepare myself to be ready to live with my parents again and that the time had come for them to be in on the big decisions I would be making for life. I didn't understand what she meant. When I asked, she said, "Like going to college, getting married and so forth."

I just sat and starred at her a few seconds, then told her I had no such plans anymore. She smiled warmly and told me not to be so sure of it. The last thing she said was, "The next time I talk to you, I want you to tell me that you have made a few friends. My momma will be happy to help you with it. Maybe a couple of girls for a sleepover?"

I nodded, and she gathered up her things and went to say goodnight to her parents. Hurriedly I gathered up my books and papers and fled into my room, closing the door behind me. Shutting out the world and all its drudgery, shutting out the voice in my head, which told me I just wasn't good enough. I sank to the floor with my back against the closed door, my knees drawn up, using my arms for a pillow and wondering why nobody really loved me. Why I wasn't cherished? What had I ever done so wrong that I couldn't find any lasting happiness? Why did every last bit of joy I ever had flee away in a moment?

If it had not been for Serandica Pappas, I might not have found my way back from some of those dark moments. She brought me back, each time I sank into a low place, by telling me that very soon, everything would be alright. One particular time, she said that we must find Justus. Then we would both always be happy. I didn't understand what she meant but it made me feel better.

The next morning at breakfast, I asked Mrs. Jones who she thought I should invite over. She knew everybody in the community and their children and it was her house I would be asking someone into, so I figured asking her was the best thing to do. She wasted no time in telling me that she thought Joyce and June, twins who lived about a mile further on down the road, would be a very good choice. She even suggested asking them for a sleepover on the week end.

Joyce and June were in my homeroom, but they were not in any of my other classes. We had spoken to one another on occasion when I had attended church with Mr. and Mrs. Jones. They seemed nice enough. They weren't in with the more popular crowd, which I wanted no part of. I knew if I didn't ask right away, I wouldn't ask at all, so I walked up to Joyce, who was straightening up her locker in the hall and told her that Mrs. Jones had told me to invite her and June for a sleepover the coming weekend, adding that she thought I should get to know some of my schoolmates a little better. Joyce smiled broadly and said that she and June had dates on Friday night and they had to stay home on Saturday nights, so they would get up for church on Sunday morning.

I asked if they would like to come on Saturday night if Mrs. Jones arranged with their parents to bring them to church on Sunday. She told me it wouldn't hurt to find out, that she and June loved getting away from their parents and younger brothers as often as possible. We went our ways saying, "See you later alligator" and "After while crocodile."

I thought to myself that had been easy enough. After school, I hurried in to ask Mrs. Jones if she would be willing to call their parents on our behalf. She was a sweet little woman and said she would be happy to do that. Sure enough, at supper, she said the girls would be there after lunch on Saturday. I wondered what we could do while they were there, other than sit around and talk. She told me we would think about it and plan up something fun to do.

I had taken what Ginger would call a baby step in the right direction. That night before I went to sleep, I tried to wrap my mind around her suggestion that I pay my parents a visit. When I couldn't come up with a plan for it, Serandica Pappas told me to, "Just do it" and spread her hands as if to say, "That's all there is to it."

I smiled to myself and tried to think of something to do when the girls got there on Saturday. I slept more peacefully that night than I had in weeks. The next morning, I got up feeling refreshed and content, but quickly checked myself by remembering a joke I had once heard. I thought, "Cheer up, things could get worse." I cheered up and sure enough, things got worse. Serandica Pappas had said, "It's easy, just do it. Take one baby step after another and soon you will be there."

So that was what I started doing, but in the back of my mind was that nagging feeling. It told me, "Hope for the best, but look for worst."

Over the next couple of months, Joyce, June and I became good friends. Occasionally, we invited other girls in for our regular week end get to-gathers, but the three of us were a good crowd and most of the time we spent together was ours for sharing secrets, planning things to do and learning to cook and sew.

The fashion magazines, which Ginger had left for me to look at, were the best. She knew I was interested in art and fashion, so she tried to inspire me to think of it as a career option. My mind wasn't ready to plan a career or anything which would keep me from feeling free to do whatever I pleased. I wanted to experience life in all its dimensions and I didn't want anybody trying to steer me one way or another. It was my life and I wanted to keep it that way.

Joyce and June had plans of getting married, having their own home and babies. I confided in them that I too had made those plans, but the only person I would ever consider a life together with had made other plans that didn't include me. In my mind, there would never be anyone I could trust again. I was going to finish high school, then travel around, working at all kinds of different jobs and living the life I wanted to live.

My two friends could never understand why I would want to live such a life. They were constantly after me to date some guy or another. No matter how hard they tried, they were not able to change my mind. They loved teasing me, telling me that I was going to become the youngest old maid anybody had ever seen. It went on and on, "How are you ever going to know if you like anybody else if you don't ever allow anybody else to come near you?"

My mind was made up. I would never allow myself to be hurt by anybody, in any way, ever again. Forever meant forever to me, even if it didn't to others. My mind was on the here and now, not some time way far in the future. Every time I looked in the mirror and saw those pin points of light in my eyes, which J.C. had said were our souls, one his one mine, I remembered I had his soul even if I didn't have his body anymore, and that was both a blessing and a curse. My whole being ached for him. I suffered severe mental anguish. I clung to Serandica Pappas's promise that everything was going to be alright. I kept on surviving.

JUST IN TIME

May was swiftly drawing to a close. Ginger showed up early on a Wednesday, which was unusual for her to do. Ordinarily she came on the weekends or late in the afternoon. I was getting ready to leave for school and hesitated about coming out of my room when I heard her in the living room talking to her parents. There was no way I could avoid her. The only door to my room opened into the living room. If I didn't leave soon I would get detention for being late to school. I opened the door as quietly as I could and had almost made it to the front door.

Ginger looked up from her papers and said, "There you are. I was beginning to wonder if you might still be sleeping. Come over here. I have to discuss something with you."

Trying to get out of it, I said I would be late for school if I didn't go then. She said what she needed to discuss with me was very important and she would drive me to school when we were done. She patted the sofa, indicating that I should sit beside her. I plopped down, mad as a hornet.

First of all, she wanted me to know how proud of me she was for keeping my grades up. Her mother had told her the twins and I had become good friends and that was what she called taking a big step.

"What have you girls been up to?" she asked, sweetly. I told her we did all the things that other girls our age did, hang out and have fun.

Boom! The bomb fell. Didn't one always fall just when things began going well and I was the least bit happy?

"You will be in your junior year next fall. It is in your best interest to make up with your parents and go home to live with them over the summer. I have previously mentioned it to you and you have been given ample time to think it over. It is now time for action. Your parents love you. Things just got out of hand for a while. They realize they were too hard on you. They were just afraid their little girl was trying to grow up too soon. Give them a chance to make amends. They have promised me that they will allow you more freedom now that you are a bit older."

Steam was about to pop out of both my ears, but I kept my temper under control. They had finally worn her down. She was taking their side.

Ginger continued, "Going home to live with them over the summer will have you already settled in when school starts in the fall. Your mother thinks it will be alright for you to work as long as you keep your grades up. The half day program is open to students who need to work. They have moved into a larger house, you know."

I didn't know, and I didn't care if they had moved into a castle. I was not going to move back in with them if there was any way on earth I could keep from it. Oblivious to my unconcern, she kept on, "You will have your own entrance to the house from the front porch. The room they have chosen for you is the only bedroom in the front of the house. You will have access to the whole house all the time. There is a door from your room into the living room and one into the hallway leading to the back of the house. The bathroom is just behind your room with easy access from the hallway."

So, they had it all planned out, did they? They know I haven't been working so they've got me where they want me. I felt my chest getting tight. I slipped my hands under my thighs to keep them from making fists. My teeth were clenched. I could hear the grinding. It was difficult to breath.

Ginger may have noticed but she continued nonetheless, "Your parents are handing you an olive branch. Their offer is a good one. You would do well to accept it."

I sprung to my feet and yelled at her, which I had never done before, "I will never, ever, go to school in Fort Worth again!"

I hurried into my room slamming the door behind me and threw myself across the bed. I was gasping for breath. The asthma attack had become full blown. Ginger came in, sat on the side of the bed and started in again. Her voice was loud and sharp, "Now you listen to what I am telling you. I've seen other girls in almost your same situation who felt they could make it on their own and failed making things worse for themselves." She started emphasizing her words, "Do not blow the opportunity your parents are offering you. Don't fool yourself into thinking you can manage on your own. Whether you realize it or not, you need your parents and they need you. They need to know that they have done everything in their power to keep you going straight."

Her voice softened a little, she must have noticed my difficulty breathing, "Things just got out of hand for a while. Give them a chance. Thing will be better this time."

I pulled myself up from the bed using the corner post and stumbled toward the door and out onto the front porch falling into the chair by the front door. I could hardly breathe at all. She said she would get my medication and some water and was back quickly with it. I finally got the pill down and sat staring into the distance, trying to get my mind on anything except what had been said to me over the past half hour.

Mrs. Jones came out with a steaming cup of black coffee. She told me to sip on it but be careful or I would burn my mouth. What I really wanted to do with it was throw it on her daughter. Mrs. Jones pulled up another wicker chair and sat beside me. She took my hand and patted it. I felt no animosity toward her. She and her husband had been very good to me and I appreciated them. Ginger leaned against the support which held up the roof over the porch. Her arms folded together, not speaking, which helped tremendously in my calming down enough for the pill to start working.

When she thought I had sat quietly long enough, she turned around with her back against the porch support. Her arms were still folded. She crossed one foot over the other one and started all over again.

"I have vacation time coming up. After that, I will be available for client phone calls. Think about what I have told you and make preparations accordingly. Don't let me find out that you have run off again. J.C. won't be here to come to your aide if it happens again. Think how disappointed he would be to find out that you had messed up. He has made a big sacrifice for you, young lady. You owe it to him keep your life going straight. You owe it to your parents. You owe it to my parents and you owe it to me. I understand that you have had it hard at home in the past. I know you hurt when things don't turn out the way you would like them to but living in a dream world won't fix it. You must learn to live in the real world. The real world is very demanding. To survive and do well you must have a good education."

I was crying rivers again. How many times had I heard those same words from J.C.'s mouth. I wanted a good education, but I would never get it in one of those big city schools. No matter what I had to do, I would not go back there.

Ginger checked her watch then said she had to be on her way. Mrs. Jones stayed with me until she was sure I felt well enough to be left alone. She said, "I have to go in and start lunch. Papa's been working in the garden all morning and he will be ready to eat at twelve on the dot."

That made me smile knowing how set their routine was. In a few minutes she came back out with a bowl of blackberries with fresh cream over them. She said, "You never ate a bite of breakfast. Those will tide you over until lunch."

I thanked her and slipped a spoonful into my mouth. Heavenly! She said, "Everything is on simmer in there. The breeze is so nice out here I will wait until you finish the berries and take the bowl back when I go to check on things."

She sat quietly for a few minutes while I enjoyed the delicious berries. Finally, she said, "I hope we can find someone to take some of our fruit and vegetables this year. My pantry is full. My freezer is full and so is Ginger's. Papa has a green thumb you know. I can't see us buying another freezer. We would just have to get rid of it when we move into the retirement center."

My hand holding another spoonful of berries was almost in my mouth when I heard what she had just said. I put the spoon of berries back in the bowl and ask her what she had said. She told me again adding, "A while back, Papa wasn't feeling too well, and he started worrying about how I would manage if something were to happen to him," she made a face and said, "you know."

She paused, then went on. "In case you haven't noticed, Papa and I are getting on in years. He asked Ginger to look into some of those places and she did. He has already made plans to sell our dear old home place." She looked around fondly then smiled and said, "I have never gone against Papa. That's why we have had a long and happy life. Most of the time he is right in the decisions he makes."

She took my hand and gave it a good pat, "We had hoped that you and J.C. would get married and take it off our hands but that seems out of the question for now, so we will do what Papa thinks is best."

She took the bowl of unfinished berries from my hand and went back inside. I sat staring at the sky for a long time thinking about what she had said and about J.C. and wondering where he was and what life had been like for him since he went away.

How wonderful it would have been sharing the Joneses happy old home with him. What on earth would have been better than that? I thought about the way Ginger had spoken to me, as if I were a spoiled child. I was as much an adult as she was. If she only knew. Then I wondered what she would have had to say about that.

I had completely forgotten about school! Mrs. Jones came to the door to say that lunch was about ready, and I should come in and eat with them. I told her I really wasn't hungry because of the asthma medication and thought maybe I should at least try to make my afternoon classes.

She said, "I called the school when Ginger was getting water for your medication. They are not expecting you until in the morning. You just rest and collect your thoughts. That was quite an ordeal Ginger put you through this morning. Papa and I love you. We are on your side."

She bent down and placed a little kiss on my forehead then went back inside. My mind was telling me that I had better figure out how to avoid going back to live with my parents. I kept running into dead ends. My mind was a complete blank, so I blamed that on the asthma medication. My eyes were stinging, and my chest was aching from trying to hold back the bitter tears which seemed to always be ready to pour down my cheeks. I took a few deep breaths, letting each one out slowly, and that helped a little.

Joyce stopped the truck by the gate, jumped down and dashed to the porch. I could tell by the smile on her face that she was extremely happy about something.

"Shame on you, playing hooky from school," she teased, then stopped suddenly in front of me and asked, "What's wrong? What is going on?"

I shook my head and she understood the meaning. She sat on the porch swing. Gave the porch a kick with her toes to get the swing going then turned sideways in it putting her feet up and letting the swing do its own work.

"Maybe you don't feel like talking right now but that gives me a chance to tell you what I came to let you know."

She put her feet back on the porch to stop the swing then leaned forward and said, "Guess who's getting married next month?"

"What?" I mumbled. Somebody getting married was the last thing I wanted to talk about at the moment.

"You won't ever guess, so I am going to tell you. I am getting married!"

The only person she had ever talked about, in a way which would lead a person to think she would marry him was that guy Eddy. She jabbered about him constantly. What a good kisser he was. What a great car he had. How everybody always catered to him, whatever he wanted. Not feeling any happiness of my own was diminishing any I had for Joyce getting married. I said, "I hope you and Eddy have a great life together."

"It's not Eddy," she said, slyly, "Eddy and I are just special friends. We um...comfort one another. You know."

I didn't know. From some of the things she and June had told me, it seemed to have been more than comfort.

"My fiancé is a man I know from church. We have been seeing one another in secret for the past year. Well, June knew but nobody else did. She covered for me when I went to meet him."

My mouth was still hanging open. Joyce went on unperturbed by my expression. "Mom and Dad like him. He runs his own business as a dry wall contractor. He owns his home and drives a new truck."

When she stopped for a breath, I said, "What about Eddy?"

She raised her eyebrows and told me that she had told Eddy a month ago and he was actually happy for her. She added, "Eddy's not marriage material. He is a long way from being ready to marry anybody."

I could not shake off the feeling. How could anybody, thinking of marriage to one person be so lovey-dovey with another, and I told her so. She got up, stepped off the porch, looked back over her shoulder at me and said, "Everybody is not as old fashioned in their thinking as you are."

She climbed into the truck and took off leaving a cloud of dust behind.

Good thing I had already taken asthma medication.

The telephone in the kitchen had been ringing almost constantly. The Joneses must have left the house while Joyce was telling me her news. By the time I got to the kitchen the phone had quit ringing. There was a freshly baked berry pie on the table. It had been cut and a couple of slices were missing. I felt sure Mrs. Jones had left it out for me to help myself. I cut a piece and stood savoring the smell of it. The phone started ringing again, making me lose concentration on the pie. I grabbed the receiver and said, "Jones residence"

June's voice asked, excitedly, "Have you heard the news?'

I told her that Joyce had just stopped by and told me. I was happy for her, but I could not wrap my mind around her keeping up the good time girl thing with her friend Eddy. June giggled, "Not that! The news about Eddy's mother, Polly, opening the old cafe out on the highway! She is going to hire a couple of school girls to help her and I was thinking you and I should go out there and get those two jobs. How about it?"

"Sure." I said, feeling a bit excited for the first time in a while.

"Be out by the gate. Joyce just got home. I am on my way." June said. I placed the receiver in its cradle, ran to check my hair, dabbed on a little make up and lipstick. I was by the gate when June got there. She made a rolling stop. I hopped in and off we went. June might not have been the safest driver, but she knew where she was going and the shortest way to get there. On the way over, which took all of two minutes, I smiled to myself. I had never even once thought about anybody in that wild crowd the twins ran around with, having a mother.

The front door of the old cafe building was standing open. The screen door screeched as we went in. Joyce called out. "Anybody home?"

A curly, slightly gray-haired head popped around the corner where the kitchen joined the front. A short, medium built woman with clear blue eyes and a lovely smile came out to meet us. She was wearing a pale pink uniform, a pink and white apron and white shoes similar to the ones I still had from working at the lunch counter in the city. She said, "What can I do for you girls?"

June didn't waste a second. She said, "Better yet, it's what we can do for you. We know you are in need of help and we are here for the jobs."

Polly's smile broadened, she had small pearly white teeth. There seemed to be a twinkle of mischief in her pretty blue eyes. June went on, "We've met before. I am Joyce's' twin."

Polly said, "I thought I recognized you from somewhere."

She walked over to one of the tables, pulled out a chair and motioned for us to join her. Not waiting to see if Polly wanted to say more, June went on, "We are two hard working girls," Thumbing over at me, she said, "That one has worked at one of the biggest lunch counters in the city and I am a very fast learner."

Polly looked at me and said, "Can that one talk?"

We all had a laugh at that. I told her when I got started I was usually hard to shut up and June liked to talk so much that I just let her go on with it. She wanted to know how we heard about her needing help so fast. She said, "The ink has barely had time to dry on the lease!"

June said, "Your two sons, Eddy and Bunkie!"

Polly got up, poured herself a cup of coffee and brought a couple of frosty root beers for us. We thanked her and sipped on them while she put sugar and cream in her coffee. Polly said she was opening the place on a very small budget. If we were willing to work hard and help her get the place ready to open that she would give us free meals and pay us five dollars for an eight-hour shift. She said that while it didn't seem like much, it was the best offer she could make us. We would receive our first pay at closing time the first full day the cafe was open which, she hoped would be on Friday of the next week.

She sipped at her coffee while June and I were looking at one another trying to decide if we should grab the jobs or not. It didn't take me but a couple of seconds. I said, "Sounds good to me."

June was quick to follow. We all sat sipping our drinks. The deal was done. Finally, I asked, "When can we start?"

Polly wanted to know when was the last day of school. We both said, "This coming Friday!"

"Well, come in on Saturday morning after you are done with school and we will get this place up and ready to go."

We thanked her, chugged the rest of our sodas and ran to the truck both giggling with excitement. We had done it! We had summer jobs.

On the way home June told me that she was going to try and get her dad to let us use the truck to go back and forth to work. I suggested that she tell him we would put gasoline in it as soon as we got our first pay. She said, "And, we will wash it and shine it up."

It was and old worn looking truck, but it ran well and got the girls where they wanted to go and back. In the nineteen-fifties that was all kids wanted, a way to get out of the house and have fun. I told June that I hoped he would let us use it but even if he didn't I was going to that job if I had to walk every step of the way, there and back.

The Joneses still were not back. I spent some time going through the clothes in my closet. I found three inter-changeable outfits that would be good for work, then dug out my white work shoes and polished them. Cutoff jeans, old blouses and tennis shoes would be fine for the days we were helping with clean up and getting the place ready to open. Suddenly I remembered the pie! I hurried into the kitchen poured myself a glass of milk and dug in. I hadn't been that hungry for months. By the time the they came home, I had taken a bubble bath and had rolled my hair on big curlers.

I started planning how to persuade my parents to let me stay in the country. I had it! I ran to the phone and dialed their number. Momma answered the phone. I told her that I was going to have to make up some classes I had missed because of asthma attacks and I could not come home until those classes were completed. She didn't say anything at first. I asked if she was still on the line. She wanted to know how come I had been having the asthma attacks so much. I lied and said it was the stress of thinking about having to go to school in the city again. She said alright but as soon as those classes were done with I was to let them know so they could come and bring me home. I went to bed glad to have a short reprieve. I was going to need the help of my friends when the time came.

June and I worked to the point of exhaustion that first week. Our mothers would have said we used a lot of elbow grease. We cleaned and painted walls, scrubbed the floor and cleaned and arranged tables and chairs. We even hand printed menus. There were napkin holders, sugar dispensers as well as salt and pepper shakers to fill.

Polly liked music and June liked to dance. The juke box man told Polly to mark the quarters she put in it with finger nail polish and he would give them back to her each time he came to take the money out. She would also get a percentage of what the box had in it. We had plenty of music while we worked. Rock and roll music was just becoming popular so there was a lot of that on it as well as some rhythm and blues and downright tear jerkers which I couldn't stand to hear. I usually went outside for a breath of fresh air when one of them started playing.

Polly had made some pretty cafe curtains for the two big front windows out of the same pink and white checked material she made some adorable table cloths to be used with linen napkins on Sundays only. Everything was looking really good when we finished the work on Thursday. After that we unloaded supplies and put out all the condiments. There was a candy case on one side of the register and a cigarette and cigar case on the other. Polly bought several kinds of candy and gum as well as a few cartons of the most popular brands of cigarettes and a few boxes of good cigars from one of the salesmen who came around. We put them in place then stood back to admire our work while Polly told us how everything was going to be priced.

She said she was going to be too busy in the kitchen, so we would have to wait tables and settle up our own tickets. Several times she reminded us to be careful while making change and that we should always initial our tickets. If there was a problem she would come out and help with it, but she felt confident that we could take care of most of it with no trouble. She wouldn't tell us how much it would be but, there would be a bonus for the one who had the most sales at the end of every month.

She said, "Push extra cheese or ice cream for pie a-la-mode and recommend the pricier items on the menu when people asked what the best thing on the menu is." I had heard all that when I worked at the lunch counter. It worked.

Once in a while when we were really tired and on our way home, we talked about how all our classmates, including Joyce, were on vacation and having fun while we worked. But we were a couple of girls on a mission to springboard ourselves into a working world where money would take us where we wanted to go. Neither of us knew for sure where that was but we had time to decide.

I knew I wanted to stay independent now that I had become that way without wanting to be. It had been thrust upon me, so I was going to embrace it. I was going to do just what J.C. had suggested, experience the world in my own way. The one thing I was sure of was that I did not want to be like everybody else, and I already had that going for me.

Polly had asked June if she thought Joyce would want to help with the opening. June assured her that her twin would be happy to help. I wanted to know how she could be so sure without asking. She told us that Joyce had been mad because she hadn't been invited to go along to ask for the job. Standing with a hand on one hip twisting to the music and snapping her fingers on the other hand, she said with a smirk on her face, "I told her, we thought you were too busy with your wedding plans to go to work at a real job."

June had a way at making people laugh. She went on to say that her sister must be enjoying her fun with the crowd because she had put her wedding off until Thanksgiving. I thought, "lucky Eddy!"

It had all been planned. Polly's daughter Maxine, or Mackie as everyone called her, who was a couple of years younger than June and me, would run the dishwasher and sterilizer keeping everything clean and ready to re-use. Bunkie was going to help Polly with the cooking and plating. Eugene, another son who was a couple of years younger than Maxine, could bus the tables, keep the floor clean and he and Bunkie could keep the trash emptied. Joyce would come in with June and I to help get the front set up for opening at six thirty Friday evening. Polly said she had gotten some flyers printed up and Eugene and some of his friends had been putting them out during the day for a week. There was a big opening night special placard in one of the front windows. We hoped for a successful opening to guarantee our payday.

By noon Friday, Polly, her daughter Mackie, June, Joyce and I were busy as bees getting last minute things done. We had extra gallon jugs of tea ready to pour into the urn. Extra coffee filters filled and ready to slip into the brewer. We had wrapped all the knives, forks and spoons in napkins and made sure there were plenty of toothpicks out. We helped Polly in the kitchen, put liners in all the trash containers and made sure there was plenty of toilet paper and paper towels in the bathroom.

Still, no Bunkie and Eugene. Polly said she should have made them come in with her. She had tried to call the house, but the phone was constantly giving a busy signal. She said one of the little boys had probably knocked it of its hook while they were playing. I mouthed to Joyce, "Little boys?"

Joyce grinned broadly and held up four fingers, then closed her hand and opened two fingers. She lifted her eyebrows and made a big shrug. I thought "Poor Polly! Eight kids!"

By five forty-five, people were already lining up outside. The parking lot was almost full. No other help was coming but we made up our minds to get it done the very best we could. The place smelled wonderful. Everything had been precooked and kept at the right temperature on the big steam table in the kitchen. It's a good thing too, Polly not having any help. We girls had filled big cake pans with ice and laid out tomatoes, lettuce and pats of butter which made it easier for Polly.

The opening night menu offered choices of Momma's country fried chicken, chicken fried steak or a hamburger plate. The sides were mashed potatoes or home fries, green beans or English peas, glazed carrots or corn. There was also a choice of hot rolls or cornbread. Dessert was fresh peach cobbler or chocolate cake. Drinks with the special were tea or coffee. The hamburger plate was served open faced with the trimmings on the side. Five dollars a plate! It was good food and a good deal. The customers all seemed to be enjoying themselves. Even the ones who had to wait a few minutes.

When Polly put the closed sign on the door, we noticed her face was flushed red. We figured she had gotten too hot working so fast and furious, but Mackie confided in us, by whispering, "Momma's mad at the boys for not coming to help us. They are going to get a piece of her mind when we get home."

I said, "Why do you think your dad didn't make them come and help?"

Mackie shook her head, drew her mouth up at one corner and said, "He was probably too drunk," then she hurried into the kitchen with her mother.

Joyce said, "That's probably right. The boys talk about him getting drunk on the way home from work every day."

I was appalled. Poor Polly! Working so hard and those big old boys and sot of a husband wouldn't lift a hand to help her.

'Little Eugene would have probably come and helped if somebody would have brought him." June said, then she lifted our tired spirits by saying, "Eugene is a little cutie pie. I would marry him if he was old enough."

105

We had to giggle but tried to hold it down for Polly's sake. We all got busy and cleaned the place up, shipshape and ready for next morning. Before we left for home, Polly handed us all pay envelopes Mackie's eyes lit up. "Me too?!" she squealed then hugged her mother tightly.

"I couldn't have done it without my girls. I wish I could pay you more. You are all worth much more but right now I hope thank you and hope to see all of you in the morning will be enough." Polly said, earnestly.

We took turns giving her hugs and telling her she could count on us being there. We were tired, but our pockets were full of tips and we each had a fat pay envelope.

I had to voice my opinion on the way home. It had not been right, those boys not coming to help their mother. How come the much-adored Eddy hadn't been included with those who were to come help? Joyce set me straight quick, "There's things you don't know. Eddy has been through hell the past couple of years. He was badly burned in a fire at his aunt's house. He laid in the hospital, not days but weeks in the burn center. He was just getting up and around when his oldest brother, who had been living in California, came home. Eddy, his brother Roy and the one from California went out for a drive, just to get Eddy out of the house for a bit. They were in Roy's car and Roy was driving. He took a curve a little too fast and the car went off the road, took out a row of fence and posts and rolled three times. Roy was killed instantly. Eddy had bad cuts, bruises and broken bones. He was in the hospital for over six weeks. The whole family, even his aunts, uncles and cousins are so glad he made it through, all they want is for him to stay alive."

The truck had been stopped a few minutes. I got out closed the door then said, "And this is the guy you and June brag about driving down the freeway at over one hundred miles an hour with? He must have a death wish. Sleep on that!" and went in the house.

I was too tired to care whether the twins were offended by my words or not. I opened my pay envelope. Polly had been as good as her word. She had paid double shift wage for each day I had worked. Including my tips, I had almost a hundred dollars for the week of long hard work. In the nineteen-fifties that wasn't bad pay for a school girl. I was going to save every penny I possibly could, ensuring myself against going back home to live.

Business at the highway cafe just kept getting better. Polly's good food, reasonable prices and hospitable ways kept them coming back. June and I liked to believe that we too were a big part of its success. We worked hard and tried to keep our customers happy. We knew from the tips we found left on our tables that the customers appreciated our way of taking care of them. Joyce worked hard but she didn't have the ready smile and quick movements June and I seemed to be blessed with. We kept the amount of tip money we each made to ourselves, but June had seen Joyce count hers and they were nowhere near the amount of her own. Joyce may have been a slow mover, but she got the job done right, and that was an important part of keeping customers. Matter of fact, there were a few who always sat at the tables they knew were hers.

After the third week Polly told us that a couple of her neighbor ladies needed jobs and she had hired them to work evening shifts so that we girls could have off some time to run around with our friends. She said when school started in the fall, the women would trade out and work the morning shifts and we could have the evening shifts as long as we made good grades. I was disappointed, and I told her that I still needed to work all the time I could because I was facing supporting myself. Her eyes were once again questioning but she didn't ask for an explanation when I didn't offer one. She said she would keep it in mind. The twins, on the other hand, were happy. They were already planning to go to the drive-in theater on Friday night.

Mackie looked worried. She asked, "Me too Momma? Do I get to be off evenings too?"

Polly assured her she would be off the same time we were. She was going to bring Eugene in to take care of the dishwasher on Mackie's days off.

On the way home, the twins begged me to go with them to the drive-in movie on Friday night. Just the three of us, they said. We could make it a celebration of our hard work the past three weeks. When I saw they were going to keep on at me, I gave in and told them I would go, with one condition, that they would agree to help me out when the time came for me to persuade my parents to let me remain in the country and go to school. They agreed so fast that it surprised me. I had expected them to try and get out of it.

When I got to the house, Mrs. Jones gave me a message from Ginger. I was to talk to my parents over the Fourth of July holiday while she was away taking the rest of her vacation. The papers had to be signed by the judge and she was not putting the paperwork in his hands until the Monday following the holiday, which was coming up in two weeks. I would have that much time to make my case to my parents.

Mrs. Jones had told her that I was working regularly. She and Papa wanted me to stay on with them as long as possible. That was great news to hear! I stayed up most of the night planning what to tell my parents and the best way to go about telling them. Asking was out of the question. I was not going to beg. I was going to tell them straight out that I was going to stay in the country, work and finish school there.

Friday night June and Joyce were there early to pick me up to go with them to the movies. I had been actually looking forward to it. Maybe an evening out with the girls would make me feel better. I was still feeling lonely for J.C. when I wasn't busy at something, and what could a night out with a couple of friends hurt? He had probably forgotten he ever knew me. After all, he didn't have a soul anymore. He had given it to me, so his body was probably out enjoying itself.

Drive-in movie theaters were the "in thing" with high school kids and young adults at that time. They were filled every weekend. Car loads of rowdy young people thronged the drive-in theaters. The price was a flat amount per car load, so people packed as many in as they possibly could. The concession stand was where the people who ran them made up the difference. Popcorn, pizza, hot dogs, candy and fountain soft drinks were food young people loved.

The movie hadn't started when we got there, so we decided to go to the concession stand. Joyce locked the truck and we hurried to get our food before the movie started. We bought popcorn and sodas first and decided to sit out on the patio adjoining the concession stand to eat and watch the movie. There were no tables, just rows of lawn chairs. There were a few other people gathering to eat and watch the movie. It would have been a pleasant place to watch from if a cold front hadn't blown in.

We sat eating and giggling, wishing we had bought hot chocolate instead of soda. A brisk north wind had come up. None of us had brought a wrap. It had been a hot day and we weren't expecting it to get so cool that late in the year. We were about to go back to the truck for the rest of the show when some guy popped into the chair next to Joyce, put his arm around her and gave her a big squeeze. Suddenly there were two more standing in front of June and me, which infuriated me because I was just getting interested in the movie. The tallest one of the three pulled June to her feet and they took off in a run.

Just as I was about to say something about people standing in front of me when I was trying to see the movie, the guy with his arm around Joyce told the one in front of me to sit down. He said, to no one in particular, "Pee Wee and June won't be back 'til the show's over," then flopped down in the chair, looking at me with a big grin on his face and said, "Hi."

My mouth was still open when Joyce chimed in, "That's Clarence, we all call him Bunkie, don't ask why, I don't know, that's just what everybody calls him."

Then she pointed with her thumb at the one next to her and told me he was her friend Eddy. Eddy nodded at me and said, "Clarence is my brother. I'm the big brother."

Clarence then chimed in, "Hey! Hey! Hey!"

By that time, I was not seeing the movie, I was seeing red. Standing up, making sure I was standing in front of Clarence so that he couldn't see the show, I boldly asked Joyce for the keys to the truck. When she asked why I said, 'It's getting pretty cold out here," and to my complete surprise, she gave me a big smile and handed me the keys.

Hurrying off, I didn't realize that Clarence was tagging along behind me. While unlocking the door on the passenger side of the truck, I was suddenly aware of someone standing beside me. I looked up into the still grinning face of Clarence, or Bunkie, or whoever he was. He said, "You sure are right. It is cold out here!"

When I asked what he thought he was doing following me, he replied that he thought he was supposed to. My mouth was hanging open, it was all I could do to keep from slapping his grinning face. Instead, I gave him a big push and told him to explain what he had just said. He wasn't grinning when he answered, "Pee wee went off with June, Eddy and Joyce have gone to Eddy's car, so it's only natural that I am stuck with you."

My mouth wouldn't open any wider. He said, "Hey! I don't like this any more than you do! Can't we just get in and sit down out of the cold and watch the movie. If I go back to Eddy's car now, he's going to chew me out for ruining his night."

For a few minutes I stood speechless. Then, I unlocked the door, flung it open wide and told him to help himself. Then I turned and practically ran back to the concession stand. If I had known where Eddy's car was parked, I would have gone straight to it. Fit to be tied, I flopped into a chair and fumed. I learned that night being hot under the collar helps keep you warm.

In a few minutes Clarence showed up again. Talking to him was not an option for me. He didn't let my not talking stop him. He said, "I don't even know your name. I wouldn't have even come out here tonight if Eddy hadn't told me that Joyce and June were bringing a friend who could use some male company. Looks like we both got set up, so why not make the best of it."

If glaring at a person could kill them, he would have been dead. At intermission, I went into the restroom, staying as long as I dared, hoping he would be gone when I came out. My plan was to sneak off to the truck and lock the doors, behind me. No such luck, there he was, grinning as big as ever. He wasn't a bad looking guy, actually he was handsome. He had black hair, nicely cut and combed. He was not short, but he wasn't nearly as tall as J.C. either.

His baritone voice and friendly manner might have won me over, had I been ready for a date but, I wasn't nearly over J.C., and probably never would be; there was no interest and I wasn't going to pretend there was just to please somebody else. I told myself that I wasn't mad at him, it was just that the girls had taken off on me. What had he said? His brother had told him I needed male company? That was who I was really mad at! Who did they think they were! Trying to force me into a dating situation.

Clarence was asking if I wanted a slice of pizza. He had gone in and gotten one and I, in my furious mind-flogging of my two closest friends, had not even noticed that he was gone until he spoke. The pizza smelled delicious, but I wasn't going to be bought with a slice of pizza. Ignoring him, trying to get back to my pity party, I shook my head and pretended to be watching the movie. He said, "If I hadn't come out here with Eddy, you wouldn't be stuck with me. If I had brought my own car, I would have been gone already"

At that very moment, I remembered the keys which Joyce had relinquished so easily. Without even thinking what the consequences might be, I asked would he be willing to help me teach my two friends and his brother a lesson. Grinning wider, he asked what I had in mind. Jingling the keys, I said, "Let's move the truck!"'

His eyes lit up with mischief and he said, "Let's go," and we ran as fast as we could for the truck. When we got to it, he said, "Give me the keys."

J.C. Had taught me to drive a car, but I had never been behind the steering wheel of a pickup truck, so I handed him the keys. He started the engine then said, "Why don't we do one better? Why don't we take the truck and go home?"

I asked if he was joking and he said that he wasn't. I thought about it for a minute, then I said, "Let's go!"

He didn't turn on the lights until we were out of the screening area. Down the road we flew, talking like we had known each other always and making up scenarios about what they would say, what they would do, when they didn't find us or the truck. At one time I thought we should go back. What if Joyce and June were left alone out there? What if Eddy and Pee Wee had let them walk back to the truck alone not knowing the truck wasn't there? Clarence said it wasn't his first rodeo, that his brother and Pee Wee wouldn't dare let the two girls walk alone. He made a face, "They want the girls to think they are being gentlemen, but I know all they want is another kiss and a promise."

I couldn't resist asking if he knew that from experience. His answer was that they had learned it from him. "Taught 'em everything they know," he said, then laughed.

He was friendly enough but a little conceited. We laughed and joked all the way back to my house. Then it hit me! What if the girls dad found out? I almost panicked. Clarence said, "Don't worry about that, their old man won't know. He's out of it by this time of night. Like I said, this is not my first time out with those two, now and then they come up with a cousin who needs a date, so Eddy always drags me into it. We've set outside those two girls house trying to make good on promises until nearly daylight. That old man, nor his old lady, has ever come out once."

Again, I couldn't resist, "Why do you guys keep trying to collect?"

He laughed and said, "Who knows? Maybe one of these days one of us might get lucky," then he added, "Truth be known, Pee Wee probably already has tonight."

"Surely, you're joking," I said, but that time he didn't answer, he just kept on grinning.

Every time a car came along we were sure it was them. No such luck. I wasn't too worried about Mr. Jones coming outside to check. He and Mrs. Jones were used to the girls being there in their daddy's truck. Many nights we stayed outside late when the weather was nice enough. It was getting pretty cold. Clarence told me to slide over next to him, so we could keep each other warm.

When I declined, he said, "I'm not going to bite you and I'm dammed sure not going to try to kiss you."

Again, I wanted to slap him a good one across the face, but Serandica Pappas was whispering in my ear, "Laugh and tell him you only kiss men, not boys."

That really had my mouth open. All I said was, "That's okay, I know you haven't learned how to kiss a girl yet."

He replied, "You sure better not be thinking about giving me any lessons."

I giggled and told him I charged for my kissing lessons and he couldn't afford them. We were both laughing so hard we didn't hear the two cars which rolled up behind the truck with the lights out. When the doors to the truck flew open and I was pulled out on one side and Clarence out the other, we both almost screamed before we recognized our assailants. There were a few dirty words exchanged on the boys' side. Joyce and June had my arms behind my back and were taking turns, playfully, pulling my hair and slapping me on the head. Eddy was telling Clarence they had called the police when they couldn't find the truck because they thought we had been kidnapped. Peewee was laughing, saying "Yeah, sure, kidnapped. I told you what they were up to."

June giggled loudly. Joyce told her to be quiet, she would wake up the Joneses and we would all be in trouble. Eddy came around and said they better go. They left us standing in the yard, rolling away as silently as they had come, with no lights on, taking Clarence with them. We girls hurried inside to get ready for bed. There was a lot of questions I wanted answers to. The twins insisted, "They're just good guys and we are good friends with them, just like we are with you. Just that we don't make out with you."

Then there was friendly punches and pillows thrown. They wanted to know what I thought of Clarence. They teased and said I must have liked him a lot to drive off with him in their daddy's truck. Instead of answering I asked if they weren't mad at Clarence and me for leaving in the truck. They just giggled and told me it wasn't the first time Clarence had left with a girl in their truck. Together, they said, "This is not my first rodeo."

They giggled enough to let me know, the joke was on me. I wanted to be mad at them. Tell them off for trying to make me do something I didn't want to do but Serandica Pappas kept whispering in my ear that everything was alright, and I could not conjure up enough anger to tell my two best friends how upset I had been with them earlier. They were such good sports about things all the time. Their happy go lucky natures were beginning to rub off on me.

Before I went to sleep I thought about the day, which was yesterday by that point. Soon summer would be over. I was hopeful that fall would bring good things as Serandica Pappas had promised. I slept peacefully, knowing that I had made some new friends who expected no more from me than friendship, and I was happy again, for a change.

Business at the cafe was booming. Polly gave me all the extra work she could. I started changing my money into twenty-dollar bills. I rolled them tightly until they resembled match sticks, then kept them tight by using a tiny piece of tape at the end. I stashed them in the beautiful little music box J.C. had given me.

I had asked the twins to go with me when I went to talk to my parents and they had agreed, saying, "You practice what you are going to say to them and leave the rest to us."

The Joneses had already told me that I could stay on with them until Christmas. After New Year's they would definitely move into a retirement center. The arrangements had already been made. I would be looking for a room to rent. June even suggested my moving in with her family if and when Joyce got married. My hopes were really soaring. Polly and the other two ladies had agreed on letting us work the morning of the Fourth of July. We could have the evening off to enjoy with our family and friends.

Momma called and told me to have all my things together. They would be coming to get me to bring me home on Wednesday night before the holiday. I almost panicked but regained my confidence quickly. I told her that I had permission from Ginger, the social worker, to stay in the country and work until at least the Monday after the holiday. I was coming in the afternoon of the fourth with some of my friends to talk to them about a couple of things. I would see them then. I placed the phone in its cradle and held my breath as long as I could, praying she wouldn't call back. When the phone didn't ring again right away I let my breath out slowly and went about my business as usual.

Our morning passed quickly on the Fourth. We girls had worn our jeans and t-shirts to work that morning in order to be ready to go straight to my parents' house when our shift was over. When we got outside, instead of walking out to where the truck was parked, Joyce and June headed for a big green Buick Roadmaster with its top down. When I didn't follow June called back to me, "Come on slow poke, let's get this done so we can go have some fun."

I walked slowly toward the car. I recognized Bunkie and Eddy but the guy in the back seat resembled J.C. so much it startled me. Joyce reintroduced the boys and said that the other one was Jay, another of their good friends. Bunkie got out and let June in the back seat then he climbed in the back seat too. Joyce got in, slid over next to Eddy and patted the rest of the front seat beside her, indicating that I should sit there.

Not wanting to cause a scene I got in and quietly told Joyce that I thought we were going in the truck. She said, "No way! I barely know how to get to the drive-in movie theater and back. Eddy and the boys drive all over Fort Worth all the time. Give me that address so we can get going."

I took a deep breath and gave her the address. She showed it to Eddy and handed it back to me. The boys were more dressed up than they had been the night of the incident at the drive-in movie. They all looked nice. Polly's boys had to be good guys with her for a mom. The music on the radio was loud and I hoped they would turn it down before we got to my parents' place.

When Eddy said we were almost there, Joyce looked at me and said, "Stick to your guns. No whining or begging. Just lay it out to them and we will be on our way again."

I reminded her that it was my last chance and I had no intentions of backing down. I meant it too. My money was saved, and I would use it to make my get an away if they tried to tell me I was going to have to come back to Fort Worth.

I knew we had the right house when I saw my two little brothers playing out front. Eddy guided the big car to a stop and we all piled out. When my brothers saw that it was me, they ran and gave me bear hugs. I introduced them to everyone then asked if our parents were inside. Joyce and June followed me into the living room. The boys stayed on the porch talking to my little brothers and helping them with their yo-yo's and spinning tops.

The room was dark. All the blinds and curtains were closed tightly. The only light in the room was coming from the television set. Well good for them. They finally bought a T.V.! Loudly I said, "Hello! We are here!" as excitedly as I possibly could.

Neither of my parents took their eyes off the television set or spoke. I didn't feel like I had the right to turn on a light without their permission. I felt Joyce give me a little push forward.

I said, "Momma, Daddy, I want you to meet my very good friends who brought me here. I am sure you remember me telling you about them on the phone."

Without looking up Momma said drily, "Yes. I remember."

There was movement at the door and I turned to see all three of the boys standing inside the door. My two little brothers rushed over to show our parents how much better they were making their yo-yo's work. All they got from my dad was a gruff, "Take that back outside before you break something in here."

Momma never even acknowledged them. I decided to put introductions behind me and plow ahead. Speaking loudly enough to be sure my parents heard what I was saying, I told them that I was sure that Ginger had been in touch with them, but I wanted to come and tell them my plans myself. I took a deep breath and said, "I have a regular job in the country. I am planning on staying in the country and finishing school out there. I can keep my job and pay my own way. I make better grades out there than I ever made in school here. The Joneses want me to help them get their things ready, so they can move into a retirement center. I am good with them until Christmas."

My parents hadn't said a word, but Daddy decided it was time for him to speak up. He said, "Don't you come in here getting uppity with your mother and me. The deal was for you to come home. Now we hear you are backing out on us. Well, I'm telling you that you can stay out there and work. In the fall you can stay out there and go to school. But, by God you will come home on the weekends until you are seventeen."

The twins and the boys had been slowly moving toward the door. One by one they went out closing the screen door quietly behind them. I didn't answer him. I went to Momma and hugged her then Daddy and hugged him. My little brothers were standing by waiting their turns. They clung to me as I walked out the door. I called back through the screen door that Ginger was out of town and would present the paper work necessary when she got back. Until then, things would remain the same. My brothers were still clinging to me. I tickled them playfully and told them I would bring them something special when I came next time. Little Robert wanted to know if it was going to be a long time again. I told him it would not be a long time at all and hurried down the walk to the car.

As soon as I shut the door, Eddy drove away slowly until we were a couple of blocks down the street. He turned on the radio as the car roared onto the highway. Jay said, "Man. That was a bad scene."

I told him he was very much mistaken. It had been a good one compared to what it could have turned out to be. Bunkie said, "No wonder you don't want to live at home."

Joyce said, "They kind of sounded like our parents, huh June?" and June replied, "A *lot* like our parents."

Back in the country they dropped me at the Joneses at my request. I wasn't up for anything else and I knew all of them would be. When I said bye and started in the house, Jay called out, "Hey, wait a minute! You owe us! For my part, how about a date?"

I walked back to the car, looked him straight in the eyes and said,

"Unlike some people, I don't like going out with someone who is already attached. I learned that the hard way. But thanks again to all of you. It meant a lot to me, your willingness to help me out. I won't soon forget it."

Joyce said, "Drive on Eddy. We are done here today."

As the car rolled away I heard Bunkie say, "Let's go to the lake!"

June replied, "We don't have our shorts and you guys are in your good clothes and shoes."

"It's going to be dark soon, who needs clothes?" Jay countered, and they were all laughing.

Being back at the Joneses house knowing I was going to be allowed to stay there until Christmas made me happy enough for the moment. As soon as I was inside and started thinking about the lake and the days I had spent out there with J.C. I fell into a state of sadness. I wanted to call his mother and ask where I could write to him, but my foolish pride wouldn't let me. Mrs. Jones was tapping at the door. She opened it and came in. She wanted to know how my visit to my parents had gone and was happy they had agreed to let me stay on until Christmas.

"Maybe just for a while on the weekends will help repair the damage that's been done." She said optimistically.

She wanted to know if I had plans for the week end. When I said I planned to work, she patted me on the back and left me alone. I undressed and flung myself across my comfortable bed. Serandica Pappas stood at the end of the bed. She didn't say anything, but I think she must have hypnotized me to sleep. I didn't know a thing until the alarm went off and it was morning.

SPRING AND SUMMER

The following spring came early, according to The Farmer's Almanac. With it came the bluebonnets, honeysuckle and roses. Breathing in the fresh morning air filled with fragrance from the flowers mixed with the moisture of rain was delightful. This was the kind of weather which made people take to the outdoors. The Joneses had moved into the retirement center and I had been welcomed into the twins' house during the week, for work and school's sake. I went home to my parents on the weekends. Everything was going pretty well. I was very careful not to rock the boat!

Joyce had put off her wedding again back in the fall. I think she just really wasn't ready to give up the good times she had been having so long, but now she finally gave in to it. The beautiful Spring weather was making her want to have a wedding in the worst way. Wouldn't you know it, the whole crowd she had run around with for so long dressed up and went to the wedding! Eddy was right up front, along with Pee Wee and his new girlfriend Charlene, Clarence and his best girl Sue, and Jay with his girlfriend, who we all called Babe. I never learned her real name but things like that didn't bother me.

What did bother me was the language those guys used. Babe, according to them, was only Jay's "main squeeze." Every fellow that came along was greeted with "Yo, Daddy-O" and a serious couple was spoken of as one another s "Old Man or Old Lady."

Having been brought up in a household which forbade disrespectful language, use of liquor and beer, any smokes other than cigarettes or cigars, and no dirty jokes or porn of any kind, I found it all hard to get used to. Joyce, June and Babe had never seemed to mind it, even though they attended church services with their families on a regular basis.

Clarence called me "Miss Goodie" which was fine with me, I told him

116

that anyone who looked in the mirror and whistled at themselves while combing their hair was a narcissist, which was much worse. He and I were a sworn non-dating couple who only paired up once in a while to balance out the crowd. As much as I hated to admit it, I usually enjoyed being out with them all. We spent a great deal of time riding around in Eddy's big Buick Roadmaster convertible.

Eddy always drove, with his left elbow out and his left hand on a knob on the steering wheel, his right arm around Joyce's shoulders. Right up until the weekend before getting married, Joyce was always squished up next to him. Now that she was married, Eddy still hadn't hooked up with another girl. My guess was that he missed Joyce more than he let anybody know.

June was next to Pee Wee on the other side of the front seat, until he started seeing Charlene. In the back seat was Jay, Babe, me and Clarence, until he met Sue. Riding in that car, flying down the highway at speeds up to one hundred miles an hour was everybody's favorite thing to do, except for me. I got used to it though and after a couple of beers, which they always had plenty of, I didn't really care anyway.

Beer was something I had no taste for but felt odd not drinking when everyone else was doing it. Sometimes, Clarence would break out a bottle of peach brandy and pass it around. In those days, nobody seemed to mind or fear drinking after one another. Eddy always told us to "Pull a good one on the peach brandy so Bunkie won't drink it all and throw up, messing up my sidewalls when he leans out of the car to puke."

For a long time, I didn't know what sidewalls were, but felt duty bound to take at least one big swig of the peach brandy, because Eddy was clearly the boss, the leader of the pack with Jay coming in second, and everybody let them do the bossing around. By the time school was out in May we were all thick as molasses. I liked them as friends, even though they reminded me of that bunch of junior high kids in Fort Worth, that I had found disgusting. They grew on me, what else can I say?

Before long I was just like them except in one area. The guys had a friend who bought booze and weed for them. I could not stand him. He drove a white Ford Thunderbird with little port holes where back seat windows would have been if it had had a back seat. None of the crowd had IDs for alcohol except Eddy. He wasn't about to risk going to jail for buying and distributing to minors.

Weed was not as easily come by in those days as it is now. The buyer had to be someone known in the as a "safe sell" to get it at all. Babe didn't like him either. He was tall, very thin, extremely pale skinned with tattoos of vipers and demons up his arms. He had coal black eyes, which seemed to look right through a person when he offered, as he always did, "For a meager hundred bucks, a night of sex and pleasure beyond any experience you've ever had."

Every time the offer was made, the guys would all howl like a pack of wolves and reply with whatever they wanted to buy from him. Babe said he was a pimp, because he had offered her a huge sum of money once, if she would agree to work for him on the weekends as a party girl. Jay had threatened him for making the offer but drew up short when the guy told him that he had friends who would take care of him if he tried anything.

"It won't be pretty what happens to your old lady," He threatened. Jay said he would have done him in on the spot if it hadn't been for what he believed might happen to Babe. One night, we girls were talking it all over and I asked them if they had ever heard of the boys going to one of the parties the guy had mentioned. Joyce and June said that Pee Wee had admitted that he had. He had called Eddy and Bunkie liars when they said they hadn't been to one yet. June said Pee Wee swore that they had all gone out to the Western Hills Motel, which was out on the highway, for a party night and that the boys would pool their money and draw straws to see which one was going and the rest hung around to make sure the party boy got home safely.

Joyce said that the boys had been offered a free night now and again if they would gigolo for some old rich woman or "homo" which was a word everyone used at that time. She said she wasn't too sure that Eddy and Pee Wee hadn't done it, because they always had money, even when they didn't have a job. When I asked June and Joyce why they would hang out with guys like that, they both agreed that it was just for fun and that neither one of them were serious at all about the guys, but they just liked doing some things their parents would not allow if they knew about it all. I guess some things never change. Sometimes, Serandica Pappas would give me that stern look of hers, shaking her head and saying, "We must wait for Justus."

When that happened, I would stop going out for a while, then give in when June wore me down.

My weekends at home with my family had worked out better than I thought it would have. Most of my time there I spent with my little brothers. They were growing so fast. It seemed to me they grew a couple of inches taller every week. Their favorite thing to do was play ball in the back yard with the new ball, bat and glove I had bought for them. I have to admit, it was kind of fun pitching for them and watching them run the bases, which were about one third the distance they should have been, but what can you do when space is limited?

Once in a while our parents would come out and sit in the lawn chairs to watch. To me, that was special. It took some of the edge off the bitterness I had harbored against them so long. My sister Billie came at least one day out of the two days I was home each weekend, bringing my little niece who was becoming a toddler. She was a beautiful child. She looked like one of the new crawling, walking dolls I had seen in the toy department of one of the big stores. My sister was already talking about Christmas.

One Sunday morning I noticed Momma busying around in the kitchen getting lunch ready earlier than usual. When I asked why, she said, "Didn't I tell you? J. C.'s parents and the kids are coming for lunch today."

I said that she hadn't and asked if there was anything I could do to help. She told me to make garden salad, some sweet tea and to set the table. When I had finished doing that, I slipped away to the phone and called Polly. When she understood what I was asking her to do she gave that mischievous little laugh and said, "Alright, but you are going to owe me big time for it."

I told her I would work a double shift for free. I went back to the kitchen to see what else I could do to help Momma while I waited for the phone to ring. Daddy and the boys were out back putting up a backboard and hoop, so the boys could practice with the new basketball I had brought them. Running out of anything to do in the kitchen, I stepped out on the porch, staying near the door. When the phone started ringing, I waited until Momma went to answer it, then slipped in and up the hall to listen. She said, "Yes," silence, then, "Now, I don't know about that. We have friends coming to lunch who haven't seen her in over a year. They will be disappointed if she's gone when they get here." Again, silence, then, "I do understand that you are in a bind. I guess she can this time but don't try making a habit of it, after all, you have her all week."

Momma slammed down the receiver and went back to the kitchen. I slipped into the bathroom, washed my face, put on fresh makeup, combed my hair, then went into my room and changed my clothes. Afterward I went back into the kitchen and asked what time she said they would be there. Momma asked, "Who?"

"Wasn't that J. C.'s mother on the phone?" I asked.

"No!" she huffed, "It was that woman Polly from the cafe where you work. Said she's in a real bind. Somebody helping her had an emergency of some kind and had to leave work. She wants you to come back early to help her out. I told her it would be alright this time, but she's not to make a habit of it. She said there would be somebody here to pick you up in a few minutes."

She turned around to face me and said, "Go get me the camera."

Dutifully, I went and got it. When I handed it to her she said, back up over there by the table and let me get a picture of you. She snapped the picture, then said, When I get these developed, I will send them one of you, so they can see how grown up you are looking these days."

I asked her why she would send them a picture, when she could hand one to them the next time she saw them. Annoyed, she said, "Didn't I tell you they are moving back to East Texas?"

I thought, "Yeah, sure! They had a grandson living there with his mother!" Anger filled me as I heard J.C.'s voice in my head saying, "I don't have a child."

Just as I was about to ask her why, I heard a car horn, long and loud and knew my transportation away from there had arrived. I gave her a kiss on the cheek, said I better run, grabbed my bag on the way out and hurried to the curb where the big Buick sat with the top closed and the motor running. The front passenger side door was open, indicating that I was to sit in the front seat. I jumped in, slammed the door shut and Eddy slowly pulled the car away and down the street to the main thoroughfare.

Only then did I notice he was the only one in the car. I had been so excited at getting away from the house before J.C.'s family arrived, I hadn't looked toward the back seat. When I turned and started to ask why everybody was so quiet, I was actually shocked. In all the time we had been running around, I had never seen Eddy in that car alone. He always had an entourage everywhere he went.

Until then he had said nothing at all, so to calm my nerves, I asked how he had managed to get away all alone. He gave me a slow smile and said he had sneaked out on them. Trying to keep him from noticing how nervous I was at being alone with him, I asked if they all would be upset when they realized he was gone without them? He gave the same mischievous laugh as his mom and said, "Today, I couldn't care less. It sounded like you needed rescuing and I figured I could manage it without their help."

Suddenly, I realized that I had put myself into the very situation that I had been avoiding. Joyce's words kept ringing in my ears. She had called me a couple of times since the wedding telling me that I should get to know Eddy better.

"He likes you a lot. He wants to ask you out. A real date. Just the two of you. He's a good guy."

He wasn't taking the usual route, so I asked where he was going.

"It's a surprise," he said flashing me a quick smile and I noticed his teeth were not the shiny, blinding white J.C.'s had been.

That thought then led to another one, about the surprise J.C. had for me in the summer after my fifteenth birthday I was becoming extremely nervous being alone with Eddy, in a frightening way that I never had when I was alone with J.C. I tried telling myself that it was because I hadn't known him since I was a child the way I had J.C. I thought about how good Polly was and how Joyce and June talked about Eddy and his friends being such good guys.

His eyes were dark and mysterious. I tried not to look at him and keep my eyes open for something that would let me know where we were headed. It was a road I hadn't been on and everything was unfamiliar, which added to my nervousness. He reached over to turn up the radio and flashed me a big smile. Again, I noticed that his teeth were not very nice then I told myself that his heavy smoking was discoloring his teeth. J.C. hadn't been a smoker.

I was trying to think of anything except the fact that I was alone with a guy whom I knew only as a good friend of one of my good friends, who knew him to be a good guy. We had left the city and were out on the highway heading south. I turned sideways in the seat facing Eddy and told him that I was a person who didn't like surprises. I appreciated him rescuing me from my parents, as well as all the times he had driven with our friends to take me home to the Joneses house, but now, he had shown up alone, definitely not headed for any of the locations we usually went. I tried again, "Rally, I insist on knowing where we are going."

I had said it sternly, hoping he would take the hint that I didn't appreciate being kept in the dark. He gave that mischievous laugh again, then said I would know in about five minutes. I was, more than furious, maybe irate was what I was, but in five minutes we had better be somewhere I would like being.

He had turned off the radio and developed a frown which made his eyes look even more mysterious. We rode along with only the steady purr of the big car's engine breaking the silence. When he turned off the main highway onto a two-lane county road, I kept quiet, but when he made a sharp turn onto a dirt road, I protested with, "You need to find a place to turn around and I mean soon," hoping he wouldn't notice the panic I was feeling.

He started a slow teasing laugh, which got a little louder each time he took a breath and started again. I did not like that kind of behavior and told him so. Suddenly, the car slid to a stop. I was so angry I did not see all the cars up ahead. I did not see the house nor hear the music. My head was roaring with ill will toward my abductor. What I thought might happen next really infuriated me.

He got out of the car and started walking away leaving the keys in the ignition. I slid across the seat and had my hand ready to start the engine, turn around and head back the way we had come, when I heard June calling, "Hey, come on to the house, there's a party going on!"

Her familiar voice did not calm me. Although, I hadn't started the car, I was ready to do so and kept my hand steady on the key. When June stuck her head in the window and asked why I wasn't getting out, I could not control my anger any longer. She had beer breath. She opened the car door and said, "Come on, loosen up. Have a little fun for a change. It's a party for God's sake! What's wrong with you?"

Through clenched teeth, I asked, "What kind of party?"

She put her hands on her hips and said, "A birthday party! What kind of party do you think?"

I still wasn't convinced and sat stubbornly. Maybe she realized I was upset because he asked me if Eddy hadn't told me on the way out. When I assured her that he hadn't told me anything, she said it was his cousin Blondie's birthday and one of Eddy's uncles and his wife were sponsoring a birthday bash for her. Then she said, "Come on in, we've been to a lot of parties out here. There's nothing going on that is illegal except a little beer drinking by minors. Whose gonna know?"

Reluctantly, I tagged along behind her, through the house and out back to the patio where at least twenty people were moving and grooving to loud rock and roll music. Eddy and his cousin Blondie were dirty dancing right in the middle of them all. I couldn't stop my mouth from dropping open. Somebody handed me a bottle of beer and June made her way onto the crowded dance floor.

As the afternoon wore on toward evening, it dawned on me that Polly knew Eddy wanted to ask me out. By sending him to pick me up on his way to the party, she had given him an opportunity of time alone with me to ask. So, I thought to myself as I sat on a tall bar stool sipping on the third beer of the afternoon. I didn't like beer, but the day was hot, and the beer was ice cold. The second one I had with a charcoal grilled burger and home fries. Eddy's aunt and uncle had turned out to be really nice people. They had no children of their own and enjoyed entertaining the nieces and nephews of their families, who were always welcome to bring friends.

June came over to sit next to me. She hopped right up on the bar. She had used her head and kept her beer drinking to a minimum not wanting to go home "polluted" she told me. Her parents had given her permission to go to the party, but they didn't know there would be any drinking. I decided to ask her why she hadn't told me about the party when she found out. She said, "Honest to God, I thought you would be at your parents all day."

It was Joyce's Sunday to work at the cafe until closing and Eddy had told them the party would be over early because his aunt and uncle had to be on the job very early Monday morning. They had all decided not to say anything about the party to me because they didn't want me to feel left out, being home with my family.

I told her I didn't like them being sneaky and sending Eddy to get me without somebody with him. She looked at me curiously and asked, "Are you afraid of him?"

I huffed, "Of course not. I just don't like other people trying to pull my strings. I'm nobody's puppet."

"Is that honestly what you think or is it the beer talking?" she asked.

I reiterated, "It's not the beer. My head is clear enough to know what I want and what I don't want. If he wants me to go out with him, he is going to have to ask me himself. I sincerely doubt that I would go out with him on a real date. He seems to be a good guy alright, but I don't like the way he teased me this afternoon, not telling me where we were going. Now I feel foolish and I shouldn't have to feel that way. He could have told me, and I would have thought a lot better of him for it."

June slid off the counter and said, "I'm supposed to be out with Jay tonight. I might as well tell you that too is part of Joyce and Jay's plan. The plan was for us to switch out tonight."

I asked her to explain in more detail. As it turned out, Jay and Joyce had decided it was time to take action and help Eddy and me get together for a date. I had heard about that before from Joyce and had told her I was against such a plan. Eddy might be a good guy, but I had no interest in him or any of the other guys we ran around with. I reminded her that my heart, body and soul belonged to somebody else, and as a friend I had gone along with them all to let them know that I wasn't succumbing to depression.

June asked if anyone had ever told me that I was a hopeless case. Again, I asked her to explain what she meant. She said, "You absolutely refuse to have any fun! Why didn't you get out there and dance with Eddy? Or if not Eddy, Jay or Bunkie? Don't say you don't dance, I know you do. When Joyce and I wanted to learn some new steps, you were the one who showed us how they were done."

I told her the kind of dancing I liked to do, and the kind of dancing Eddy and the guys liked to do, were worlds apart. She hissed, "Snob."

Then laughed letting me know it was good natured ribbing. Jay sauntered over and asked if we wanted to go to the drive-in for a movie, and let the booze wear off before going home.

Answering for the both of us, June said, "Sure!

I said it was a good idea, but I was not about to go with Eddy. June said, "Fine, I will be happy to go with Eddy. Jay and I are just out on a whim, right Jay?"

He said, "That's right June bug," then he looked at me and said, "Will it get you all bent out of shape to sit with me?"

I said no, as long as it was clear that's all I was going to do. He grinned real big and said, "Haven't you heard? Babe and I are engaged?"

"So was Joyce, it didn't seem to stop her." I quipped but Jay just shrugged his shoulders, as if to say, "No big deal."

Clarence's car wouldn't start. Everybody teased, telling him to remember, he had to put gasoline in the tank. Somebody else said, "Maybe he planned on running out of gasoline, just not so soon!"

More laughing. Clarence and his new girlfriend, Sue, took it all in stride. To my surprise, Eddy offered his brother the use of the Buick, saying that he would ride back with Jay.

I'll admit it, I sometimes catch on slowly but, I do catch on. Walking with Jay out to the car, I remembered that he and Joyce had instigated a switch out plan. Joyce wasn't even there, but old faithful, Jay, was going ahead with it. When we got to the car, Eddy and June were already in the back seat, all hugged up, laughing hilariously, about who knows what. Before we got into the car, Jay bent down and whispered in my ear, "I'm supposed to call out 'switcheroo'. What do you say we have a little fun first?"

His head was still close to my face. Suspicious person that I am, I whispered back, "What exactly do you have in mind?"

"Well, June thinks I'm going to say it now."

I looked up into his face. His dark brown eyes were sparkling playfully. I wanted to be clear on the matter, so I said, "I am not going along with the plan. I never said I would." He put an arm around me, squeezed me to him and said playfully, "That's okay with me green eyes."

He still had a big grin on his face and he winked. I knew I was safe with him, but I didn't like getting drawn in on other peoples' games. Not wanting to be seen as a prude, I let him take my hand and lead me around to the driver side of the car. He opened the door and whispered again, "Stay close to me. Let's make 'em sweat."

He winked again, and I took it as it was intended. I had seen Jay and Babe together and was sure any kind of flirtation on Jays part was fake.

After he got the car parked at the drive-in and the speaker on the window, he put his arm around me and pulled me closer than I cared to be, but he whispered in my ear, "Relax and play along, Eddy doesn't know anything about the plan. He likes you enough to start getting jealous. When he and June leave the car to go to the concession stand, and they will, you and I will have our laugh."

I just nodded and pretended to watch the movie. Being so close to Jay was making me a little nervous. Every time I tried to pull away he held me in place pretty easily. Jay wasn't quite as tall as J.C., but he reminded me of him a lot. He had thick, black, wavy hair, a handsome face and a muscular build. The cologne he was wearing smelled wonderful. I admitted to myself that he would be a pretty good substitute for J.C., if he wasn't already engaged to Babe.

I had just relaxed enough to lay my head against Jays shoulder when Eddy said, rather gruffly, "We better go to the concession stand now or there will be a line so long the movie will start again before we get our order in."

Jay said, 'You two go on. We're good, right green eyes?"

I couldn't find a word to say so I just nodded and smiled. They walked away from the car, looking back a couple of times to see if we were still snuggled together. Jay didn't release his arm from around my shoulders until they were completely out of sight. I moved to the other side of the car and leaned against the door. Jay started laughing. I wondered if he was laughing because we had "Played a good one" on the other two, or at me because I got away from him so swiftly. Answering my question, he said,

"Did you notice how mad old Ed was?"

I said I hadn't noticed and he said, "He's green with envy right now."

I told him I wasn't sure I liked the game we were playing. The last thing I would want was for Babe to be mad at me. To my surprise, he said, "She and I talked it over before she left. Joyce asked if she'd mind lending me out, just once or twice while she was gone and just to make Eddy jealous. She said it was fine with her, just not to take it too far."

I told him they were all a bunch of nut cases to think they were going to push me into going out with Eddy. I told him I felt the way about J.C. that he and Babe felt about one another. He reached over, took my hand in his, pulled me back across the seat and said softly, "If you can't be with the one you love, love the one you are with, that's my motto."

We just sat looking at one another a few seconds then he kissed me, softly. I couldn't bring myself to kiss him back. It just seemed so wrong. I pulled away and stayed against the door until June and Eddy came back, both with handfuls of snacks. Jay had scooted down in the seat and pretended to be asleep. Giggling in her usual way, June said, "What have you done to him?"

Jay sat up in the seat and said, "The two of us just don't see things the same way," then he shouted, "Switcheroo!"

June didn't wait one second. She climbed over into the front seat between us and said to Jay, "Don't worry baby, you and I do see eye to eye."

He put his arm around her and she snuggled right up to him as if it was the most natural thing in the world. When the front door of the car opened, I almost fell out on the ground. I caught myself and turned to get out of the car, repulsed by the promiscuous behavior June was displaying toward Jay. Eddy was standing at the car door. He said, "Switch has been called. You are going to have to sit in back with me or move over, so I can get in beside you."

I thought it might be a good idea to move over and let him in front with the rest of us. That way there wouldn't be enough room for more hanky-panky than I was willing to deal with. June turned her head toward me and said, "You two get in the back seat. Jay and I have plans for the front seat."

I looked up at Jay and he was shaking his head no. I scooted over next to June and Eddy got in beside me. He put his arm up over the back of the seat and said, "Jay, we better get these girls home, they've both got to be at work early in the morning."

June's "Aww, no!" made us all laugh. I decided to ask Eddy if he had found work yet. After all, his mother had said he and Clarence were going to have to find work soon. I was feeling bold. We were all tight packed in the front seat and headed home. He said he hadn't gotten anything for sure but had at least one good offer at a furniture factory. His mother had worked there once and had put in a good word to the guy who was the boss. Then I asked how he managed to always have money for spending when he wasn't working. I knew he didn't want to answer that question, but it was my way of putting him on notice that I was the kind of girl who wanted to know a lot about someone who planned on getting a "real date" with me.

'That's kind of a long story," he said. I told him I had time to hear it and he said, "Well, I guess nobody's told you but it's like this, I had a couple of pretty bad things happen to me awhile back. For a long time, I couldn't even sit up in bed, much less walk. The first was from being burned badly on my right side in a fire. The second was an awful wreck. My oldest brother and the one just older than me, Roy, and I were all out riding around on some of the back roads. My brother Roy was driving, we were in his car. He was hitting some pretty high speeds. We had all been drinking. I hadn't been out much in such a long time, it was fun being out with them. My oldest brother, Cecil, had been out of state a couple of years and was going to leave out again the next day. Anyway, Roy couldn't get the car straightened back up from a curve in the road. We flew off the road, tore up a hundred or so feet of fence posts and barbed wire and landed upside down in a field full of cows. My brother Roy was dead. Killed instantly."

June and Jay had been completely quiet. I knew Eddy must be telling the truth, there were tears in his eyes. I felt so bad that I had asked, but he still hadn't answered my question about the money. I didn't want to seem cold hearted, so I wasn't about to ask again. After a minute, he started talking again. "All my aunts and uncles started giving me money when the fire accident happened. They kept it up after Roy died in the wreck and I was hospitalized for a long time. I don't ask them for it. They just give it to me. I guess they don't know of anything that helps more."

I asked about his other brother. He said, "Cecil barely had a scratch on him. He left for California as soon as Roy's funeral was over. I couldn't even go to my own brother's funeral because my injuries were too bad."

At that point Jay jumped in, "Old Ed was out of commission so long, we started thinking we might be going to lose him too. But he's a tough cuss. Finally pulled out of it. That was just a little over a year ago."

June asked if I remembered the guy who rode the Harley up on the school grounds every day at lunch but before I could say that I did, she said, "That was Eddy's brother, Roy."

Jay stopped the car by the front gate at the Joneses house. Eddy took a deep breath, released it, got out and asked if he could walk me to the door. I said goodnight to June and Jay and walked slowly with Eddy to the porch. He didn't come up on the porch. My heart had softened considerably for him after hearing those sad events. I went back down the steps to where he stood. The porch light was on and I could see the pain lingering in his eyes.

126

My heart went out to him. I had never felt such compassion for another person. I touched his arm gently and told him how very sorry I was for his loss, kissed him on the cheek, then watched as he walked back to the car.

Alone in my room, I kept thinking about the things Eddy had shared. I thought about us all in that Buick, speeding down the highway and around the curvy back roads at the lake, and wondered why he drove the way he did knowing the same thing could happen again. Then it hit me, he actually had a death wish, and didn't care if he took all his friends with him.

Instantly, Serandica Pappas appeared. She was looking pitifully at me. Finally, she spoke her usual words, "We have to find Justus," then she said, "You must help me find Justus."

My mind was so full of what Eddy had just told me that for the first time, it annoyed me that she kept on about her Justus. When I started getting ready for bed, she disappeared. Needless to say, I slept fitfully, tossing and turning, I couldn't get comfortable and I could not get Jays words to stop ringing in my ears, "If you can't be with the one you love, love the one you are with."

I could still feel the softness of his kiss on my lips and wondered why.

Business was booming at the cafe. No wonder, it was a pleasant place to eat any meal of the day. Polly knew her business well. She always took a few minutes out of the kitchen during each shift to circulate among the customers, asking them questions about their preferences, and finding out how they were being treated by the waitstaff. She heard few complaints, but she was quick to call all of us on any she did get.

People were generous with their tips and that made it all worthwhile. I was concerned about Polly. She put in way too many hours at the cafe. I couldn't help wondering why. We had all learned how to take care of the place. I could cook almost as good as she could, having learned from her and one of the women on the evening shift was an excellent cook. She had shared some of her recipes with Polly, who used them to liven up the regular menu every Sunday.

She worked seven days a week, sixteen and eighteen hours a day. She didn't even go to the bank, she sent Joyce most of the time. June and I wanted nothing to do with the money, other than put it in the register. In my opinion, Polly should be the one out front taking care of the register, but she told us we each had to use a special key and make our own change. It was a good idea. We knew she wanted everything coming out of the kitchen up to her standards and we all appreciated that she trusted us with the money when she was busy.

One thing she did do, she emptied the register on each shift after a big run was over, leaving only enough for making change up to fifty dollars. Nobody knew where she hid the money in the kitchen. We all agreed it was better that way. I was still getting paid cash at the end of each shift and I too had a special place in my room where I hoarded money like Scrooge. Serandica Pappas was the only one who knew where I banked, and she wasn't going to tell anybody.

Many nights, I kept it by my pillow, rewinding and listening again and again until I fell asleep. There was over three hundred dollars stashed away safely there, along with the handwritten note from J.C. which said, "You are my little sweetheart and I will love you forever."

Each time I added money, I took the paper out and held it close to my heart, crying until Serandica Pappas showed up to comfort me, and remind me about her Justus. I was beginning to understand how she felt, not being able to be with the one she loved so much. When Jay's words, "If you can't be with the one you love, love the one you are with," popped into my head, she disappeared immediately.

I wondered what it all meant. I wondered where in the world J.C. was, what his life was like in the military, and why I never got a letter. I felt sorry for not talking to him before he went away for basic training, but my selfish, childish, heart was so broken, that I could not see the "big picture" as he had called it.

I should have stayed when his parents came for lunch at my parents' house and asked his mom for an address so that I could write to him and say I was sorry, but I was sure that his parents and my parents were behind his doing what he did. I didn't want to see them or talk to them. I had nothing solid to base it on except what I felt in my heart, and Serandica Pappas always agreed with me on that matter.

The last week end of summer I went clothes shopping for school. For the first time in a couple of years, I was on a city bus, headed uptown. I had a few things in the closet which were plenty good to wear another year, but I could not resist the new straight skirts, sweaters and penny loafers. I had seen Eddy's cousin Blondie in a couple of those tight skirts, doing the twist. My figure was as good or better than hers. She was actually a little on the chubby side. Not much mind you, but I had lost my childish chub and was proud of it. All that hard work was paying off in more ways than one.

I had negotiated with Momma to let me go and shop alone for my own things, after all, it was my hard-earned money I would be spending, and it wasn't costing my parents a thing. When I offered to go along with her on Sunday to shop for my little brothers' school things, which I was going to help pay for, she turned me down which hurt my feelings considerably.

She wanted to wait until a couple of days before school started then find some sales, she told me. She said if I could help with paying for their new shoes and haircuts that would be enough. I wanted to help so I gave her fifty dollars, which she snatched out of my hand as if she was afraid I might suddenly change my mind. She didn't even say thank you. Later, I made sure to tell Ronnie and Robert that I had given Momma the money. As usual, they gave me a big hug and said thank you.

School got off to a grand start with an assembly in the auditorium, then hurry and scurry of getting to and from the lockers in the hall and into home room. I was a junior at last! The first day getting used to the classes went well for me, but immediately after that first day, everything started going downhill. I was having trouble concentrating at school. It was hard for me to study much at night, I was so tired after work. At the end of the first six weeks, my parents announced that a letter had come from the school indicating that I wasn't doing grade level work.

They didn't say any more about it until it was almost time to go back to the country. Eddy and June or Jay and June had been coming in on Sunday afternoons to pick me up. I would hang out with the crowd until bedtime, then hurry and try to do any assignments I needed to turn in on Monday before getting to bed.

To me it wasn't a big deal, after all it was only the first six weeks of school. I got into my first argument with my parents since I started coming home on the weekends. I had tried hard to hold my tongue, but that day it got loose.

"It's mostly that stupid math!" I yelled at Momma.

She replied, "Don't you talk to me in that tone of voice," then she added, rather calmly, "If you can't keep your grades up, you will have to quit working at that roadhouse and come home to finish school."

I said flatly that I wasn't quitting my job and the cafe was not a roadhouse. It was a nice, clean, pleasant place for people to bring their families to eat. My mouth just couldn't stay shut. I told her, if they had ever one time come out there to eat, they would know that it was not a roadhouse. Momma was not one to be bested on anything. If she felt like she was losing in an argument, she always started throwing dirt.

"You *could* use the time you run around with that bunch of heathens to study. God only knows what you have been up to with that bunch. I've got a good mind to have your Daddy go out and tell them all to keep away from you when they pull up and honk that horn! Yes, that's what I'm going to do. We will pick you up and bring you home. You've got six more weeks to get your grades up. You better get them up and keep them up or you will not stay out there any longer!"

Until then, Daddy hadn't said a word. He had sat with his eyes glued to the television set. I was telling Momma that I would get my grades up and that she could quit worrying about it when he stood up and told me to shut my mouth while I was ahead. He said there was nothing he would like better than to go out and tell my friends where to go.

The look on his face was the same look he had when he used the belt on me. We stood staring at one another a couple of minutes. His look was daring me to say another word, but I couldn't let it go. I told him they had to quit treating me like a child. I was going to be seventeen soon and I was a young woman with a real job, making real money, paying my own way.

Momma got up, stood between Daddy and me and said, "This is the last slack we are going to give you. Get the grades up in the next six weeks or else."

Her look told me that I was going to be very sorry if I kept on. I ran out of the room and into the back yard. Ronnie and Robert had been listening at the back door. I held them to me and we were all crying when the car horn sounded. I asked them to please run around the house and tell my friends I would be right there. They took off around the house in a run. I went as quietly up the hall as I could, grabbed my bag and was at the car before Daddy came out of the house.

My brothers had already run toward the back of the house. I slammed the door shut and Eddy took off. He had seen my face and heard whatever my brothers had said, and realized a swift exit was best. Out on the highway, I saw that we were alone again. I was trying to get my face straightened up, but it wasn't working. Tears kept coming as soon as I wiped them away. He said, "Come over here," and patted the seat beside him.

At that point, I didn't care where I sat. All I wanted was to feel better about what had just happened at my parents' house. He didn't ask, he said, "Let's ride out to Eagle Mountain Lake."

I told him I was not up to a party at the moment and he said, "No party, just you and me. We can sit out there and talk it over."

I was still upset and found myself saying, "Sure, why not."

When we got to the lake, he got out of the car, opened the trunk, took out a cooler chest and set it on the hood. He took out a couple of bottles of beer and opened them with what he called his church key then handed one to me and got into the car on the passenger side.

Instead of moving closer to him. I slid into the driver seat. He just smiled and took a big swallow of his beer. I swallowed a big mouthful. It was cold, sudsy and didn't taste so bad. The day had been scorching at one hundred degrees. He said, "Doesn't taste half bad on a hot day."

I nodded, and he continued to make conversion, "Looks like Summer might last into Fall."

Again, I nodded, and he said, "Are you ready to tell me what was going on back there at your parents' house?"

I took a deep breath and blurted it all out. I was crying again. He moved over beside me, scooted down in the seat a little, told me to relax and put my head on his shoulder. I told him that I did not like people telling me what to do. He said, "Okay, if that's the way you see it, but, I'm just trying to help you unwind."

He downed another swallow of his beer. I sat wondering if I should drink anymore of mine. Finally, I told him I was afraid I was being lousy company for him and apologized. He sat back up in the seat put his arm around me and told me not to ever think I was lousy company for him. He said he was happy just to sit and drink his beer, if that was all I wanted him to do. I wasted no time in telling him that suited me because I wasn't up to anything but figuring out how I could make my grades and live at the twins' house until I finished school or at least until I was seventeen in November.

He wanted to know more about my situation. I told him all I felt like he needed to know, then asked him to tell me more about his family. He talked about his brothers and sister, his step-dad and how his momma was the best mother on earth. He said she was like her father, his grandad, had been, good natured, loved kids, and he didn't mind admitting she was his best girl until I came along. He gave that little mischievous laugh that I had heard before, not only from him but from Polly too.

He finished his beer and asked if I wanted to go sit by the water for a while. He took the cooler out of the trunk and headed for a grassy spot on a little rise. We made a pit stop on the way, then settled down on the grass.

He handed me the second bottle of beer. I sat looking at it, one in each hand. I decided to finish off the first one. While I was doing that he told me he was sorry I was having so much trouble with my parents. He wanted to know if it was with one more than the other. I told him it was both of them. He confided in me that he had never seen his own dad, at least not that he could remember.

His step-dad had raised him and his brother Roy. His brother Cecil was told to leave because he didn't like their step-dad and didn't feel that he treated their mother right. He said Cecil showed up now and again, but always got into a fight with their step-dad and was always told to leave, which he seemed happy to do.

While he was talking, looking out across the lake I glanced down at his right forearm. He was wearing a white t-shirt which left his whole arm exposed. All the guys back then, had a pack of cigarettes, rolled into the sleeve of the t-shirt, because there were no pockets in most of them. Usually, they also had a book of matches from their favorite hangout spot in the cellophane wrapper around the pack of cigarettes. I pretended not to notice his scarred forearm. I thought the permanent scar my little brother Ronnie had from the front of his chest to the middle of his back, because of the heart surgery, was the worst I had ever seen, but Eddy's forearm and part of his upper arm was marred terribly. I wanted to reach over and tenderly run my hand up and down his arm, but something kept me from touching him.

When I looked up, he was watching me. He turned his arm one way and another, held it up as if wanting to take a good look at it himself and said, "I know it looks pretty bad but not near as bad as it did. My right leg is in

L.A. LAYNE

the same shape, but they both work alright. I probably would have died if it had not been for my Aunt Elsie. She's a nurse you know."

When he fell silent, I asked if he liked his step-dad. I had never heard Polly mention him. He said no, he tolerated him because he had to.

We sat until it was dark, baring our souls to one another, drinking beer and smoking cigarettes. I had been around smoking all my life but until that evening I hadn't taken up the habit. When Eddy lit two and handed one to me, I took it, puffed on it, without inhaling the smoke. Surely that couldn't hurt anything. After the sixth beer, anything seemed to be alright. I was tired of fighting it all. I just wanted a little relief from all the stress and pain. My mind told me one thing. My body kept telling me something else and Jay's words echoed in my head, "If you can't be with the one you love. Love the one you are with."

We were both laying on our backs, looking at the stars, trying to find the little dipper. The big dipper wasn't hard to spot. Maybe it was all that beer. He rolled closer to me and said, "There it is. See?"

He was pointing to the sky just over my head. I tilted my head back trying to see the constellation and was surprised when he kissed me. It wasn't a tender kiss. It wasn't a demanding kiss. It was like an asking for another kiss. Like a hungry, needy kiss. When he kissed me the second time, I kissed him back. Mine was an "I'm not too sure, but I guess it's alright, after all, we've really gotten to know one another tonight" kiss.

A few more beers, a few more kisses, a little more necking and petting, then he told me that he didn't just want to go steady. He didn't want to play any more "switcharoo." He wanted me to be his girl and his alone.

My head was swirling. I didn't remember that I was in love with J.C. and I sure didn't see or hear Serandica Pappas telling me we needed to find Justus. With every kiss, all the plans I had ever made disappeared from my mind. Eddy was there, he was real, and his kisses were good.

The one thing that kept repeating itself in my drunken mind and body was Jay's words, "If you can't be with the one you love, love the one you are with" and that was how I became known as "Eddy's girl" from that night on.

My parents pestered me constantly about my grades. Between school, working at the cafe and spending time with Eddy, I now did very little with the usual crowd. When things got too heated and I told Eddy I was afraid I might get pregnant, he told me that wasn't likely to happen because of his injuries from the fire. He explained to me in detail about the doctors informing him that he shouldn't expect to father children and asked if talking to his Aunt Elsie would ease my mind.

I still wasn't convinced and told him that I wanted to get married if he was going to keep up his constant sexual advances. He said he would make me a deal. He would buy me an engagement ring if I would finish school.

132

He said it would be impossible to get married in the state of Texas before I was seventeen, without my parents' consent. His plan was to get the ring, ask my parents' permission and if they wouldn't allow it, to wait until I had my birthday in November. He said, "One way or another, I want you to finish high school."

I had heard that before, but that seemed a terribly long time ago.

The little gold ring was nothing fancy, but I wore it proudly, as if wearing it and being engaged to be married gave consent to do anything I wanted and as much as I felt like.

Halloween weekend, I asked Eddy to take me to my parents' house, to tell them about our engagement. We got all dressed up and arrived at their door happy, hand in hand and got the usual greeting from Ronnie and Robert. Then we went inside to tell my parents our news.

I don't know if my happiness set them off, or what. We told them our plan and I went over to Momma first, proudly displaying the ring on my finger. I told her that Polly was giving us an engagement party at the cafe and we wanted them to come and bring my brothers.

She never looked at the ring, she kept starring at Eddy. At first, when she made no comment, I thought she was speechless because she was surprised. More nicely than I had ever heard him speak in a very long time, Daddy said, "Come here sugar girl, let me get a good look at that ring."

Eddy was still standing just inside the door. My brothers ran to have a look. Just as I stuck my hand out for Daddy to look the ring over, he grabbed my hand and before I could pull my hand away, he snatched the ring from my finger, threw it across the room at Eddy, stood up and said, "Get out of here you little hoodlum, and don't bother coming back."

My little brothers were clinging to me so tightly that I couldn't move easily. It all happened so suddenly, it seemed like I was seeing it all in slow motion. Eddy picked up the ring, stepped outside the door, put his foot against the screen and said, "She's my girl. I'm going to marry her whether you like it or not, you haven't seen the last of me."

He walked to the car and drove away. I was still trying to get past Daddy and out the door. He grabbed my arm, pushed me back over to the couch and down beside Momma. He stood there glaring at me. I glared back and knew it was the last effort I was going to make trying to be civil to him.

Momma said, "So that's why your grades have been falling. Well, I told you we were tired of your excuses. The last time you started that stuff it took almost losing the best friends we ever had to keep you from making a fool of your silly little self. That one found out what he got for it and this one will too if you don't straighten up and fly right."

There it was, now I knew for sure what I had thought all along was true. I looked at Daddy and saw the guilt in his eyes, without caring what the consequences might be I asked, "What did you do to cause J.C. to join the army?"

Momma told my brothers to go out back and play, that she and Daddy had some things they wanted to talk to me about by myself. Reluctantly, they went. As soon as the back door shut, she said t Daddy, "Do ahead, tell her Reagan."

Daddy sat back down in his chair, calmly as if nothing had happened, lit a cigarette and said, "I told J.C. that he keep away from you until you were at least twenty-one years old. I told him in front of his parents, so he knew I meant business. I told him I would carry out what had only been a threat until then. You are under age, so I said your momma and I would file charges of statutory rape against him and to make his choice, go to the army or go to jail"

My eyes were burning with tears, my chest ached as if I would never be able to catch my breath again. Struggling to my feet, I ran into my room, closed the door to it behind me and fell across the bed, sure that I was dying. After a little while, Momma opened the door and came in. She said, "That's enough of that stuff now. You asked for it then and you are asking for it now. Get your bags packed and be quick about it, or tomorrow that Eddy is going to be given the same choice."

Feeling I had an ace up my sleeve, I said, 'that won't' work with Eddy, he has injuries from being burned in two bad fires and a horrible car accident. He has already tried to join the army and they wouldn't take him for those reasons."

Momma huffed, "Well then, I guess he will find himself in jail if you don't get your stuff packed in the next few minutes." I told her that everything, besides my gown and pajamas, were at the Joneses house and I would have to get them from out there. I was thinking about the money in the music box. Let them take me away somewhere. If I could get my hands on my money, when I turned seventeen I could go on however I chose.

"No," she said, "we are not taking you anywhere but to the bus station. In an hour you will be on your way to my sister Venus's house in East Texas. You can stay there until you come to your senses. After we get you on that bus, we will go out and get your things and send what we think you need of it to you."

Getting on that bus was one of the hardest things I had done in a long time. Daddy took me by the arm and led me a few feet away. He said, "Don't go getting any foolish notions about getting off the bus and making any phone calls, that hoodlum will be in jail before morning comes if you do. Don't entertain the idea when you get there either. I mean business."

I knew he would do what he said, if he could be so mean to a friend, he sure wouldn't mind doing so to someone he didn't like.

There were very few people on the bus going east. I had taken the first seat across from the driver, I tried to think about anything besides what I had been told by my parents, but it wasn't working. I felt no remorse for any of my behaviors.

What J.C. and I had together was romantic and passionate. What Eddy and I had was completely different. It was deep rooted desire. Bodily release of pent up longings and frustrations from our early years. We had things together that were common, such as my asthmatic past and his injuries. Two people who could have died very young but were saved for something special down the road.

I longed for what I had with J.C. until my whole body ached. Eddy had told me that he longed for someone of his very own. He had grown tired of the party girls. I, too longed for someone of my own with whom I could share my longings and desires. My mind was still full of J.C., my body was with Eddy. "If you can't be with the one you love, love the one you are with."

The night was stormy. Lighting flashed from all directions. I was almost hypnotized by the huge wipers pushing away water from the windshield of the bus. Serandica Pappas appeared between me and the driving rain on the windshield. Smiling, she said, "Now we can find Justus."

I blinked away the tears in my eyes and smiled back at her, then closed my eyes and fell asleep. I dreamed of J.C. being at his parents' house when I arrived in East Texas, and thought how strange it was, that I hadn't remembered they had gone back there to live. I dreamed of Eddy, out with the crowd again, the Buick speeding down the highway, and I wasn't with them. Joyce was sitting next to him and she was wearing my ring.

Mommas sister, Aunt Venus had four girls, all older than me, except her youngest who had a speech impediment and seemed younger than she actually was because of it. I hadn't been around my aunt and her family for such a long time that I had forgotten what a nice, sweet person she was. Seeing her in her white uniform, waiting with her husband Albert, to pick me up at the bus station, it made me think about how much I was going to miss Eddy. He was always talking about his Aunt Elsie and her family. She too was a nurse.

Waiting my turn to step out of the bus, I wondered why I had never mentioned to him that I also had an aunt who was a nurse. She said, "You and I will go on to the car, Albert can wait for your bags."

I told her there was no need for him to wait because I had no bags. The smile disappeared from her face. She said, "You are going to stay awhile with us, aren't you?"

We all started walking to the car and I told her truthfully that I had no choice in the matter. Not wanting her to think I was being rude, I told her I was very happy she had allowed me to come for a visit. Thinking Momma might not have told her why I was there, I asked. She said, "Honey, all your mother said was you needed time away from Fort Worth, we don't care what the reason is, we are glad to have you, but you may have to wear some of the girls' clothes since you didn't bring any with you."

On the way to the house I told them my parents were sending my things separately. Neither of them voiced an opinion. It wasn't far to their house from the bus station. After living in the Fort Worth area, my home town looked like a tourist stop, blink your eyes and you might miss it.

My aunt had just finished a long shift at the hospital, but she insisted that I eat a sandwich. Her oldest daughter, who still lived at home and had never married, came in and ate with me. She was my sister's age.

Long after her parents went to bed, we sat in the living-room in the dark talking things over. I held nothing back. I knew she would understand. She said, "While you don't have Billie to talk to about things, I will be your confidant. I think my parents have the right to know the truth of why you are here, but I won't mention what you've told me if you don't want me too."

I said that I planned to tell them at some point any way because I too felt like they should know. She gave me a pair of pajamas and we said good night. I wasn't that sleepy, having slept most of the way there on the bus. I pulled the afghan from the back of the sofa over me and tried to go to sleep again. It didn't happen. I lay awake wondering what was going to happen next and hoping they wouldn't try to force me to go to school. As far as I was concerned, I was through with a formal education.

Finding a job there shouldn't be too hard if they had a drugstore lunch counter or cafe. After all, I had a lot of experience. But that was only plan B. Plan A had formed in my mind while I was on the bus. With any kind of luck, Momma would send my things right away. If she didn't look to carefully, she would also send my music box.

Knowing Momma, I figured she wouldn't miss a thing. If only I had the money with me. Serandica Pappas kept me company until dawn. She didn't say anything, just sat at the end of the sofa by my feet and stared at me.

A week passed before my things arrived in cardboard boxes. My uncle had picked them up at the bus depot. They hadn't even bothered sending them express. Of course, that would have cost more. What did they care if I had to borrow clothing from my cousins? My hopes soared as I dug through the cartons for my music box and the freedom it held for me. Finally, I placed every last article onto the floor. There was no music box.

My heart sank. I should have known. Resigning myself to the fact that payment for all my hard work was gone, I got busy putting everything away in the closet space my cousin, Myrtle Lou, graciously allotted me. She said it would be best if she shared her room with me since she was privy to my reason for being there. She also told me that it wasn't necessary for the other girls to know.

She had been sharing her room with her youngest sister, but she along with her mother thought it would be best for her to share her room with me. She said, after all, I have been assigned to keep an eye on you. She made a face when she said it, so I knew she was just trying to be funny. Her little sister had been moved in with her middle sister for the duration of my visit.

Myrtle Lou had her own car. She worked for a factory in town that manufactured ladies under garments, everything from bras to garter belts. She offered to try to help me get a job there for which I was grateful. It would only be part time at first, but some money was better than no money.

I was putting away the notebooks and school items on one of the closet shelves when I ran across the sealed envelope. It was business sized. Knowing I had nothing like that at the Joneses house, I turned it over. There was a note in Momma's hand writing that said, "FAMILY PICTURES." Smaller print read, "Give to Venus. I've called her to let her know that I've sent this in with your things."

It felt pretty bulky. I figured Momma had made copies of some of the old family pictures she had kept in an album to share with my aunt and her family. When I handed her the envelope, my aunt told me that it was a mystery to her. I stood waiting as she eagerly tore the end of the envelope and poured out its contents on the kitchen table. Both our mouths flew open at the same time! In a folded sheet of notebook paper was my money, which Momma had undoubtedly pressed with an iron. It fell onto the table. We stood speechless, until my aunt picked up the folded note and read aloud, "Venus, this money is for you and Albert, to help pay for our daughters keep. There will be things she needs. I know you will use it in the best way."

I shuffled through the money. It was my money alright. The exact amount, in the same denominations. I fled the room. I wanted to run out the door and keep on going. Why? I kept asking myself, as I walked. Why did my parents treat me the way they did?

What made them deprive me of the last bit of joy I had? Why hadn't I died as a small child, never to have known anything at all? Ever.

A car stopped at the corner. It was Myrtle Lou. She tried joviality, "Hey chick! Can you give me directions to the GRANDEE?"

The Grandee was a local night spot, known for its clientele of hookers. It took the edge off the bitterness in me, just long enough for me to get in the car and reply, "From how far out of town are you?"

My cousin was old enough to have had a few dealings with some of the ups and downs of life. She had a great sense of humor that I had never seen in any of her family members. Sometimes I wondered which of our ancestors she was like. She loved living on the sunny side, learning all the newest dances and teaching them to the younger girls in the family. She wasn't a raving beauty but, her choice of good make-up, always well kept hair, lovely clothes and shoes, along with that great personality, surpassed beauty.

If she wasn't the happiest, go luckiest young woman in town, she sure had everybody fooled. She practiced regular church attendance with her family. Sang in the choir as well as the town choral group, comprised of male and female barber shop quartet singers. Her work as a line inspector at the lingerie factory, where she landed her first job right out of high school, was one of the top paying jobs in town. Traveling was her hobby. Occasionally she accompanied the other female singers of her choral group on an all paid cruise. Her reply to anyone daring to ask about her ironclad decision to remain single was, "Why would I want to mess up a life as good as mine with marriage?"

All that was well and good but Mommas way of letting me know she had found my treasure trove upset me so much, I wasn't sure I could tell her about it. She mentioned casually, that her mother said I seemed to be upset about the money Momma had entrusted her with.

"Why not," I thought, "I've told her everything else so far."

When I finished explaining why I had run out of the house she drew down her mouth, shook her head in disgust and said, "Sounds like something your mother would do, but don't worry, our moms may be sisters, but they are different as night and day. That money is going to be there for you when you need it. Meantime, I came to find you, because I have news I think you will really like. You can come to work with me Monday. That is, if you don't mind working on the assembly line."

I told her I was a fast learner and would be happy for any job I could get. Thanking her would not be good enough for me. I was ready to show her that I could do anything I set my mind to

AN IMPORTANT DECISION

November seventeenth of that year was my big day. Even though I longed for J.C. in my heart, I also missed Eddy and all my friends from Fort Worth. I would not allow myself to write to any of them or even give them a call. My heart was set on keeping my troubled life away from them all. J. C.'s parents lived only a few blocks away, but I could not bring myself to face them after what my parents had done to them. I was sure they didn't blame me, but there was just no way to undo such a hateful deed imposed on their son.

Work at the factory was fast and furious. Orders were being shipped out all over the world. Christmas was on its way and Thanksgiving was just around the corner. I was resolved to make an effort to look at life in the same way as my cousin 'Boo', which was Myrtle Lou's nickname. Approaching every new day as a joyful challenge. Keeping my mind on making an affordable gift list, and sticking to it, helped tremendously.

On Saturdays, Boo and I would make excursions into some of the larger towns in the area, expressly for Christmas shopping. Her outlook on life in general was contagious.

The Saturday evening of Thanksgiving week when she suggested we meet a couple of guys for dinner and drinks. Their choral group had been hired to entertain a convention of supper clubbers and a friend of hers had a couple of friends with no dates for the dinner and dance after the show they were all in had finished it's run for the night.

Knowing the crowd that she associated herself with was a sophisticated group, I felt uneasy about taking her up on it. Sure, I could drink and dance but somehow, I couldn't wrap my mind around being out with people of her group's social graces. When I told her how I felt about it, she said, "Pshaw! You are as good and refined as anyone in our group. Don't ever put yourself down on a lower level than you are. Not for any reason. Do you hear me? It's okay. If you don't want to go. I attend this kind of thing two or three times a year just to keep from getting small town stale. But for God's sake, don't think so little of yourself that you put yourself into a non-participant in anything but work category."

I thanked her for her vote of confidence but still declined. She said, "Don't worry, I won't hold it against you, but I meant what I said, every word of it."

Two weeks before Christmas, I mailed gifts home for my brothers and my little niece. Shopping for them had been fun. Although Boo reminded me that I should forgive my parents and at least send them a Christmas card, I refused. As for my sister, she hadn't bothered even calling or writing a letter. What did she care about me anyway? She had a husband and child to think about. I didn't know her phone number or her address, she had never bothered giving them to me and I certainly wasn't going to ask for them.

Gifts for the family members in whose house I was now living was easy. Their tree was beautiful, decorated with ornaments lovelier than I had ever seen. Everybody gathered around the tree early on Christmas morning, even though we had all been at the church late on Christmas Eve. My uncle had gotten out of bed much earlier than the rest of us. He had put on coffee and hot chocolate and made his special festive grapefruit halves with simple syrup poured over the loosened wedges and sprinkled liberally with granulated sugar then topped off with a maraschino cherry in the center. They were not only tasty but pretty, too.

In the oven he had made what he called baked French toast. It was divine. To make it he cut several slices of stale bread into cubes, layered them in the bottom of a buttered casserole dish, placed cream cheese among the cubes then poured a mixture of beaten eggs and milk with a pinch of nutmeg thrown in and topped it with bits of the Christmas ham. It baked to a perfect golden brown in the oven pre-heated to three hundred and fifty degrees for twenty minutes and was then served warm with warm buttery maple syrup.

Hearing him do his Christmas ritual, as he called it, describing what we were having for breakfast in the manner of a Cordon Bleu chef, was interesting and fun. Our mouths were watering for the sumptuous feast which we devoured with abandon, not caring that maple syrup and butter dripped, here and there, down the fronts of all our brightly colored house coats which he had given us after the midnight church services.

Uncle Homer said everyone had been allowed to open one gift with the condition being that the one gift was from him. He had carefully selected the housecoats, making sure he found a different color for each of us, including Aunt Venus. They were soft and comfortable as well as pretty.

We had such a good time teasing him and telling him how sly it was of him to make that deal with us all, for we each were allowed to open one present, but he was getting to open one present from each of us to show appreciation for our gift from him and the gourmet breakfast he was going to prepare the next morning.

Christmas at that house was the best thing that could have happened to finish the horrible year I had come through and brighten my hopes for the future. It was one of those scenes which seems more like a beautiful dream than reality. I never realized until then how wonderful family life done the right way could be. I wanted that Christmas to last forever and I knew without a doubt that it was the kind of Christmas I would strive to have the rest of my life.

It felt so good to be happy again that I had not had one thought of J.C. or Eddy during the next couple of days. It shocked me so much that I had not thought of them that I locked myself in the bathroom and cried like a baby until Serandica Pappas came to comfort me.

"What is wrong with me?" I asked as softly as my trembling lips would allow. How could I be so callous toward two young men whom I loved dearly? Serandica Pappas said, "Come, we will find Justus, and everything will be wonderful!"

That was exactly what I needed to hear. What was I waiting on? I was seventeen and had my own money again. I was free to do whatever I pleased. Leaving Serandica Pappas in the bathroom, and hurrying out to find Boo, I almost knocked one of Aunt Venus's favorite lamps off the little hall table where it shared space with a telephone. Straightening everything back up, I ran across an envelope shaped like a Christmas card with my name on it. There was an address which I didn't recognize as one belonging to any of my friends or relatives. I did not recognize the handwriting and there was no name with the address. I rushed back into the bathroom, locked the door and ripped it open in such haste and carelessness that I didn't notice tearing through the address. As soon as I saw it, I knew who it was from.

A lovely thin gold ring with a topaz birthstone was taped with clear tape to the inside of the card. Underneath was a note, "Sorry I missed your special birthday. Wish I could have been there to celebrate it, and Christmas, with you. I can only say Happy New Year and mean it with all my heart."

I cried great heaving sobs, as I placed the ring on my right-hand ring finger. Then I held it to my cheek, wet with the tears which had been welling up. I heard knocking at the bathroom door, but I could not make myself get up and open it. I could not answer when a voice asked was everything okay. My ears would not hear clearly who was asking. My heart had come up into my throat it seemed.

141

Finally, I got up to open the door. It was my aunt. She said, "Honey, what in the world is wrong?"

I stammered that nothing was wrong. Then I showed her the card and ring. There was a puzzled look on her face. She said, "There's no name on it, who is it from?"

Only then did I realize, that perhaps Boo had not told her all she had learned from me. I lied and said I didn't know. She looked the envelope over, noticing the post mark was an out of the country one. She said, "I wonder who sent this?"

I shrugged my shoulders, indicating that I didn't know. I was still afraid of things my parents might have in store for later use, that I didn't dare say more. That night I lay awake until the wee hours of morning, wondering how he had found out where I was.

The next day, I saw Boo looking fondly at the little topaz and gold ring. She had such a smug look on her face, I knew she must have had something to do with my getting it. Feeling bold enough by that time I said, "I know you had something to do with this getting to me. I thank you and love you for being so thoughtful of me."

She made a face and said, "Whatever are you talking about?"

I told her not to deny it, she was the only one who could have gotten word to him. She gave me an understanding smile and said, "What better gift could I have given you? After all, he and I went to school together. We graduated the same year. It was easy. I called and asked his mom for the address. The next step is yours. Momma always says to be sure what you wish for because you might just get it."

I didn't understand the meaning of the saying attached to the rest of what she had said. After a few minutes, I asked. She gave me a sympathetic smile and said, "I felt the same way about a guy when I was fifteen."

Most of the time, Boo and I did our running around together. I never heard her ask her sisters to come along. On the other hand, I never heard them ask to go. Why would they ask to go with us when they each had their own car? Dee had finished high school two years after Boo. Jo was graduating in the spring and received her car keys at Christmas. Baby rode around with everybody in the family. Uncle Homer said the gas station attendants bowed to him when he went in to pay the bill at the first of every month, to which his family of young ladies responded with laughs.

They were all such a special family, that I started being thankful to God that my parents had sent me to live with them. Aunt Venus, Uncle Homer, Boo, Dee, Jo and Baby were my extended family and they had all worked their magic on me. They were all beautiful in looks and deeds and I couldn't help wanting a family of my own, who in turn, would be like them.

January had been extremely cold. We did very little until the third week in February when Boo called me aside to ask if I would like to ride over to

Tyler to see a movie. It was mid-week and it surprised me, for we never went out of town on a weekday evening. She said she was so tired of being in the house that a drive on a clear evening would probably do us both good. I had been feeling a little cooped up myself.

On the road we turned up the radio and sang along. I liked the freedom of being able to just get in a car and go, without being asked where I was going, with whom and being told what time to be home. Even though I was a full eight years younger than Boo, I saw myself as a mature, experienced young woman, but as I found out later that night, I was still only a teenager who thought she was a mature woman.

Boo said she could understand what he meant and hoped that I would come to understand as well. She explained that the big picture was the future, and all the things we do, or don't do, early on effects the outcome of what happens in the future. She said, "In the case of you and him, every effort either of you made at the time, would make the future, the big picture, a better one."

I told her it sounded good, but the future was far away as was he. She reminded me that the future is all the time after the present. The future is now. It all sounded like sophisticated intellectualism to me, so I always changed the subject when morals and ideals were involved in our conversations.

The movie wasn't as interesting as it sounded. I was looking all around the theater, instead of at the huge screen which gave off all the light there was in the seating area except the tiny running lights up each side of the isles, when I saw two figures walking slowly toward the front of the second isle over and looking this way and that as if they were trying to find someone.

At first, I figured my eyes were playing tricks on me because of the lack of lighting, but I kept watching their silhouettes and then I was sure. It was Eddy and Jay.

I grabbed Boo's arm and whispered that Eddy was on the next isle over. She shushed me and said, "Don't be silly, he has no idea where you are, and I certainly have had no part in letting him know."

I let her arm go, jumped up, trampled on the feet of those sitting between me and the isle on our side of the building. Once in the isle I ran as fast as I could up to the entrance, out into the lobby and almost into the arms of Eddy. I was so happy to see him. He quickly clamped his arms around me and gave me a long kiss, which I returned eagerly. Then Jay had to have a turn. He gave me a big bear hug but released me pretty quickly.

I turned to see Boo, the look on her face was one of anger. I introduced them to her and she still didn't respond. Eddy said, "Well then let's go."

He put his arm around me and pulled me close, I put my arms around his middle and we started toward the doors to leave the building. Boo, jumped in front of us and said, "Oh no you don't!"

She gave me a hard pinch on the upper arm, which made me yelp like a hurt puppy. She looked Eddy straight in the eye and told him if he thought I was going with him anywhere at the moment he had better think again. Jay started laughing. He was a good-natured guy and never liked having trouble with anybody, but the look on his face said, "What do you think you can do about it if she wants to go?"

Instead, he said, "Come on shorty, let's all shake this joint and get something real to eat. I'm starving. This idiot (pointing to Eddy) wouldn't even let me stop to pee."

Boo turned on him and said, "Watch your manners!"

Jay just shook his head and started laughing again. Boo started walking as fast as her wedge heeled shoes would go toward the street doors. We all followed along quietly. Once we were outside, and a few feet away from the ticket booth, she whirled around, put her forefinger in Eddy's face and demanded to know how he found out where I was.

Jay just couldn't stop himself from laughing again. His car was parked at curb side, so he opened the door and motioned for Eddy and me to get into the car then he spoke loudly to Boo and said, "You too sister."

When Boo flatly refused by telling him that neither she nor I was going anywhere with a couple of thugs my mouth fell open and must have exposed my tonsils. Jay slapped his leg and said, "If that don't take the cake. First, we were hoodlums, now we are thugs. What do you say we all just go get a beer and stop the nonsense?"

Boo, not one to be bullied, said, "We came here in my car, and we are leaving in my car."

The look on her face told me to do as she said, or the police would soon be involved. Her hands were on her hips, her handbag dangling beside her leg. I had never seen her so mad. I told Eddy and Jay to follow us. Jay said, "Nothing doing unless she cuts us some slack."

The laughter was gone from his face and I saw in its place the look of a hungry, determined young man bent on having his way in the matter at hand, which for him was getting something to eat. With all the swagger of John Wayne, he walked over to Boo and said, "In case you haven't noticed, little sister, I am three time as big as you are. I am a man. Whether you like me or not, whether you think I am a thug or not doesn't matter a whit to me. When A man is as hungry as I am, he might forget that you and green eyes over there are a couple of ladies. He might just throw you over his shoulder and take off with you whether you want to go or not!"

By this time, he was standing in front of her looking down at her. She, her face as red as wine, which did not look good on a person as white skinned as she was, looked up at him and said, "You just try it!"

Jay started laughing again and I have to admit it was pretty funny at the moment, but Boo was dead serious. He said, "Would you rather I turned you across my knee and spanked your bottom until it gets as red as your face?"

His laughter should have let her know that he was joking. Evidently, she saw no humor in anything he had said. She actually moved into him enough that her breasts were against his belt buckle. She threw one arm to the side pointing toward the stream of people coming out of the movie theater, clenched her teeth and told him to take a good look around, she said, "Think about it buster. You are in my territory. You two don't look anything like anybody else here. All I have to do is yell rape, and I will, if you make one tiny move. Don't even blink an eye."

Jay quit laughing. In a very soft manly voice he said, "I believe you would."

They stood staring at one another. Finally, he said, 'Ma'am, please be good enough to let me buy supper. I don't mean any harm. Old Ed over there is so in love with little green eyes he is not going to leave here without her. He made her a promise to marry her when she turned seventeen. If my information is right, she is seventeen and a few months over. We may look like thugs to you ma'am, but we are just a couple of hard working, fun loving old boys from the city. No matter how long you and I stand here and threaten one another, he's going to marry her. He has a decent paying job and he's ready to settle down and be a family man. The only thing that will make him turn around and leave is if she says she doesn't love him and doesn't want to marry him. Now you go on and ask her, if you think you need to."

Boo had stood quietly while he talked, but she hadn't moved a bit. She looked over at me, took a couple of steps backward then asked, "Well? What do you have to say about it?'"

I said I thought we should go get something to eat. I told Eddy that he and Jay should follow us. I would go in Boo's car so that she might calm down a little more. He held me as if he couldn't bear to let me go. He whispered, "Tell her not to try giving us the slip."

He was smiling so I knew he was only being playful. I walked across the street with Boo to her car. She started the engine then said, "Juke joint I guess," and headed for the one farthest away thinking they probably didn't know where they were going.

I told her that they were not thugs or hoodlums as my parents had put it themselves. They were a couple of really good guys, who ran around with a few more just like them. They were friends who stood together when the going got tough for one or more of them. She wasn't convinced. She told me she was going to call her parents when we got the cafe. She said, "You better use your head and not your other thing in making this decision. You know what can happen if you act too quickly. There is another guy who calls you sweetheart and professes his love for you who is doing something he probably hates in order to make the big picture a better one."

She said I had to be strong and wait long enough to be sure, for my hearts sake. If you are not true to yourself, you will never be happy or successful. It had started falling on deaf ears. Eddy loved me. He was willing to take any chance he had to for me. He wanted to marry me right then, not off in the big picture someday.

At the cafe, she went straight to the phone booth at the outer corner of the building. When Jay got to the parking lot he pulled into a spot almost in front of where Boo was in the phone booth. They both got out and came to the car. Jay told Eddy to take me on inside and he would keep an eye on "Shorty." I said, "She is not going to like that Jay."

He agreed that she might not, but he didn't want to go in leaving her outside alone. Eddy said what happened to "hungry man"?

Jay replied, "Haven't you heard? Man don't live on bread alone. She might be a feisty little thing but that's a dark corner down there."

I reminded him he was a long way from Fort Worth. He said, "Towns may be different green eyes, but people are the same everywhere. I will make sure no harm comes to her. You two go on in. Ed order what I told you I wanted on the way over here. Maybe with any kind of luck, it will be sitting on the table when I get there."

We sat in one of those booths that take up the corner. Eddy insisted that we sit on the outer part of the seats instead of sliding over to the middle. He said that Jay and my cousin might want to get to know one another better. I assured him that Boo was not one bit interested in getting to know Jay. He said, "Maybe not, but it won't hurt to watch the show."

I couldn't help but enjoy his humorous nature. Eddy had a way of seeing things which was unique. It was one of the qualities I admired in him. While we waited, and Eddy held my hand tightly in his and me squeezing back on it, my mind was whirling with the things Boo had said on the way over. I knew in my heart that it would be now or never. Jay had been right, I knew them both that well. I knew they hadn't come to kidnap me, as my cousin seemed to think. It was a sure thing. If I said go away, come again some other day, I would never see Eddy again.

What we had together wasn't what most people would call a perfect relationship, but it was a good one. Boo and Jay came in the cafe at just the right moment. The big picture my mind was painting wasn't a nice one. When I shivered thinking about it, Eddy asked if I was cold. I said a little, but the hot food would soon warm me up. He leaned into my ear and whispered, "Let's go out to the car and I will get you warmed up good."

I slapped him on the upper arm and told him not to even get started with that tonight. The mischievousness went out of his eyes. I knew then he wasn't joking about what he had said. Not that I didn't want to feel his body close to mine. Not that I didn't care about him anymore. It just seemed like one of those things I wasn't ready to give in so quickly about, in present company. I also knew if he was disrespectful of me about it in any way that I would turn him down. I was not a party girl and I didn't plan on being treated like one anymore.

I heard Eddy ordering and wondered why the waitress had walked away from the table without even asking for my order. The waitress brought the food on two huge trays. Boo refused to eat anything asking only for a cup of coffee. She scooted away from Jay to the middle of the booth and scowled at him when he started to move closer. He said, "I just didn't want us to have to yell at one another to hear what was being said."

She said, "Why don't' you eat your food that you were starving for and forget about talking."

The guys scarfed down their food as if they hadn't eaten in a week. I ate a bite now and then and took a sip of soda with it. At one point I asked Eddy how he found out where I was. He sat back, wiped his mouth, ran his tongue over and around his teeth a few times, then said he had gotten Joyce to sleuth for him.

The minute he said Joyce my mind started painting dirty pictures of them. Making out, laughing about it, even though Joyce was married. When I realized I hadn't heard a word he was saying, I asked if he would repeat it. He looked at me in a strange way and started over. "Joyce agreed to help me right after that night at your parent's place when your daddy ordered me out of the house."

I heard Boo make one of the snorting sounds she often made when she didn't like what she was hearing. Eddy continued, "She and June got busy on the old couple you lived with. By the way, they asked us all to a Christmas party at the new place," he gave that little laugh that I loved so well and went on, "It wasn't all that bad. We dressed up and were on our best behavior, like regular ladies and gentlemen. We had that old couple eating out of our hands, didn't we Jay?"

At that point, I told him I didn't want to hear anymore. Boo spoke through gritted teeth that she was ready to leave but Eddy went right on. After all, there was no way for her to get away from the spot she was perched in, unless she went under the table or over the top. I looked for her to take either path, at any time.

"It wasn't as bad as it sounds, we weren't disrespectful of them. We just wanted to pander to them enough to get the information we needed."

I saw it coming and said I had heard enough and looked at Jay, knowing he would not try to keep us there. He got up, threw some twenties on the table and walked toward the door. I saw him talking to Boo and wondered what he was saying to her. When Eddy and I got to the car, Jay said he was going to ride with Boo. Eddy and I could take his car, so I could decide if I was going back with them or not. Then Boo told Eddy to stay in front of her on the highway. Promising that she would be watching every moment, adding, "Don't even think about trying to ditch me."

Eddy told me about his job at the furniture factory and said it was possible to advance and make good money. He had missed me terribly. He had given it a lot of thought and decided we should go ahead and get married and he didn't mean later. He didn't ask if I had been seeing anybody and I didn't ask him. He held me close, left hand expertly guiding the car down the highway. I told him about my job and the happiness I had gotten used to living with my relatives. He said he had not had one happy moment since he saw me last.

His plan was for us to drive from my aunt's house straight on to Oklahoma. He had learned of a place there where we could get married, no questions asked, day or night, no matter what time. It was legal.

When we got back to the house, the whole place was lit up. Everybody was up waiting for us. I learned that the guys had gone to the house first. Baby had answered the door and told them Boo and I had gone to a movie in Tyler then my uncle had gotten to the door and demanded to know who they were and what they wanted. They had told him. Aunt Venus had come in and listened to what they had to say. After she and Uncle Homer had conferred a few minutes and decided to call my parents, she told Eddy that they would not stand in the way if that was what I wanted to do, but my mother was her sister and she had to let her know that he was there, and marriage was on the table.

Uncle Homer wouldn't let them leave until she had made the call. I figured that would settle it, the highway patrol and every other law enforcement officer between there and Fort Worth had probably been alerted as if we were a bunch of criminals.

It went quieter than I had expected it to go. Aunt Venus said it was up to me, I was welcome to stay with them as long as I wanted to, but the young men must leave the area if I chose to stay. She wanted that clear, for my mother's sake. Eddy agreed, then it was all up to me.

All those faces looking at me, waiting for my decision, was awful. When the silence became uncomfortable Boo said, "Remember, love is what counts, you know where your heart is."

I still wasn't ready to answer, Jay said, "You're not living unless you're lovin' green eyes."

Then Eddy said, "Without you, I have no reason to live,"

I did not understand why he said what he had but it touched me deeply. Without giving it one more thought, I said I did want to marry him. To give me a few minutes to get my things together.

The phone rang, I held my breath. I heard Eddy's voice saying, "We don't need anybody to go with us, it's all arranged. She's seventeen now and she's not yours any longer. She's been my girl for quite a while, now she's going to be my wife, and nobody is going to get in our way."

I couldn't help wondering who he was talking to. My aunt's voice on the phone answered my question, "Oh Ruth, why don't you just let them go on and get married without interfering. If they've done the wrong thing, they will be the ones to pay the consequences."

As I walked back into the room, I could see my aunt holding the receiver a couple of inches away from her ear. When she placed the receiver back on the hook, she looked at Eddy and said, "Young man, I do not envy you in this endeavor. If you two really love one another, you are both going to have to be big enough about it to look over what has happened in the past and make this a new beginning all the way. Ruth has decided that she, Reagan and the boys are going with you, to make sure that the marriage is legal. If you do not go back to Fort Worth and work together with them, she and Reagan will file kidnapping charges against both of you boys."

Uncle Homer said he felt that going back and getting it right would be the best thing to do. He said that marriage is a wonderful occupation when done right and we should consider the alternatives. Even Jay said, "Ed, we've been pals a long time and I am involved in this up to my neck. What can it hurt now if her old man and his old lady want to see their daughter get married?"

Eddy asked my aunt if she would call my mother back and tell her for them to be ready and waiting when we got to their house because we were going to be married before the sun rose again. After our goodbyes to them all, Aunt Venus made the call and we were on the road to becoming Mr. And Mrs. Eddy Layne and so it was for the next twenty-three years.

PART II

FEBRUARY NINETEEN FIFTY-SIX

I was seventeen and married. Eddy was four years older. We took our vows seriously. We both understood that ours was a union of commitment to one another. We didn't talk about love, the future or children. We lived in the moment, for the most part. Working, running around with our friends and making whoopee. Each time Eddy reminded me that I was supposed to go back to school and get my diploma, I hedged. I wanted to work and help save money toward a home of our own. At first, he refused until I reminded him that I was married to him, but I still had time on my hands and needed to work in order to keep my sanity. Of course, he wanted me to work for his mom again, but I was of another mind about it.

Polly was a wonderful person. I loved her as a friend as much as a mother-in-law, but I wanted to be free of our family ties. When I told him so, he looked at me as if I was a stranger. He could not imagine the two of us, being alone together somewhere away from our families. I tried to explain to him that I wanted the two of us to do things the way we wanted to do them and not always be trying to please our parents. Our parents were still treating us like children when we were adults.

Our opinions on the matter caused considerable disputations between us. There were other things too. Eddy didn't talk to me like he did when we first met. When his friends were around, he was the happy go lucky guy he had always been. Alone with me, he became quieter and almost sullen it seemed. He seemed happy enough in bed, but everything else was kind of ho hum. Working was my way of dealing with everything. Eddy worked hard too. He liked gathering with his friends and cousins after work, drinking beer and running around. I on the other hand, reminded him that he told me he was ready to settle down. I used my time after work, cleaning our tiny apartment, doing laundry, my nails, my hair and cooking what little food we managed to keep in the house.

One night, after a round of drinking, we were in bed. I was sure Eddy was asleep for I heard him snoring. He hadn't made his usual sexual advances which led me to thinking he might have been up to something. Heaving loudly, I turned over, pulled up the covers and had a good cry. It wasn't that I wanted constant attention from him, but a lot more than what I had been getting lately. I knew I was through with the running around and partying and had believed that he was too.

Through my tears I saw Serandica Pappas sitting on the window sill near my side of the bed. She too was crying. She had made no contact in months. To tell the truth, I had been so busy working that I hadn't even wondered why she hadn't shown up. There was something so comforting about her presence, whether she was crying or smiling. I waited, hoping she would say something to encourage me. Finally, I asked in a whisper if she had found Justus. She shook her head no and raised her head to speak, but suddenly disappeared. I let out a big sigh and started to turn on my back when I noticed Eddy, leaning on an elbow, staring at the place where Serandica Pappas had been sitting on the window sill.

I lay very still, waiting for him to say something. He finally turned his face to me and said, "If I hadn't seen it with my own eyes, I would never have believed it."

He didn't kiss me, he didn't ask me any questions, he just lay back on his pillow and shook his head side to side in a negative manner. I wanted to know what he saw, so I asked him what he meant when he said he wouldn't have believed it.

He described her in detail. He had seen Serandica Pappas! I didn't know whether to be happy about that or pretend I hadn't seen anything. He got back up on his elbow and asked who Justus was. Half afraid to confide in him I kept my mouth shut. Eddy got out of bed, turned all the lights in the apartment on and got a beer out of the refrigerator. He came back, sat on the side of the bed and looked at me with his hazel eyes turning so brown and dark that it scared me.

"What was that and who the hell is Justus?" He asked tersely. Deciding it might be time to tell him about Serandica Pappas, I sat up in bed and started to tell him when just behind him, she appeared again shaking her head and giving me that look of hers that said, "No." I took a deep breath and told Eddy that he had been drinking too much and must be seeing and hearing things. He said, "Nah, uh-uh, I heard you ask her if she had found Justus and why have you been crying?"

I told him that I missed him when he was out with his pals. He reminded me that I was the one who had chosen to stay home and on it went until time for us both to get ready for work again. Eddy never asked me again about that night, but it made a profound difference in him. He started coming home right after work. He took up fishing at the lake. We spent many evenings out by the water. Sometimes he caught fish and sometimes he didn't. I always took along something for us to eat just in case, but the best meals we ever had together were the ones when he caught a few good fish and I cooked them at the water's edge.

Sometimes we stayed out just laying on our backs and looking at the stars and constellations. One night, I asked him why he hardly ever talked to me the way he did before we got married. He said he figured we already knew everything there was to know about one another so there really wasn't anything to talk about was there?

In a way, I agreed with him. We didn't have a lot in common after all. But it was on those nights, out by the lake, just the two of us, that we found something beyond words, beyond love. It was more like a complete understanding of one another, which needed no words. We both just somehow knew that we were supposed to be together.

Everything had been going well until one night, right after we had finished eating supper, my parents showed up at the door. They had just come for a visit they said, and I was happy they had finally decided to come by. It had been a hot day. A nice breeze was playing with the curtains. I suggested that we all go out and sit on the porch. Everybody except Momma and I were already outside. I was waiting for her to come out of the bathroom. My back had been hurting all day, but suddenly it got worse. Momma came to the front door and opened the screen to go outside.

She said loudly, "I've been meaning to tell you. I got a phone call from J.C. It was kind of funny. He said he was on leave in Hawaii before coming back to the states. Since you are older now, he was going to arrange it so that you could come there and the two of you could be married and honeymoon in Hawaii."

I fainted and knew nothing for a few minutes. Everybody was huddled around me on the floor. Momma was explaining to Eddy that she had told J.C. that she didn't think my husband would like that. Eddy's face had that hard, dark look that I had seen many times before we were married, and I didn't like it.

At that moment though, all I could think about was the pain which was tearing through my lower body. Not only in my lower back but in my abdomen. I felt nauseated. They helped me up, but my knees buckled. Eddy rushed me to the hospital where it was determined that I was having a miscarriage. All I knew was the pain was unbearable.

The next three weeks were spent at home. I wanted to go back to work but the doctor at the hospital advised against it. Visits from family members were no help to me. I didn't want to see any of them. Eddy was more withdrawn and sullen than he had been since I met him, and I did not understand why.

His closeness at the time would have helped my feelings tremendously. I couldn't feel anything but sorrow for myself for what I had just gone through. It was such a shock to my system that I couldn't feel the sadness I should have been feeling at the loss of a precious life which had left my body in such haste and caused me such agony.

Then there were the snide, rude remarks from Eddy's aunts and his cousins. "Must have been somebody else's, Eddy can't father children." On and on it went, until I wanted to run away from it all. When I had heard all I could stand, I decided that Eddy would go with me to the doctor referred to me by the intern at the hospital. He didn't like the idea of having to take off work to go but he did it because I was so upset at the remarks being made by his family. It didn't matter to me what they thought, I knew I had not been with anyone except Eddy and I did not like it that they would be trying to make him think I had.

As it turned out, the doctor determined that he was producing a very low sperm count which would lead an untrained person to think such things. He told Eddy that he had a fruitful little wife and we might expect to have another pregnancy someday but to try to wait at least a year to get serious about it.

I couldn't tell whether Eddy was happy or not. He just sat with a blank look on his face. I had not expected to have children with Eddy, and after what I had been through was not looking forward to having any in the near future. After that the hateful remarks stopped but nobody made any apologies either.

One Saturday, I was cleaning the apartment when Eddy came home. Having felt better the past week, I was looking for something to keep me busy. I had pulled things out of the closet and was going through them. I ran across some old pictures of J.C. and me, which I had kept in a shoebox, along with the beautiful little music box and had a cry over them.

Eddy walked into the room, snatched the box up and started looking at the pictures, his face taking on that look. He tossed the box at me. I barely caught the music box before it hit the floor. He growled, "Let's get something straight right now. You are my wife. You have no business keeping pictures and stuff which remind you of your old lover. You said you married me and said you love me. If that is true, take the box of stuff right now and put it in the dumpster. If you want him still, get on out of here and go to him."

My heart hurt so badly I could not speak. How could a person throw part of their life in the trash? I knew he meant it. I took our vows seriously and wanted to remain his wife, but I knew I would never be able to put J.C. out of my heart. What the two of us had together was special. I knew Eddy and I would never have that same kind of romantic love.

What he said was true. I was his wife and would remain his wife. So, I walked to the dumpster and threw the box in, but I never, in all the years of our marriage, forgave him for making me do that. If I said I didn't grieve over letting go of those few precious things, I would be lying. Eddy's eyes were always on me, so he knew when I cried and exactly what it was about. To this day, I still cry about it.

Without Serandica Pappas, I would have never lived to this great age. She was always there to comfort me and give me hope, by reminding me that she and I would one day find Justus, and everything would be wonderful. She was so beautiful and convincing, I couldn't help but feel better.

A PRETTY FLOWER

In November of the following year, after suffering much pain from a breech birth with an episiotomy, I gave birth to our beautiful baby girl. As soon as I saw her the first time, I knew she was worth the pain. She was perfect! The best thing that could have happened to me at that time in my life. To this day, I still feel the same way my first born.

Her name was as beautiful as she was. I had known it would be the right name, if our child was a girl several months before the birth took place. I had seen a rose bush with only one lovely rose on it. As soon as I saw it, I loved it and wanted to pick it, take it inside and put it in a vase. Something would not allow me to do that. Serandica Pappas appeared, telling me to leave it there and watch it blossom into a mature flower and I would find it more beautiful than the bud.

The bud was fresh smooth and tender. Dewdrops were clinging to it. The color was vibrant yellow with a blush of peach. It was absolutely the most beautiful flower I had ever seen. When we heard the Native Indian name, that meant a pretty flower, I realized the flower was an omen and the name was the one which would belong to our baby.

As soon as I saw her I knew we had chosen the right name, for she was indeed my very own pretty flower. Her delicate skin with its faint touch of peach, her golden hair with its blush of red, her whole tiny body, unfolding, just like that beautiful rose. She will forever be my pretty flower, **MARSHEILLA.**

Eddy was a proud father. His face lit up for a change when he came home from work every day. He didn't like to pick her up, he was afraid he would hurt her, but that didn't last very long. After a few months he would put her on his shoulders and prance around the house like a pony. He promised to buy her a baby grand piano when she got old enough to take piano lessons. He would roll around on the floor, tossing her into the air and she loved it. I loved watching him play with her. She was Daddy's little girl until the next year in November, when our first son was born.

JUNIOR

My labor was easier and much quicker with our second child. He too was perfect. I had been thinking of names but hadn't settled on one. Trying to discuss a name for our first son with Eddy was next to impossible. When I brought up one I really liked to go on the birth certificate, Eddy refused it. He would not hear of naming him anything but Jr. When I was told that our son was to have his father's name, I objected. Not that I didn't like the name, I just thought our son should have his own, special name. This child of ours was special and he needed a special name. Though I fought against it, Eddy insisted and so it was placed on the birth certificate, **WILLIAM EDWARD LAYNE, JR.**

I knew giving in to it was the right thing to do. But in my heart, I could only call him, "my sweet William." He was his father's first son, but he was also my first son and I felt cheated for not being allowed to have a part in naming him. In many ways he was like his father, but he was also like me.

From the moment our son was born Eddy took him in hand, showing him off, buying special toys such as a football and a fishing pole with a toy fish hanging from a toy hook. As far as he was concerned our little girl was mine and our little boy was his. It always broke my heart watching her compete for the same attention her brother received from his dad. After all, she was our first.

With two children under age two I could not think of going back to work. The loss of wages from my employment began to be noticed. I worked hard trying to keep the costs down at home. Instead of using a diaper service, I washed diapers in the bath tub. I learned to cook a decent pot of red beans and fried potatoes. On special occasions a fried chicken or a few pork chops.

Our babies did not eat baby food. I boiled eggs and pureed the yolks, made oatmeal cooked until it was soft enough to slide down their little throats and used canned milk, diluted with water and a little dark Karo syrup to keep their little bowels moving right. I potty-trained them both and by the time they were a year old, they knew to use the potty, at least most of the time. They could talk in sentences by the time they were a year old. Nobody ever talked baby talk to them. We all talked to them like we talked to one another and they learned it quickly. After all, they were the two cutest, smartest babies that ever lived, at least until their little sister was born.

By the time our third child was born, we had moved to West Texas. Eddy had been working at a foundry in Fort Worth. He had held on to his day job at the furniture factory and worked the evening shift at the foundry. He would come home late at night looking like he had just walked out of a coal mine. The only white was the white of his eyes, with a little gray around them where he had worn goggles while at work.

I had no washing machine and those coveralls were not coming clean without one. Momma was not about to let me wash them in her washing machine, so I had to go to his mother's house to do laundry. He would leave the children and me there on his way to work at the furniture factory, pick us up on his way to the foundry, drop us off at home, eat a quick bite of supper and off he would go again.

I didn't like it one bit but could see no way we could manage otherwise. Momma wasn't willing to keep the babies, except every once in a while. Eddy's mom couldn't because she was still having to work herself, so my trying to go back to work was out of the question.

Momma had a way of letting you know things in the most infuriating way possible. One Sunday after lunch, they dropped in for one of their impromptu visits. Things had been going pretty well between us and I, as usual, was unprepared for the news she was bringing. My sister, her husband and my little niece had moved back to West Texas. The tiny town had only a grocery store and a gasoline station, according to Momma. She was always calling them and then coming by to let me know how things were going out there in the middle of nowhere, as she called it.

This particular afternoon, the only time Eddy, the little ones and I had together to enjoy one another all week, she wanted to let me know that my sister had invited us all to come for a visit. Momma couldn't wait to go see the place her other daughter was now calling home. Daddy said he wasn't too crazy about making the trip, but my brothers were ready to hit the road. Eddy said there was no way we could go. He had to get in all the hours at work he could. Momma said, "By the way, our old friends are wanting to pay us a visit the same weekend."

I heard what she was saying and told Eddy it would be nice to take the children and go with my parents. He didn't like the idea of my going and taking the children. It seemed settled until Momma said, "Well, that might work out fine, J.C. is out of the service and wants to come with them to meet Eddy and see your children. They can all stay at our house while they are in town and we are visiting your sister and her family. That way you and Eddy can have them over here, or you can all go over there. That ought to work out just fine."

The look that came across Eddy's face was one I had never seen before. I would have sworn it looked like panic. He didn't say a word. He got up, went into the kitchen and opened a bottle of beer. Daddy told Momma that he didn't think Eddy liked that idea much.

At that moment, I may have had the same look on my face as Eddy. It frightened me a little to think about us all being together in one place. I went into the kitchen and asked Eddy, if he would change his mind about letting me take the kids and go with my parents to visit my sister. He took a long drink of his beer, looked at me with a frown and said, "You mean you don't want to see him again?"

I was quick to tell him that I did not care for Momma's arrangements. She called from the living room and said they had to go, and they left before I could get back in there. Eddy followed me into the living room, sat down in his chair, leaned back looking as if he was in deep thought. I took the kiddos, got them ready for bed, sung to them until they fell asleep, then went back to find Eddy still in deep thought. He asked, "Do you really want to go visit your sister?"

I told him I would love to go see where they lived. Even the town we had lived in, when we were in East Texas had a population of about three thousand. I reminded him that he had been working awfully hard for a very long time with no time off, no vacation or anything. I said that I wouldn't go unless he went too. I reminded him that my sister had said there was a river only a half mile from their house which was full of good fish.

Later, when I thought he had gone to sleep, he rolled over, propped up on his elbow and said, "You are right, I do need some time off and I'm due it. Find out for sure when your parents are going to leave and make sure to get the directions in case we get separated from them."

Our visit to my sister and her family was only the beginning of our life in West Texas. After that visit, fishing on the Brazos had hooked Eddy. With the first five-pound catfish he caught on that visit and its delicious fried goodness, along with homemade hush puppies and tartar sauce, came a love of the place that lasted the rest of our married lives together.

In a few weeks' time, we too lived in that quaint little town too. My life had become a very busy one. Along with my two children, I kept my niece while my sister and her husband were at work and then I started keeping my brother-in-law's sister's little girl as well.

Eddy rode back and forth into Abilene to work with my sister and her husband. I kept the only car we had in case of an emergency with any of the children. They were all good, but a big handful for one person. As if that was not enough, in a few weeks Eddy's parents came for a visit and Eddy's three younger brothers wanted to stay with us. Polly and her husband would not tell them they couldn't, and neither would Eddy.

So, there I was, with my own two children, my little niece and her little cousin and Eddy's three younger brothers. The oldest was ten, the other two were eight and six, and I was five months pregnant.

A SHINING STAR

The cooking, house cleaning and taking care of children, left me little time for anything else. Eddy's little brothers ended up with us longer than I had expected. They cried so much when I told them it was time for them to go home that it touched my heart. Eddy wanted to keep them with us and send them to school in a small town instead of the metroplex, but I knew my limits and told him so. It was a sad trip taking them home, but it had to be done.

It was on that trip that I learned of my parents' plan to move back to Abilene. Daddy had been offered a very good job by his old boss and friend in Abilene and Momma said she wanted to be closer to her grandchildren. By the time our third child was born, my parents and brothers were there to help with the children until I was up to it again. I have to admit, for once in a very long time, it was a relief, having them there helping out.

I knew before she was born that this child would have a special name. One that meant something different than second daughter. Just before she was born, we were sitting in the yard, enjoying the summer night air. I lay back my head on Eddy's shoulder and sat gazing at the stars thinking of the first night we had been alone together at the lake in Fort Worth. Looking into that night sky and letting thoughts run through my head was as good as it got in those days.

Suddenly, a star I hadn't noticed seemed to pop up and shine forth brilliantly. It seemed to rotate and sparkle, like a beautifully cut diamond. The star somehow made me think of a jewel. At first, I thought that might be a good name if the baby was a girl. But Serandica Pappas appeared at just that moment and shook her head no. I took a deep breath and let it out, choking back tears. Serandica Pappas had reminded me that it was the same star J.C. and I had exchanged our personal vows under.

Eddy wanted to know if I was alright. I told him I had been thinking about Jewel being a pretty name if the baby was a girl. One of my aunts, Daddy's youngest sister was named Jewel. The beautiful star made me remember how pretty she had always been. I showed him the star. He too thought it must be a special star, for he hadn't seen it until I pointed it out to him.

A few days later, we both heard, yet again, a native American Indian name for a bright star and knew it would be the right name if our baby was a girl. When she was born, I knew instantly the name was perfect. That tiny bundle of beauty was and will ever be, our very own bright star shinning in our hearts, **TAHLONAH.**

GALVESTION

Our children thrived on the fresh air and good food which we had in abundance. By nineteen-sixty, we had acquired a five-acre piece of property with a five-room wood frame house on it. The first thing I noticed when we arrived to look the place over good, was the little white church across the highway. Across the top of the entrance was a red neon light which read, "JESUS SAVES." We thought that was the most unusual thing we had ever seen.

At night, when there were no other lights around except the stars, that light shone brightly in the night, not only for us, but for all who traveled down that highway. To this day, it shines forth that wonderful news, reminding us to thank God for the greatest gift ever given to the people of this planet.

We loved our little home, with its spindly young trees. There were a couple of pecan trees, a couple of peach trees, a pear and a mimosa along with lovely wisteria and honeysuckle vines. At night, we could hear coyotes yowling in the shin oaks which bordered the property. That took some getting used to, but we all dearly loved living there. The first year did get pretty lonely for me at times, though. Work was not an option for me at that time with three young ones at home. I spent my time caring for them, doing laundry, cooking and keeping the house. Eventually, I started a vegetable garden and Eddy bought a few chickens from some people down the road. We were all in good health and good spirits. Even our relatives, who visited now and then poked fun at us, saying that we couldn't be farmers because we had been city dwellers too long. I noticed it didn't keep them from showing up and eating the veggies from my garden and the eggs from our chickens!

My parents moved to the gulf coast. Daddy's brother Johnny, the one who had owned the farm we had lived on in East Texas, was in the business of building homes. Hurricane Carla had hit the gulf coast with a vengeance. Uncle Johnny needed help with the reconstruction work. The pay was too good for Daddy to refuse, so off they went to the gulf coast.

Momma wrote often, telling us how the storm had ruined hundreds of houses there. In one of her letters, she had to tell me that J.C.'s parents, and he, had moved to the area as well. His dad worked at one of the ship yards and J.C. had a good job at one of the chemical plants. She said they always asked about my sister Billie and her family and me and mine.

Eddy never cared to hear about the goings on of anything but what was happening with us at the moment. We were either painting the house, roofing the house, working in the yard, on the car or mending the fences around the property, so I didn't bother sharing that particular bit of news with him.

Eddy wanted to buy some other animals. One day he came home with a Shetland pony for the children. They were all so happy over that animal, until he proved to be a biter. He didn't want anyone riding on its back, so he would bite at whoever was trying to ride him. That all ended when Eddy's family came for a visit and the bigger boys rode him and somehow taught him not to bite.

One Monday morning I noticed several cars at the church across road and my curiosity was roused. All week they were there. I watched as a crowd stood for a while in the church yard and visited, laughing and talking to one another and it made me feel rather lonely. We had made no friends and there were few neighbors in the area. I was at the kitchen sink when Serandica Pappas appeared. She motioned for me to follow her. She said, "Come with me and see."

The children had gone out in the yard to play so I figured she wanted to show me something they were up to. I remember going out the door and into the yard, but nothing else until I realized I was across the highway, hurrying my children along into the church yard where all the people were turning to see who was coming up. Something told me to hurry, because they were all about to leave.

A short bald-headed man was rushing toward us and the others were meandering along behind him. I noticed they were all smiling at us in a friendly way. My heart felt warm and happy as if they were people I already knew. The bald-headed man said, "The angels are ringing the bells in heaven. We have been praying for the Lord to send us whoever was in need of our help and praise God, he has heard us, and you and your children have come to receive His blessing!" and all the other people said, "Amen!"

It was as if I could actually hear those joyous bells ringing in heaven and I knew we were among genuinely loving and caring people. I had never felt so safe and happy. The children were already running about with other children their ages, laughing and happy.

I learned there was a revival going on at the church. We were invited to come to the evening services which would run from Monday evening through Sunday evening. I promised to be there, took my children and went home a changed person it seemed. A person with new found friends, a young mother who had somehow gotten across that busy highway with her three young children to a company of Christian people who were good and ready to become our friends and neighbors.

All day that joy clung to me and the kids. We were the happiest little bunch and when Eddy came home we couldn't wait to tell him about our day. We were all trying to talk at once and Eddy looked overwhelmed by what we were saying and how happy we were. We had met him at the car, he hadn't gotten out, but had opened the door. The children were up in his lap, smothering him with kisses and I was eagerly waiting my turn. Finally, he put the kids on the ground, finished getting out of the car, gave me a good kiss which I returned happily, and asked, "Now, what is all this about"

He was always welcomed home from work but not in such a happy manner. I told him everything that had happened, and he just shook his head as if he couldn't believe what he was hearing. When I told him that we were going to the evening service, he flatly refused to go. He said, "You and the kids go if you want to, but don't get started on me. Nobody goes to churches except a bunch of hypocrites."

I told him he was wrong. The people we had found were good people who were ready to be our friends and neighbors. He didn't argue. He said all he wanted to know was what was for supper.

While we were eating, the kids kept talking about their new friends who they would soon be going to school with. Eddy told them he was glad they had made some new friends. I hoped that he would change his mind about going to the evening services at the church. He didn't, until the very last night, when he came in and sat down beside us mid-way through the service. I was so happy, I cried. When the invitation was given, I took our children and headed forward to join the church and Eddy followed. That night was the beginning of a new kind of life, which we enjoyed. We were happier than we had ever known we could be.

In the months to come, we had our new friends over to visit and we in turn, visited with them. Sometimes four or five families would all get together at one house. The women would all prepare food and the men would play ball or some other games with the children. After the meal, which was usually served in the yard, the kids would all run off to play together and the adults all sat around visiting. Those were special, happy days and evenings which changed our lives completely.

Eddy kept bringing in livestock. He wanted the children to learn about the animals and have pets. In Fort Worth we had visited the zoo often, taking the little ones to see the animals. We now had a cow and calf, hogs with piglets, chickens with baby chicks, a pony, some sheep and a dog.

Life just kept getting better and I was so happy that I had to write and tell my folks about it. In one of her letters back, Momma said it sounded wonderful, but they missed us and hoped we would come for a visit. I mentioned it to Eddy and he said no way, but the more I thought about it the more I wanted to go. Momma said they would send bus tickets for the children and me to come if Eddy didn't want to go.

He finally agreed, and one-way tickets arrived. Eddy laughed about that and said he guessed they were planning to try to keep us there. Not to worry, he assured me, he would send money for our tickets back home when he got his next paycheck.

The bus trip there seemed as if it would never end, but finally, after leaving before daylight from Abilene, the bus we were on pulled into the Texas City station at sunset. My parents and my two brothers were there waiting for us. We were a tired little bunch but happy that we had finally arrived. The first thing we all wanted to know was how far was it to the ocean. When my dad said it was only a few blocks, it seemed strange that we could not see it. My parents took us down to the water.

I had never seen the Gulf nor any part of the ocean. I always thought all the ocean water would be the lovely colors of dark and light blue with a few white caps. The gulf water was as green as a field of wheat. Disappointment would not be the right word for how I felt about the color of the water. More like surprise. The children, of course, wanted to get right into the water. There was no beach area at that location, so Daddy promised to take us to the beach at Galveston to.

My brothers had been many times and told the little ones how much fun it was going to be. As it turned out, Uncle Johnny and Aunt Else were the ones who took us to Galveston. Uncle Johnny had some business to attend to over there and wanted to see the children and me, so off we went.

In those days the beaches were not so crowded. We were able to walk along the water's edge and even find a few shells. Aunt Elsie stayed with us while Uncle Johnny went to take care of the business matter. When my kids wanted to get in the water Aunt Elsie said they must not, Uncle Johnny would not like all that damp sand brought back into his new car. So, we didn't have much of a day at the beach after all. We ended up getting hot dogs from a vendor which almost proved to be too messy, but somehow, we were allowed to ride back to my parents' house in that fine new car.

Later, I told the children that we would get their daddy to come with us next time and they could play in the water all they wanted. My plans were to stay two weeks. Every morning while the children were still sleeping, I would get up early, just as dawn was breaking, practically run the four blocks to the water's edge and watch the sun come up.

It was so beautiful, I wished I had brought some art materials. The cameras we had then just did not do those lovely sunrises justice. One morning was exceptional. The water and light were silhouetted just right, giving off hints of silver with black silhouetted objects such as a pier and some boats. I had never seen anything like it and never have since. What a painting that would have made!

I never tried to paint it from memory, I knew I could never capture that moment on canvas. That quiet time, so early in the morning, renewed my spirit and refreshed my body. I would not have missed it for anything.

The following weekend my parents took us on a tour of the area. They drove back to Galveston to show us all the old houses and huge trees covered with hanging moss. They took us to visit a battleship docked permanently and open to visitors. They took us down to The Strand to buy souvenirs, for which I had no money, but not back to the beach. Momma said it was awfully crowed on the weekends. It was a fun day nonetheless and we were all tired at the end of it.

Coming into the house from my early morning walk on Monday, I heard Momma talking on the telephone with someone. I didn't want to interrupt her conversation, so I sat down quietly. She said, "Oh sure that might be fun. Come early though so we can make a day of it."

When she had put the receiver down she turned and said, "You will never guess who is coming over for a visit Saturday."

Thinking it might be Uncle Johnny's daughter, my cousin Mary Francis, I said it would be nice to see my cousin. We were both in grade school the last time I had seen her. Momma, almost gleefully, said, "Guess again!" and when I couldn't think who it might be, she couldn't play her game any longer, she told me it was J.C.'s parents, "All the boys are coming with them. Doyle is over from Houston and J.C. Is living with his parents again."

She went on about what she needed to get from the grocery store for the special lunch she wanted to prepare. I left her making a list and went into the bedroom, picked up the phone and called my sister in West Texas. We still hadn't had a phone put in, so I prayed for her to be home. When she answered I was relieved and told her that whatever she did to please get word to Eddy to send money for our tickets by Western Union the next day and not to ask why, to just do it and I would explain later. When she was sure none of us were sick, she said she would call her husband at work and tell him to see that Eddy sent the money. Then she told me she was off all week and I should call back and let her know when to meet the bus.

I didn't tell my parents about the call. The next morning after I took my walk, I went to the store near the bus station, where I had seen a Western Union sign in the window the day we had arrived. Sure enough, the money was there. I went into the station, bought the tickets for a bus leaving at ten a.m., hurried to my parents' house, threw everything into our bags, got the children up and dressed them.

They were whining, as kids do when they are not ready to get out of bed. When Momma came into the room asking what on earth was going on, I told her that we were leaving on the ten o'clock bus and she threw a big fit and told me I could not do that. I said, "Watch me. It has been a nice visit so far, but I have to go home today."

Of course, she had to know why, so I told her. She acted as if I was the most horrible person in the world, not wanting to be in the company of such dear friends. I knew there was no time for a drug out explanation, so I picked up the bags, took my children and walked to the bus station. When the bus finally came I got the children seated and quiet and the bus pulled out of the station and headed north. I took a deep breath and a sigh of relief, for once again I had been able to avoid seeing J.C. and knew in my heart that I had done the right thing.

I never told Eddy or my sister the real reason I wanted to come home early. I just said that I was ready to leave, that Momma and I had not agreed on a few things. Later, Billie said Momma had told her and she too thought I made the right decision.

A STRONG OAK

There is something to be said for becoming parents, home owners, and church goers. Those three things made us better people. We learned from our experiences and became mature in our thinking and our ways. Life was as good as we were able to make it, and that was saying something for two people who had no expectations in their youth. We had both been sickly, I with asthma, Ed with his afflictions from the burns and car accident. Two people who were adrift, going nowhere in particular, brought together by forces of nature and spirit, which neither of us fully understood.

Ed went about his work without complaint. He said he was happy, just being a husband and a dad. Our little home and family was enough for him, it seemed. I was happy just being alive and strong enough to take care of our children and keep things going around the house, but there was a part of me that wanted more. I wanted to paint, write, learn to play music. I wanted to do crafts, make pretty things for the house and to sell my work.

My church activities and the children took up all my time. I was the only female in the community who had a driver's license and took it upon myself to become the driver for all the other women and their children when they had doctors' appointments and shopping in Abilene.

In the spring of nineteen sixty-two there was an outbreak of measles in the community. In those days women and girls were not vaccinated against what seemed to be mostly a childhood disease which took care of itself with the right amount of care. I remembered clearly having had those ugly itchy spots and staying in bed in a darkened room when I was in the first grade.

Our children came through the outbreak with little trouble, other than the itching, which I tried to soothe with calamine lotion. When I woke up with my body covered with an itchy red rash, I was shocked to say the least. I became quite ill, nauseated and running a high temperature. After the third day of it, I went to see the doctor. Not only did I have measles, I was three months pregnant!

In all the busy goings on, I had lost count of time and had no idea that I was pregnant. I argued with the doctor that I couldn't possibly have the measles, because I had experienced a good case of them as a child. He said that was usually the case, but sometimes, when the body was run down, a person could indeed have a second occurrence of measles. He then suggested that I talk it over with my husband and together we should decide whether to abort the pregnancy or not, explaining that in my case, an abortion would be legal.

I did not understand why he would suggest such a thing and asked him why he had. He told me that there was a chance my baby might be born with one or more deformities, ranging from mild to extremely severe. I left that office with a strange sense of "Why me? What had I possibly done to deserve such judgment? What was I supposed to do?"

All my life I had heard that abortion was wrong. In my heart, I felt that was true, but how could I bring a baby into the world with a monstrous disability of some sort? What kind of a life could such a child enjoy? The rest of my day was spent in a stupor. I hardly remembered picking up the children from a neighbor's house. I guess by sheer will power I kept my head until Eddy came home from work.

Without allowing the kids their usual welcome Daddy home from work routine, I told them I needed to talk to Daddy about something very important and told them to stay outdoors and play for a while, then they could come in and give Daddy all the hugs and kisses they wanted while I made dinner. They ran off to play without asking any questions.

I met Eddy at the car and told him immediately that we had a huge problem and it must be taken care of as quickly as possible. He tried to lighten up my mood by teasing and joking with me as was his usual way of offsetting problems.

"Eddy, this is something very serious and we have to discuss it now," I told him firmly, so that he wouldn't rush off to get his welcome home from the children. He sat down, pulled me into his lap and said, "Now what is it that can't wait to be said?"

When I had finished telling him, his face took on that dark look that I had never learned to discern, and he sat quietly, without a word for some time. He pushed me up from his lap, got up and walked toward the house, then he turned around and asked what I thought should be done? I started crying and stammering and trying to tell him how I felt. When I had finished by saying that I did not know what the right thing to do was, he said, "You should."

I told him that my heart told me to keep the child, but my mind was asking "What if"? He replied, "There is no what if. The baby inside you is our flesh and blood. That child is ours to take care of no matter what condition it comes out in," then he calmly walked over to our other children who greeted him with happy shrieks of joy.

I knew in my heart he was right, and it was settled. Over the next six months, I prayed daily for God to help us face whatever His will for the baby was and give me strength to raise all my children in the best way possible. The church had special prayer meetings for the welfare of our unborn child and I am here to tell you that those prayers were heard and answered. Our tiny baby boy arrived in November, three pounds and three ounces. Other than being tiny, the doctor could find nothing else wrong. He quickly started gaining weight and everything worked the way it should. I will forever give God the glory for our second precious son, **ALLYN BARACHEL,** *"A strong oak that bows only before God."*

I wondered if the name I had chosen for our tiny son was the right one. Before long, I knew the name was the right one. He was strong, healthy and ready to live. Through hardships, trials and temptations, he has lived up to his name. He is, and will forever be our strong oak, bowing only to God

A SPECIAL MESSENGER

The years which followed were filled with the usual growing pains of family life. Eddy continued to be a steady worker, quickly finding his way to the top position of any job he had. Even then there were times when I had to return to work to help meet all our financial obligations. Growing children, in school and out, required money which in those days didn't seem to go far enough, no matter what our incomes were. Although we lived in much better circumstances than our parents had done, and enjoyed the middle-class life we led, we never could manage to get ahead.

In nineteen seventy-three Eddy became acquainted with a business owner in the area who made him a very good offer to run an egg farm. I did not particularly care for it, but knew my husband was ready for more than the usual work by the hour job. He wanted to feel the sense of real accomplishment which the new business would provide.

The owner lived out of town where the home office of the operation was located and needed someone to act as his business partner for the local branch. There were two separate living quarters on the property, as well as an operation involving forty thousand cage layers. Fresh eggs were a booming business and Eddy welcomed the challenge. The eggs were gathered on conveyer belts into the processing plant where they were candled, cleaned, graded, sized and packaged.

Eddy was overjoyed because there would be work our whole family could do together. The money was more than we had imagined. The three older children were in high school and the youngest in sixth grade. They all liked the idea of having their own money. The two oldest were already feeling liberated by being allowed to set up separate living quarters in the second building, which was located only some twenty feet away from the main dwelling.

My only objection to our new employment was the teasing and unkind remarks we were letting ourselves in for and it started immediately. Texas was famous for The Chicken Ranch joke. The joke being that a farmer had turned a huge profit by offering the services of his daughters to the men folk round about in exchange for a few chickens on each visit. The farmer then sold the eggs making a good living as he had several daughters who were visited often.

Eddy tried to calm my hysteria of being put into a situation which would make us the butt of such vulgar comments, by saying the place was an egg farm, not a chicken ranch. To make bad matters worse, our oldest son found a T-shirt with a caricature of a lecherous looking fellow handing an armload of chickens to a scantily dressed young lady. The shirt said it all and I was furious every time he wore the thing, but he thought it was funny.

At any rate, the work was steady and productive. We supplied eggs to all the grocers, cafes and schools for miles around. I did all the office work and candled eggs when I had time. While I oversaw operations, Eddy took care of the routes and orders. Our children learned every aspect of the work. By the time the two oldest graduated high school, we were financially able to put them into their own new vehicles which delighted them enough to stay on with us awhile longer.

I had hopes for them to go to university. Eddy was just happy they had graduated high school, knowing their prospects were much better than ours had been, at their ages. They both said they would look into college after a year off from school. So, it was that we all remained, living and working in the egg business. Everything was going so well we had to hire extra workers and add another delivery truck.

Somewhere along the way, Eddy started drinking heavily. I did not realize what was going on for a while, because he had also started spending a lot of time at the homestead, adding on to the house and turning it into a huge house for us to go home to, when we were ready to retire. A place with plenty of room to house our children and hopefully our grandchildren.

When he started coming home later at night, I began to question his staying up so late, then trying to run the route the next day. He told me not to worry about it, everything was running like a well-oiled machine. When I started noticing the smell of hard liquor on his breath, he just laughed and told me that some friend or another had stopped off to see how the work on the homestead was going and had offered him a drink.

I didn't like it, even though we had stopped attending church when we took on the egg farm. It got worse by the week. To make it worse, I had not been feeling right. With Eddy gone so much, I figured the added responsibility on my part was the cause of my not feeling top notch. My health had been good over the past many years. I was still a young thirty-eight-year-old and my youngest child had become a teenager. Life was too good in general to let my health get in the way of my work.

I went for a visit to our family doctor who insisted on me having a thorough, physical. When he told me that I was not sick, I was pregnant, my chin almost hit my knees. How could it be? I had not had a full monthly period in the past few years and figured menopause was setting in early, for which I was actually glad. But another child? I was too shocked for words. Not only was I pregnant, I was five months pregnant. The doctor suggested that I slow down on my duties at work and take it easy for a change. Little did he know that in my situation that was not possible. I worked right up until time for our fifth child to be born.

Eddy was overjoyed at having a new baby. He said it made him feel young again. I reminded him that he was still a young man, to which he replied that there were days when he felt very old. I thought that was a strange thing for him to say, but never thought to ask why he felt old. We discussed names for our new baby. He said if the child was a boy he would like to name him Charles Steffen. He said that was a good strong name for a boy and that it was his lawyers name. He hoped, if the child was a boy, he might become a lawyer.

If the baby was a girl, I was to choose the name. I gave the naming of our child a lot of thought. After some research and decided on, **STEPHENIE LAYOYCE**, *"A special messenger of joy."*

The first name was spelled with an 'e' because, Serandica Pappas had reminded me that her Justus's last name was Stephenoupolis. It just stuck with me. When she was born, I knew the name was right. Our little 'special messenger' arrived in good health and ready for life.

She was beautiful. The first time I heard her cry and saw her little face, all shiny as if it had been sprinkled with fine silver and gold glitter, I knew she was bringing me joy. To this day, every time I hear her voice and see her face, I know I named her correctly, for she does indeed always bring me a special message of hope and encouragement; a message of love and expectation of all that is new and significant to life. She is and will forever be our special messenger of joy.

NINETEEN SEVENTY-EIGHT

I found it extremely hard to write about this chapter about of our lives. Even though everything at work was running well, there was something wrong. I knew there was but could not put my finger on it. Our two oldest were running around at night in their new vehicles, with their friends. Like Eddy, they too were coming home later and later. Our middle daughter was not yet in on the running around so much. We spent many evenings at home together, just she, the baby and me. Eddy had started taking our youngest son with him to help with work at the homestead. He said he was teaching him how to get things done out there since our oldest son had no interest in helping anymore.

Each evening, after the baby was put down for the night, my daughter and I would eat our dinner, watch a little television and go to bed. Each night, the hour of Eddy and our youngest son coming home got later. One night I told my daughter that I was going to look for them. She stayed with the baby and I headed for the homestead. Mid-way there I spotted the egg delivery van coming toward me. I thought to myself, "Dear God! Eddy is driving drunk with our son in the vehicle!"

By the time I got to the cross over and headed back, the van was almost a mile ahead of me. It was after midnight and there was not much traffic. I floor boarded the accelerator and came up behind the van which was weaving from lane to lane. I blinked the lights a few times then honked the horn with no response. I was afraid to pull alongside for fear of having a collision with the veering van. There was a huge truck stop just up the road. To my great relief, the van pulled off the main highway into the parking lot of the truck stop coming to a sudden halt. I got out of the car and ran to the driver's side ready to give my husband a few strong words about his actions. Imagine my horror when I opened the door and found our youngest son, who was not even old enough to have a learner's permit, at the controls.

Eddy was in the passenger seat, drunk. I pulled my son out of the van and told him to come with me. I yelled back at my husband to go into the truck stop and drink coffee until he was able to drive himself home. Back at the house my fury overtook my fright. I told my son that he could not go with his dad any more. It was too dangerous for him. Of course, he could not see the harm. He said his daddy needed his help and he had to go with him. I loved my husband, but I loved my children even more and I knew there was no way that kind of behavior could continue.

When Ed finally made it home, I confronted him. His answer when I said that we had to get this straightened out right now, was to ask what there was to eat. At the moment, I didn't care if he ever ate again or not. My fury turned to aggression and I accused him of not caring about us all. I told him that he would have to stop what he was doing, or I would take my children and leave. He sat quietly a few minutes then got up and went to bed. I got no sleep that night.

Hot coffee was waiting when he got up. Instead of either of us going to work, we sat at the table and stared at one another until he said, "Have it your way then," and got up and went to work as usual.

Things were not the same. It was as if everything was falling apart and there was no way I could stop it. Every day turned into a yelling match with either Eddy or the two oldest. We were both working overtime and Eddy was not happy. We thought moving back to the country would be better for the whole family, so we decided to give up living at the egg farm and move back home. We had saved enough money to get by on until we could find other work.

Eddy had been having a lot of trouble with his back, but he kept applying for ordinary jobs. Finally, he landed one in Abilene. After only a few months he was hospitalized with a slipped disk from lifting heavy bags of sand. He had taken a job as a sandblaster. It was good pay but hard work. After the surgery on his back, he was not able to go back into that work again.

In the months to come, Eddy was in and out of the hospital for pneumonia several times. Then we learned that our oldest daughter was pregnant, and she wouldn't come home. We had no idea where she was nor who she was with. I was getting a taste of what I had put my parents through when I was much younger than our daughter was at the time.

When she finally did come home she went to work at the hospital as an aide. Eddy was sick a lot and as much as we wanted to be good parents, our relationship with our children soured. Our oldest son was using his dad's new truck and totaled it. We were thankful he was not hurt and continued as we always had.

179

In nineteen seventy-seven when our baby was only eighteen months old, just before Christmas, Eddy was hospitalized once again. I knew there was something more wrong with him than pneumonia. I insisted on him going to the hospital in Abilene. Reluctantly, he agreed. After a week of tests, we learned that he was in fourth stage with cancer. It was terminal. He could not possibly live more than a few weeks. He was to remain in the hospital for he was too weak to be moved. They would keep him out of pain and with any luck, he would not suffer too much.

We had seen his mother waste away to sixty pounds of skin and bone, suffering terribly the last few months of her life from cervical cancer. I prayed for him not to have to lay and suffer the way his sweet mother, Polly, had done.

His family was to be called in if they wanted to see him before he was unable to respond to them. It all happened so fast. After the initial shock, one of the doctors told me to go and make arrangements for the time was at hand. It was the hardest thing I had ever had to do in my life, but with God's help and Serandica Pappas beside me, I got it done.

January fifth nineteen seventy-eight, one week before Eddy died, our daughter gave birth to our first grandson. His grandfather saw him one time before he slipped away on January twelfth. It was a tragedy and a blessing. That little blessing along with our own baby daughter who was eighteen months old, were the most wonderful gifts God had ever bestowed upon me. Taking care of those two little ones kept me sane, otherwise, I might have slipped into an irrevocable state of depression.

My children were constant reminders that I still had them, even though my husband of twenty-three years was gone. It is to all of them that I am writing these memoirs, to let them know that they were all special gifts and blessings to their father and me. Their strength was what I clung to when he was gone. I admit, they gave to me much more love and attention than I gave them. For that I am truly sorry. I never realized any of their pain of loss. Only mine.

When all had been said and done and I finally came to my senses again, and all that mattered to me in the world was my children, their children and all ours to come in the future, it was perhaps too little, too late.

PART III

WHAT NOW

Everything seemed to have happened in what felt like the blink of an eye and we were jettisoned into the future and it was nineteen ninety-five. My children and I had somehow survived the years following Eddy's passing. I had become a grandmother several times over and my own youngest was off to college. For the first time in my life I was completely alone, except for the constant visiting of Serandica Pappas.

While holding down a full-time job, I enrolled in community college. I needed to sharpen my computer skills. My concentration was on Psychology. I needed help in understanding myself and others. I knew I was miserably lacking in that area. The classes I enjoyed most were English and Creative writing. Of course, the majority of the students were fresh out of high school. It took some doing on my part going to classes with all those young people. It didn't take me long to figure out that none of them cared less about an older woman in the class room. Most of them were only there because their parents expected them to be learning how to make something. It seemed that sleeping in class was their idea of how that was achieved. I also learned that the professors couldn't care less as long as the lecture halls were full, which insured their salary.

A couple of older ladies who lived in my apartment building were members of the local Writer's Guild. When they learned that I was taking some creative writing courses they invited me to accompany them to a few of their meetings and perhaps later join the group. It was an interesting crowd of women and men of all ages. They met once each month, talked about what was new in the literary world and offered suggestions as well as reading and criticizing one another's' writing endeavors. A few of them had some success with publishing and were willing to help others succeed as well.

I had written a little poetry, as well as a couple of books that I had never figured out how to get published. When the guild members were asked to submit their poetic works to a reliable publishing house out of the country I jumped at the chance, got mine together and submitted them along with all the others. We were told not to expect too much. Even though people in other parts of the world were more inclined to purchase books of poetry, it was still a long shot.

Feeling a need for a change in the way I wore my hair and some clothes that made me look more polished, and professional, I dug into what little reserves I had and came up with a new hairdo which cost a bundle. It was now dark auburn with copper highlights. New shoes and a couple of handbags, and a few items of clothing to go with them didn't seem such an extravagant thing to do. After all, it had been years since I had done anything for myself. I felt like I was worth it after all.

When the guild offered special rates on a group tour of the United Kingdom, I was glad I had gussied up a little. They made the trip sound so affordable that I knew I had to go. Carried away with anticipation. I mentioned to Serandica Pappas, one evening when she put in an appearance, that I was planning to go abroad. As she had done for years, she smiled, clasped her hands together beneath her chin, and said what she always had said each time I found myself wondering what I was going to do with the rest of my life. As she had from the beginning, 'we must find Justus'. When she stood next to my chair I realized I had never entertained the idea of asking her how I might help with that.

I plopped down lazily into the big overstuffed chair. Took a deep breath and told her I would love to help her find him, but my children needed me. When she shook her head, I asked, "How can I possibly help you find him? I have no earthly idea where he might be."

I knew my voice sounded gruff, but I was tired and wished she would just tell me what I was supposed to do to help find her Justus. She smiled, her green eyes almost the color of emeralds sparkled, as she looked away into the distance she said, "We must travel."

I reminded her that I had just finished saying that I was going with the group to London and would not likely have time to go running all over the world looking for someone having very little money for to do so, especially when I didn't even know where she wanted me to go. I went into my bedroom, opened the closet door and started examining garments hanging neatly on the racks. Serandica started pulling out articles of clothing and throwing them onto the bed. Excitedly she said, "Hurry! We don't have much time!"

Something inside me said, "Go with it," so I picked up a comfortable, long skirt and a long-sleeved blouse, changed into them, fixed my hair, put on a pair of comfortable shoes and walked with her back into the living room. She opened the front door, then motioned for me to follow her and got into the car. I got into the driver seat, started the engine and backed into the street. Before long we were on the highway. It was still daylight but almost dusk. I said, "I think you should tell me where we are going."

She just kept smiling and pointing ahead. I glanced at the gasoline gauge and was relieved that it indicated a full tank. After a few minutes, Serandica moved to the edge of the seat as if she was looking for something. Before I could ask, she said "Take the next exit."

I asked no questions, just did as she said feeling comfortable letting her make the decisions. Soon we came to a huge Truss bridge over the highway. Just after we crossed the bridge she pointed to a small road ahead and said, "Turn there," which I did, realizing I had no idea where we were.

The road we had turned on to, was paved and led to a boat ramp at the end. I turned into a parking area and turned off the key. I was going to ask why we had come there but she had already opened the door and was walking toward the boat ramp. I called out to her, but she motioned for me to come with her, so I reluctantly followed her down to the water's edge.

"It is almost dark! What are we doing here?" I asked. She looked at me as if to say, "Don't you know?"

There was a canoe tied to the pier, off to the side of the boat ramp. She got into the canoe and started singing, "Row, row, row your boat gently down the stream."

Concerned at this point, I asked again, "What are you doing?"

She motioned for me to get into the canoe. I said, "No way. You of all people should know better than to ask me to get into a canoe. You know I am terrified of small boats and deep water!"

"The water is not deep. It is a good boat and besides, I am here." she said, brightly. I wasn't about to get in that thing, but she coaxed, "You must. I promise, I will not let anything happen to you. Fear is what is holding you back. Come now."

She held up both her hands to me. I stepped into the canoe very slowly and sat down. I was trembling, yet it was as if I had no will of my own in the matter. Sitting rigid, looking straight ahead, grasping the sides of the canoe tightly and knowing that Serandica was rowing the thing, I watched in unbelief as the river narrowed into a stream. It was dark, and the moonlight shone on the water, which appeared to be running slowly in the direction we were going. Serandica kept singing the row, row, row your boat song, over and over. It would have been annoying, but she sung it softly, humming part of the time.

I must have fallen asleep, for the next thing I knew, the canoe was grounded and Serandica Pappas was nowhere in sight. The full moon lit the grassy river bank which had a background of thick forest where nothing could be seen. I sat in the canoe, afraid to move, and whispered, "Serandica, where are you?"

Suddenly, there she was, on the river bank, motioning me to come to her. Shakily, I whispered the words, "Where are we? Why are we here?"

She just stood there smiling, extending her hands to me. Knowing she was there calmed my fear slightly. Rising cautiously, I made my way out of the canoe and onto the ground, but I was angry at Serandica Pappas for bringing me to such an isolated place at night. I was about to give her a piece of my mind about it, but just then I heard the faint sound of what seemed to be the wild beat of Native American drums, a sound which definitely sent my mind whirling backward into the past.

The moon gave a beautiful sheen to the water, rippling and trickling against the river bank. There was a mist shrouding the forest, which was absolutely ghostly. I shivered and rubbed my hands up and down my arms to keep the chill in the night air from making my teeth chatter.

The drumbeats got louder but did not keep me from hearing the hoot of an owl, the croaks of frogs or the chirping of crickets. Serandica Pappas pointed up river at another canoe approaching. She stood smiling as if I should be happy to see someone else arrive at this out of the way place in the middle of the night. As it came ashore I saw that there were two people in the canoe. A scantily dressed Native American man and a Native American woman dressed in deerskin. Their long hair was plaited similarly with braids draped over their shoulders in front.

The man stepped out of the canoe before it stopped moving and stood little more than an arm's length in front of me. The woman stayed seated in the canoe. I was frightened and tried to run but my feet would not move. The man was not scowling at me, his look was actually pleasant. He opened his arms in a sweeping motion and began to speak, but he did not speak in English.

Serandica Pappas translated his words. Even though I could not understand his words and the sound of his voice were very familiar.

"See all this? See how beautiful it is? Feel how peaceful it is here? I want to be in this place. Where do you want to be?" The voice was my deceased husband, Eddy's voice. I stood with my mouth open and could not speak. I kept trying to say something. When the words finally came out, all I could say was, "It is indeed a beautiful place, I can understand that you love it, but it is not my realm. My place is in the future. I will always remember you and the years we shared, as well as this lovely place. I will never forget you. Perhaps one day, we might visit one another again."

Serandica Pappas translated. He smiled, placed his fisted hand over his heart for a few seconds then extended his arm and still fisted hand outward and down river. He spoke the word "Go," stepped back into the canoe, and as suddenly as it had come it was gone, back up the river.

I turned to inquire of Serandica Pappas, but she was already in the canoe, beckoning me to get into it. I was so stunned by what had happened I just sat in the canoe not knowing what to ask. We were moving down river again, but the water was swifter, and the canoe was moving faster it seemed. I became frightened and cried out that I wanted to go home. I started screaming and closed my eyes. The canoe lifted into the air. I had never been so afraid in my life.

Suddenly everything was still and dark. I could hear soft music playing, beautiful Celtic music. I opened my eyes slowly, not knowing what to expect. In the dim light I realized that I was no longer in the canoe but in an airplane trying to figure out how I got there. It was about to come into my head when I noticed light streaming in from the window.

There was nobody, not even Serandica Pappas, in the other seat so I moved over to look out at the beautiful sunrise. Glancing downward I saw large patches of emerald green and realized the plane must be over Ireland. My heart began to pound, I had always wanted to visit Ireland! How could this be? Looking around and finding everyone else asleep made me feel lonely. That is when Serandica appeared beside me, her usual smile taking my mind off the "why" and "how." She lit up the space around us but said, "Go back to sleep, we are not there yet."

Looking back out the window I saw what looked like mountains in the distance and wondered where we were again. Then I closed my eyes and fell asleep. A voice from a speaker woke me up. It was the pilot announcing that we were in a holding pattern and would land as soon as he was given the word. Smog was causing the delay. Again, I looked out the window and was astonished to see the Acropolis standing majestically above a sprawling city of glass, concrete and steel.

My heart started pounding. I had always wanted to visit Athens. Serandica was gone again but the passengers were waking up and the stewardess was offering coffee. My thoughts were not on how all this happened, but rather how I was going to explore that ancient part of the city and the modern part below it. I watched breathlessly as the scene changed to the ocean, it's waters sparkling. I watched as it changed from dark blue green to gray with white foam as it washed shoreward. It mesmerized me.

After a few minutes I realized the plane was lower. The huge buildings of the Acropolis stood like sentries over the modern city. The sun shining brightly against the ancient ghostly monuments made me feel as if I was somehow connected with that wondrous place. The plane landed, and a stewardess handed me a bag. I tried to tell her I had not brought one, but the other passengers were already pressing against me, moving me swiftly toward the doorway and through the cavernous deplaning tunnel. Suddenly, I found myself in the terminal, which was flooded with people, all rushing to buy tickets or to vehicles waiting outside. I walked out and down the sidewalk with no idea where I was going.

Suddenly it was as if everything about me was moving in slow motion. There was a man coming toward me with open arms. I looked behind me, thinking he was greeting someone on the walkway behind me. No one was there. The man was still walking toward me, his arms open wide. It seemed like I should know him, but I couldn't make out who it was. When he stopped in front of me and said, "Welcome to the land of the living," I opened my mouth to speak but again found that I could say nothing. He took my hand and led me away into the crowd of people milling about the terminal. I was not afraid for some reason. It seemed as if I was on my way to finding out what had led me to that place and why. Everything went dark suddenly, and a booming voice said, very clearly, in English, "Choose this day."

I stopped walking and could no longer feel the hand of the man who had been leading me away from the air terminal. I could not move so I took a deep breath and closed my eyes, wondering what was going on and what I should do. When I opened my eyes again I was in my living room, in the chair I had sat down in earlier.

At first, I was sorry that what had happened was only a dream or a vision. It had all seemed so real. I was very tired. Looking around the dark room and seeing no light of any kind, I turned on the table lamp beside my chair, yawned and stretched, then got up and went into the kitchen. I had not eaten when I came home from work. I tried to shake off the things which a few minutes earlier had seemed so real. I took out left overs and warmed them in the microwave. Thoughts kept racing through my mind while I ate. Later as I tried to watch television, I wanted to call my children and tell them what had happened but decided not to. After all, it was getting late and I didn't want to disturb them.

The next morning, which was Saturday, I woke up with it all still on my mind. I lay in bed trying to figure it all out. After a few minutes, I got up and dressed, ate breakfast and started

sorting through the morning mail. I found an unusual looking envelope with out of the country markings and realized it was from the publishing house in Great Britain. I ripped it open excitedly. There was a one-page letter and a check for more money than I had made in years!

I read the letter over and over, wanting to make sure of what it said, "Royalties paid quarterly." There would hopefully be more! Although it made me feel terribly guilty, I decided to keep the news of my good fortune to myself and started packing for the group trip with the Writer's Guild. The money couldn't have come at a better time.

We flew to New York City on the first leg. I browsed the little terminal shops while on a two-hour layover before the flight to London, England. I used the time looking around, being careful not to spend too much of my money before even leaving the country. I didn't eat for fear of air sickness. Finally, we were in the air again and it was for real! I was on my way to see things I had never imagined seeing in my lifetime.

There were two sisters seated next to me on the flight who had introduced themselves as Petula and Ophelia, but I wasn't sure which was which, they looked so similar. They were somewhat older than me, but full of good attitude and fun. Traveling had been their favorite pastime over the years. There were very few places they had not been. I listened happily until the sleeping pill I had taken kicked in and I heard nothing more until somebody shook me telling me to fasten seat belts as the plane was preparing for landing. Groggy and disoriented I tried to fasten up but finally had to have help from one of the sisters. She said, "Don't worry dear, Sister and I will help you."

I thought, "How sweet they are! Perhaps I can be like them when I am that age." Upon my first glimpse at the buildings as the hotel mini bus left Heathrow, I thought they looked much like the ones at home. The only difference being the wording and some of the spelling, but as the vehicle rolled into the older part of London, I was thrilled to see places that looked more like the ones I had seen in movies and books over the years.

My agenda called for two days and nights in London before going on to Wales. I was to meet with the publisher to leave a manuscript. Hopefully my book manuscript would fetch even better than the poetry had, which would indeed make me a happy camper.

Although it was hard for me to get used to the way the Londoners spoke, I loved listening to them. Arriving at the hotel and realizing it was so near Harrods excited me terribly. I could hardly wait to go there and look around, maybe pick out a few things to take home as souvenirs.

Tea was being served, so the sisters and I sat at one of the beautiful little tables in the hotel's huge dining room along with one of the guild women. Every time the waiter passed our table, he offered us a different plate filled with tiny sandwiches and ended with scones so buttery they melted in my mouth. They weren't the big scones I made from biscuit mix at home. They were dainty and tasted much better.

It gave me great pleasure to find out the two sisters would be taking the same tours as those on my agenda. It would be more fun seeing everything with somebody else, rather than alone. We barely had time to freshen up a bit before the first tour began.

My room was gorgeous, and it was all I could do to keep from canceling on the tour and staying in the room. The sisters would be waiting for me downstairs, so I hurried around and made it back in time to load on the tour bus with them. The tour guides voice over the loudspeaker was kind of humdrum and uninteresting. It was hard for me to keep up with what he was saying as the double decker rolled along the crowded streets.

After a few minutes of trying to listen while looking to one side or the other, trying not to miss a single thing, I finally got used to his speech enough to understand what he was telling us.

"England is famous for many things. She has produced Kings, Queens, noblemen, poets and artists and many scholars. Whether Royal or Commoner, her people are her greatest resource. London is the capital city with a population of more than six million. Your first stop will be to visit The Old Lady of Threadneedle Street. She will not sew up a tear or mend your trousers, but she will help you with your money. She is the Bank of England."

The visit was indeed an experience that most, including myself, would never forget. From there we were hurried onto a boat for an excursion along the river Thames. The group wandered into the gardens which were crazy quilts of flowers and flowering shrubs of all kinds and colors. They spread all the way down to the river where our boat was waiting to take us to Runnymede, where a group of noblemen forced King John to sign the Magna Carta in twelve fifteen. From what I could understand that document served as the English Bill of Rights. From there we were taken back aboard the tour bus for a ride down Oxford Street. One of the tourists asked the guide why people drove on the wrong side of the street. He said, "Perhaps it is the wrong side of the street to you madam, but it has been the way people in this part of the world has traveled for centuries. When traveling, whether walking, on horses or in a carriage or cart, the men always carried a sword or some other sort of weapon for protection against highwaymen. Most were right handed and wanted the weapon between them and whoever meant to cause the harm or robbery."

By then the bus had stopped at Trafalgar Square where our attention was called to a tall granite column with a statue of Horacio Nelson. The guide informed us that Nelson, a tough one-eyed, one-armed British Admiral had wiped out Napoleon's entire navy at Trafalgar. Nelson had been killed in the battle. Meanwhile, Napoleon was marching with his grand army to Russia and was eventually crushed at the Battle of Waterloo. Everything was silent for a few minutes as the bus rolled past Buckingham Palace.

The guide said the standard, or flag was not flying which meant the Queen was not in residence there at the time. We did get to see the changing of the guard, a ceremony performed by men in red tunics and black bearskin helmets. At dusk, Big Ben was magnificent. On the way back to the hotel the guide spat out more history than I could keep track of. Growing tired of the tour, I had already decided it would be a good idea to bring along a small recording device and a camera on the next excursion.

The next morning breakfast was served to me in bed. What, I thought, could be better than this? The chambermaid ran a hot bath for me while I was enjoying a breakfast of poached egg on a real English muffin, a spiced pear and, upon my request, coffee, instead of tea. After the breakfast things were taken away I enjoyed a wonderful bubble bath wondering what exciting things the day would be holding for me. I dried with the plush white towels, brushed my hair and dusted on some of the lovely smelling bath powder with its fluffy puff. I had bought it at one of the little shops near the hotel. It smelled of gardenias and sandalwood all mixed together. The scent was light enough for morning use. A small bottle of perfume in the same fragrance was for evenings.

After dressing I pulled back the drapes and noticed the fog was thick outside. I chose a long skirt and matching blouse, along with a long light weight sweater. As I dressed I thought about how many years it had been since I had worn clothing like the things I had purchased for my trip, knowing I was going to spend most of what I had made on the poetry book sales, but why not? I deserved it for all the years of struggling and doing without. I was going first class all the way and had made up my mind not to have any regrets. The phone's loud clanging ring broke my train of thought. It was a message that the Palace tour would be boarding in thirty minutes. I rushed to put on a little makeup, checked my nails to make sure they weren't chipped and straightened everything. I wanted to look as nice as possible for visiting the palace.

It was more beautiful than I had expected but there was a musty smell that made my chest feel tight. I was glad when we got back outside again. On our way again, the guide once more went into his rhetoric about London being the capital of England and the United Kingdom including Northern Ireland. He said it is like no other place in the world, fifty miles inward from the sea and sprawls like an octopus on both sides of the Thames, which he again reminded us was pronounced "Tims". I turned on the tape recorder and tried to get as much of what he was saying as possible. After all, that was what I went there for, to learn something I didn't know. He went on, "The Celts called it LLAN DIN, which meant holy hill. The Romans called it, Londinuim, so that was how in later years it became known as London."

We were told that in the city itself thousands work in banks, at merchant exchanges, insurance companies and shipping houses. I learned that Saint Paul's Cathedral is the largest anywhere except for Saint Peter's at the Vatican and that the outer city bustled with a mixture of culture. In Westminster Abbey many kings and Queens had been crowned, married and buried and many other famous people were in tombs or had monuments there. Among them, in the poet's corner, Lord Byron and Alford Tennyson.

The guides voice rambled constantly. I was glad I had brought along empty cassettes to tape it all when my ears tired of listening. I just wanted to look about and see things. Even the sisters were quiet. They did seem excited that we were on our way to Madame Tussaud's Wax Museum, where we would see the magnificent life like figures of Kings, Queens, movie stars and many other famous people from all walks of life, even murderers, one of the sisters told me with a giggle. We passed Oxford and Cambridge, two of the oldest universities in Europe. We saw Bobbies directing traffic and marveled at their skill. The last thing the guide told us before that tour ended was that London was never hot. Most of the time the temperature never got above a pleasant eighty degrees. The nights were usually very cool, and a wrap was most appreciated by those who wished to venture out in the evenings.

Back at the hotel we were served lunch around one thirty in the afternoon. We had little bowls of watercress soup and those tiny sandwiches along with white wine and cheeses. I loved it all, to me it was a grand way to live. I found myself wishing that it would go on forever. After lunch I promised the sisters to sit with them at dinner and went to my room to relax and look at the brochures form the travel agency.

Wales was the next stop. My plan was to stay there for the rest of the trip. I hoped the place was like the pictures, which showed green valleys and houses of Celtic structure. Some of the country houses were built with the grayish colored rock which had been cleared from the land and surrounded by rock fences. The brochures mentioned a bustling cultural district where poets, artists and musicians hobnobbed. I didn't think I was ready for that myself but figured it would be interesting to learn about.

Time was flying by making me wish I could stay on in London longer, but I had to stick to the agenda for I had no idea how to strike out on my own and do the things I wanted to do. I was fairly hungry by the time dinner time rolled around, as I had skipped afternoon tea, and wasted no time getting freshened up and ready to go meet the sisters and find out what they had been up to.

The elevator stopped once on the way down. A tall man in a tweed jacket with leather patches at the elbows stepped in and faced forward, taking a military at ease stance. He had a familiar look about him. Actually, I felt sure I had seen somewhere before. His hair was mostly white, and he wore silver tone rimmed eyeglasses. When the elevator stopped on the mezzanine, where I was getting off, he moved aside, allowing me to step out first. I looked up into his face and said, "Thank you."

He had a handsome face and strong features. I kept thinking I had seen him, maybe on one of the tours. Everyone was being seated as they entered the dining room. I spotted the sisters who had been watching for me. They were waving from the table. Without waiting to be escorted, I hurried over, delighted to see their happy faces. They had spent the afternoon shopping and told me about the shops they had been to and how to get there in case

I decided to go shopping. I had to admit that I had been lazy all afternoon but was ready for my last evening in London. When the sisters heard that I hadn't made plans already, they insisted that I go with them to the opera. I heard them ask but had just noticed that the man I saw on the elevator was seated alone at a small table near us. He was facing me and was close enough to overhear our conversation. I had an eerie feeling when I realized he was looking straight at me. The two women were chatting happily. When the question was put to me again, rather loudly, it drew my attention back to what they were talking about.

"Lois my girl, will you come with us to the opera tonight?" I looked back at the man and his head came up suddenly as the question was asked. He was looking at me again, and I couldn't take my eyes off him. It was as if I was hypnotized. I heard the question and answered back, "Yes, perhaps,"

They both turned to see what or who had caught my attention. At the moment a waiter was talking to the man then he walked over to our table and handed me a note and said, "For you madame."

I opened it and read, "Did you ever know a J.C. Henry?"

TOGETHER AGAIN

My mouth flew open! I was afraid to think and told myself it couldn't be him. One of the sisters put a hand on my arm and asked, "Are you alright dear? You are as white as a sheet."

I handed her the piece of paper. She looked at it, then asked, "Well, do you know someone with that name?"

Breathlessly, I answered, "Yes, but it was a very long time ago"

The look on my face must have said it all. He was already up and coming to our table. The other sister asked, "Are you alright? Is that an expression of happiness or fear?"

I took a deep breath and said, "Both."

He stood beside my chair and said, "Excuse me ma'am, but I couldn't help overhearing someone call you Lois. I knew someone by that name many years ago and found myself thinking you might be the same person."

"Why, he's got the same Texas drawl as you do dear!" one of the sisters giggled, then placed a gloved hand over her mouth. I could not speak. I did not know what to say. Dumbfounded I just sat and stared at him. The longer I looked at his smiling face the more I was sure that it was, indeed, my own long-lost J.C.

When I finally found my voice again, I said, "It has been over forty years. What are the chances of us meeting here, so far away from home?"

"What are the chances?" he asked back.

The two women were patiently waiting, it seemed, for an introduction. Finding my manners as well as my voice, I introduced him as a dear friend and they asked him to sit with us for desert, a scrumptious custard with caramel sauce served with fresh whipped cream, but I could hardly taste, much less swallow, any of mine.

My heart was beating fast and my emotions were mixed. All those years had gone by, but the pain still lingering deep within me began to surface rapidly. My eyes were starting to smart, and my throat was tightening and beginning to ache.

The sisters were asking him all kinds of questions and in a matter of minutes I learned that he had retired from the military and was nearing retirement at a chemical company, where he had been an executive for the past twenty years. While listening to it all, and trying to calm myself, I thought, "Sounds like you stayed with the plan old boy. The big picture and all that."

I knew it was sarcasm but at the moment, I could not allow myself to feel anything else.

"Just look at us doing all the talking." one of the sisters said. The one who had introduced herself as Ophelia leaned toward him and said, "Your friend has a serious heart condition and is planning on taking it easy in Wales beginning tomorrow."

Again, my mouth flew open and, "What are you talking about?" I blurted out, then added, "I've not had any heart problem, at least lately."

With that the two women burst into laughter and suddenly I felt like I was back in Texas with Joyce and June. J.C. sat looking at me, shaking his head side to side.

"You are looking great. No one would ever know by looking at you that you have ever had a heart problem." He said.

Petula reminded Ophelia about the opera. They asked if I would be joining them and I said that I should spend some time with my old friend and they left us there together. We were now alone in a crowded room.

"I cannot believe meeting you here." I said sincerely.

"Me either," he said, then added, "I believe we've got some unfinished business that needs to be attended to. Don't you?"

His mouth was drawn down into a tight line when he finished saying that, and I didn't waste any time, because I didn't know how long I might have to say what I had always told myself I would say if I ever saw him again. Of course, that had been before I gave up on the idea that I would ever see him again. It all spilled out, right then and there.

"You know that saying, 'I'm sorry isn't good enough'? It's true for me, for not listening to what you wanted to say to me the night before you went away so long ago. Believe me, I have regretted it. All through the years, I have been ashamed of not opening the door that night. Only after many years did I come to realize that it must have hurt you as terribly as it did me. Please believe me, I could not help myself from doing that hateful thing. It was as if the only person I was sure of was deserting me and I had no control over keeping it from happening. I wanted you to stay, not leave me, so badly. I was too young to understand, but I do now. And you were right, and I should have listened to you."

He reached across the table, took my hands in his and said, "I know. I know, and I should have realized that you weren't able to deal with me going. I did write you letters you know."

"I never got them"

"I sent them to your mother because I knew she would read them and I wanted her and your dad to know I how very much cared for you."

"I never got a word from her except the message you sent about meeting you in Hawaii when I turned seventeen, but I had already married."

"The first few months I figured you were just mad at me. After a year went by I decided you probably didn't care about me anymore at all, so I quit sending letters, except for the card with that little ring on your pinkie for your birthday, when you were at your aunt's that time."

"I cared alright. I always cared. Several months after that first Christmas without you, Momma did give me a couple of pictures. One was of you at boot camp and another of you, holding your toddler son on your knee," I paused but when he didn't say anything right away, I went on, "In the picture of you holding the child, your wedding ring is clearly visible, so I figured that you had gone back to your ex-wife and son. I felt as if you weren't thinking anything about me anymore and the picture was proof of that."

His mouth was drawn down tightly again.

"That shows how much you really don't know. You didn't see her in the picture, did you? The ring is the one I am still wearing. The one I've worn since that night I tried to talk to you about it all. It is part of the set we would use when we were married. I wore it so that I would always stay faithful to you. We were wed in our hearts, you and me.

That picture must have been the one Momma snapped when I was home on furlough and they had the child at their house. Momma didn't want to accept that the child was not mine, but there was proof. You know how my mom always was about kids. She left him with Momma until he was a year old then came back and took him away. Momma never quite got over it, anyway, that was a long time ago."

"It certainly was," I answered smiling, "I'm sorry, I'm probably keeping you from being somewhere you need to be."

"Not at all. Maybe I am keeping you from being somewhere."

"No. I don't have to be anywhere in particular for a whole two weeks. I am on a much-needed vacation. Are you here on business or pleasure?"

"It was all business until now."

There was an awkward moment of silence between us before he went on, "I had some contacts to make in Devonshire. I've done that already, so I've time to spare. Now where did you say you were going tomorrow?"

"Wales."

I was anxious to find out more about his status, so I asked him point blank, "Are you here with someone?"

"No. I'm here all alone. I had planned to go to France for a few days, maybe visit some of the places I had been when I was in military service."

He looked around the room and asked, "Are you here with someone?"

"Not unless you count Petula and Ophelia, I only met them on the plane over."

He laughed, then asked, "Are you sure you didn't want to go to the opera with them?"

I said that it would have only been for something to pass the time, that I had rather spend the time with him.

"Are you ready?"

"Ready for what?"

"To go get re-acquainted."

We sat looking into each other's eyes a few seconds and without any reservations, I said, "If you are."

"Did you bring a wrap?"

"I'll go up and get one"

"I'm coming with you, I'm not going to let you get away so easily this time."

In the elevator we read the sign.

AFTER TEN P.M. THE LIFTS MOVE SLOWLY FOR THE COMFORT OF OUR TENNANTS.

"Probably because of the rich food and booze!" he joked.

We were at the room soon enough. I hurried, changing into to more comfortable shoes for walking. Soon we were on the ground floor and out into the night. The fog was light, and the air was cool.

"Shall we walk awhile?" he asked.

I was up to a walk and told him it would help digest the food, so off we went, strolling out to one of the crossing bridges.

"Let's walk until we get tired then take a taxi back," he suggested.

It sounded like a good plan to me. We stopped to rest on one of the wrought iron benches which were placed here and there along the walking path and bicycle lane out a way from the busy street.

"When you turned to thank me in the elevator and I saw those green eyes, for just a second, I hoped it might be you, but it was at the table when that woman called your name that I had to know."

I told him that the stance he had taken in the elevator had triggered something in my mind too. While we were resting, he asked about my husband and children. I tried to tell him without too many details about them. After all, we had only just met again, and I wasn't that comfortable about opening up to him. He said it must have been fate that we had found one another again. He had never remarried or had children.

Walking again we talked about our parents and how we had felt at their deaths. We had both had our problems with them, but we still loved them very much, even to the end. On the way back to the hotel, he said, "Shall we get a bottle of champagne?"

I thought that was a wonderful idea. We stopped in at a little package shop and he bought the champagne and flagged down a taxi.

"We walked farther than I thought we would. Are you tired?" he asked when we got back to my room. I told him that I was fine and would enjoy a glass of champagne before we said good night. I hung up my wrap and his jacket while he uncorked and poured the champagne. I had brought him to my room instead of going to his, even though we were mature, and it shouldn't matter in the least to anyone else, I didn't want anyone to see me going into his room. I smiled to myself thinking "What if someone saw him leaving mine?" then quickly dismissed those thoughts as he handed me the glass of bubbly.

"You know, we never had secrets. Do we have any now?"

I said that I had none and asked if he had any. Looking me in the eyes he assured me that he had none. I sat down on the sofa and invited him to sit beside me, which he did, but not too close. I slipped out of my shoes and propped my feet on the ottoman. He said, put your feet over here, and patted his knees. When I didn't respond he said, "Come on, put 'em up here and let me give you a foot massage."

I leaned against the end of the sofa and lifted both feet onto his knees, extremely glad I had a pedicure the day before I left home. His warm hands worked their magic on my tired feet, until it began to feel a little too good. I put my feet back on the floor and said, "It's your turn," and patted my knees.

He wasted no time getting his boots off but put only one of his feet into my lap. I worked at trying to give the same attention he had mine, but it took both hands since his feet were very large compared to mine. He poured us both another glass of champagne as I finished one foot and started the other until he began a series of exaggerated 'oohs' and 'ahs' about how good that was feeling. I shoved his foot onto the floor. He immediately put it back up and said, "No, no, don't quit now, I'm just beginning to relax a little!"

I shoved his foot down again. He sat up and said, "I haven't tickled your feet in a very long time."

Before I could make a move, he grabbed both my feet, put them between the arm next to me and his body and started trying to tickle them as he had done so many times when we were young. I tried not to let him get any pleasure out of it but before long it just tickled too much, and I was giggling like a child.

Suddenly he stopped, and I quickly put my shoes back on. Concerned, he said, "I'm sorry, I forgot about your asthma attacks."

I told him that I had not had any of the attacks in years, but that didn't mean he was allowed to start with my feet again.

"Are you sure you are alright? Your cheeks are kind of red?"

He had learned in close to my face as I told him I was fine, that I had just gotten a little warm from the scuffling and the champagne, he went ahead and kissed me. I didn't kiss him back at first, but I didn't resist either. I was a little apprehensive about it and told him so.

"There's been a lot of water gone under the bridge since we were young you know."

"I know. For both of us."

He took a deep breath and said, "I guess that's my queue to go. What time will you be leaving in the morning?"

"Very early, right after breakfast."

He put on his boots and collected his jacket which he threw over his shoulder. At the door where he paused then turned and said, "I've got an idea." He came back to where I was standing by the closet door and said, "Why don't we sleep late in the morning. I can rent a car and drive you to Wales. You can call ahead and keep the same lodging as you have on the tour agenda. As far as that goes you can cancel the tour if you want to. I can take you sightseeing."

I wanted to do that so badly but was still a little afraid to cancel on the tours. I was sure enough of him, but I was not sure of myself. In spite of my fears I heard myself saying, "That sounds wonderful, if you are sure it is not going to interfere with things you wanted to do."

He chucked my chin, kissed my lips lightly and said there was nothing he would enjoy doing more, then turned back toward the door. Suddenly I wasn't all that anxious for him to leave.

"I'm afraid if you leave, I will never see you again!"

He raised his eyebrows, "Are you asking me to stay?"

I walked toward him with outstretched arms. He held me close for a while, then asked again, "Do you want me to stay with you tonight? I will you know. I am ready to stay with you from now on. All you have to do is say yes."

I clung to him. My eyes filled with tears. Just as he had, all those years ago, he took out a handkerchief from his pocket, dabbed at my tears and said, "Now, what is that all about?"

I sobbed, "It's been such a very long time and I'm not the same person I used to be."

"I know sweetheart, neither of us are the same, but that doesn't matter to me at all. What does matter is us just being together. That is what is important to me. I thought I would never see you again, but I kept right on loving you, more than you will ever know. You have to believe that because it is true."

Tears were burning my cheeks and he kept trying to wipe them away. "Through all those years, I never got over you J.C., never."

Just then Serandica Pappas appeared between us. Her back was to me as she faced J.C. She put her arms around his neck and tiptoed up to kiss him.

"Oh, my Justus! My darling Justus."

She disappeared, and I couldn't speak. He had not reacted in any way and I didn't know if he had seen her or not. He just smiled at me. Not knowing what I should say, I just smiled back then leaned my head against his chest and wondered what was going on with Serandica Pappas calling him her Justus and kissing him.

LOVER'S LEGEND

The next morning while he called for a rental car, I notified the tour guide of my plans to travel to Wales by car with a friend and would rejoin the tour in Cardiff. The car was a convertible. I had never seen anything quite like it. It had a black canvas top that could be folded back and buttoned down. The top was up because the morning mist was still heavy. The body of the car was white with a long front end and a short back end. Most of our bags fit but we had to send a couple of the largest by packet freight. They told us not to worry, the bags would probably arrive at the hotel in Cardiff before we got there.

It took a while to get out of the city, out where I could breathe easy again. I had become tense and quiet, but J.C. talked and pointed out things and places of interest as if he had driven on the wrong side of the streets always. By the time we crossed into Wales the sun had come out and shone brilliantly on the lush green countryside. Every once in a while, we would see a cow grazing or a small herd of sheep. People waved when we passed, and we waved back.

Before we got to Cardiff we stopped and put the top back and stretched out our legs. One of the locals was entertaining a small crowd of tourists so we hung around awhile, listening with the others.

"To call Wales part of England is unforgivable and there is an ancient enmity between Wales and England. One would not be popular if one called a Welch person English! You'll instantly be aware that Wales is very different. The road signs are bilingual, and you will wonder where all the vowels went to when you try to pronounce the Welch version! One will also notice that an English-speaking Welch person speaks English fluently.

You can expect to see the site of King Arthur's round table and the birthplace of Merlin the famed magician. Wales chose a bright red dragon, known as 'The Red Dragon of Cadwaladr' for its emblem. Merlin spoke a prophecy that there would be a long fight between a great Red Dragon, Wales, and a Great White Dragon, England.

There is one place you simply cannot miss seeing, it is a craggy rock known as Madogs Island, it is near Llandudno sea side resort. There is a big flat rock on which has been inscribed, 'Prince Madog sailed from here to Mobile, Alabama' which brought forth the legend that Madog discovered America."

Everybody laughed, as did he, before continuing his tale.

"Now some of the English took that legend as a historical fact, especially when they were trying to lay claim to the new world. They even produced some explorers who swore they had discovered Native Indian tribes with Welch habits of living and Welch words in their language. One time, the English went so far as to try to prove that Montezuma was of Welsh decent.

Wales is full of strange stories and the landscapes are often swathed with an eerie mist which makes it easy to believe in strange happenings and unearthly creatures. It is no wonder the writers and musicians love it so much."

He then dismissed the crowd by saying he wished all an unforgettable adventure. We decided to go on to Cardiff for to spend the night then do some sightseeing in the morning. Back on the road, we noticed that many of the houses were painted in very bright colors.

"Some paint salesman probably made a lot of money around here!" J.C. joked.

When we stopped near Cardiff for lunch at a pub called The Dragonfly, we learned that a town called Llanymynech has the border between England and Wales running through the center of it.

"There is a church yard with a cemetery where bodies are buried with the head in Wales and the feet in England," the pub owner told us, "It is a great tourist attraction but not too good for the pub owner because the line runs through the middle of the establishment and he has to pay taxes two ways, Welsh and English!"

We also learned that a ferry runs from Holy Island on the Menai Straight to Dublin Ireland. J.C. suggested I leave the tour group that planned to head north to Llangollen the following day. We could take our time sightseeing in Wales and then take the ferry to Dublin and on to Limerick. He didn't have to twist my arm. I was enjoying being with him. The publishers e-mail note had said, "Contact upon arrival."

J.C. suggested we could try to find out if someone was willing to rent out their house for a few days. Having planned to spend time in some nice hotels I didn't much care for the idea, even after he explained that in that part of the U.K. people would sometimes rent out their dwelling for a good price and simply go stay with relatives a few days. He said successful musicians, artists and poets were their best customers. I thought he must be joking until he laid out some American money on the table and told the barmaid we were looking to rent a small country house for a few days and did she know of anything? She grinned and said, "Well now, aren't you the lucky ones. I just happen to have one that should suit you well."

"Of course, we will want to see the house before we agree on the rent," J.C. said.

"Indeed," she said and walked away until we had finished our meal. J.C. asked her where the house was located, and she handed him a piece of paper with detailed directions and an old fashioned looking door key.

"Have a look. If you like it go ahead and unload your things. I will be down later to collect rent."

As it turned out, it was just down the road about a mile. The house was small but not bad. There was one large room with several windows which reminded me of a sun room I had seen once. The windows were curtained with country floral drapes tied back with sheer solid colored panels in between. There were large vases of fresh cut flowers. There were wicker chairs with wicker foot rests and a wicker table with wooden chairs. The little house was clean and cozy. The kitchen was very small, but that didn't really bother me. I wasn't planning to be doing much cooking. Behind a large room divider, we found the bathroom with a huge old fashioned clawfoot tub, plumbed in on the side. The only thing I did not see was a bed. We opened double doors which we thought might be a closet where a roll away bed was stored and that turned out to be where the Murphy bed was located.

Just then the screen door slammed and the girl from the pub walked in.

"I've come for the rent," She announced, sounding completely sure of herself. J.C. Asked her what she was asking for a month and held up his hand when I started to protest. She said, without hesitating, that it would be five hundred American, cash. He opened his wallet and shelled the money right out.

"Towels and bed linens in the chest," she said and pointed toward a large chest of drawers, "When you are ready to leave, give the key to the bar keep if I am not there. He is my Da."

She was gone as suddenly as she had arrived. Noticing the bare mattress and empty towel racks made me wonder why the girl had taken nothing with her when she left. I found the closet with no clothing in it and the clean bed linens were in the chest of drawers, along with an assortment of kitchen towels, but there were no clothing or shoes of any kind in the house. I mentioned it and J.C. said, "I didn't hear her say she lived in the house, she said she had a house. She probably rents the place out all the time. A lot of tourists visit Wales you know, like the group you were traveling with. A lot of vacationers and honeymooners who want a secluded place for a while."

I started pulling out linens and towels, but he said, "Let's go outside and look the place over good."

It was still light enough to have a good look around, so I followed him out protesting that he had given the girl a month's rent when we were planning to be there only a few days. He gave me one of his light and easy little laughs and said, "The price would have been the same had I said a week."

"How do you know that?"

I did not realize that he had traveled extensively in his work. He explained that it was quite natural for people in that part of the world to let out houses. It's not as expensive as it is to stay in hotels. It was a precursor to what is now called Air BnB.

"In the work place, those of us who travel a lot save the expense money and use it for other things, like good wine."

It made sense when he explained it that way, so I turned my attention to the pond a short distance from the house where he was pointing, showing me the ducks floating around on it. At that moment I realized I how very much had missed in my life and how ready I was to catch up on it all.

We picked up some maps to plot our course and learned that Llyn is Welsh for lake and that one small lake in the area is bottomless and home to a monster to rival the one in Loch Ness. Over the next few days we traveled all around visiting vineyards, taking back with us several bottles of wine sampled the cuisine, bought breads and cheeses, and drove everywhere there was a drivable road. On the map we found Horseshoe Pass, a spectacular winding road leading down into Llangollen, which was in a beautiful vale. Across the road there was a huge banner that read

LLANGOLLEN HOSTS INTERNATIONAL FESTIVAL of MUSIC and DANCE

We attended the music festival, or eisteddfod, in Llangollen joining in the parade of locals and visitors singing, dancing and playing musical instruments.

On our way to Holy Island, just across the Menai Straight and next to the Britannia Bridge, we found the town with the longest one-word name in Europe.

Llanfairpwllgwyngyllgogerychwyrndrobwllllantysiliogogogoch.

When we asked at the souvenir shop about it we were told that it meant, 'Church of Saint Mary in the hollow by the white hazel near the rapid whirlpool', and 'Church of Saint Tysilio by the red cove' but for short the locals called it Llanfair PG. By now we had learned that the people of Wales are not only very knowledgeable about their country, but they also have a wonderful sense of humor.

We took the ferry to Dublin and had a wonderful time browsing the shops and seeing where the most beautiful crystal was made. We spent a day on the Waterford Crystal and Kilkenny Rail trip. We strolled the cobblestone streets taking in the cathedrals and abbeys, then explored Kilkenny Castle. Later, we arrived at the Waterford Crystal Factory where the guide took us through the process of crystal making and I learned the famous New Year's Eve ball that is dropped in Times Square each year was made there.

The following day we drove to Limerick where we visited St. John's Castle and St. Mary's Cathedral. J.C. had a couple of business friends who invited us for lunch. They had a lovely home and invited us to stay with them for a few days. I politely refused explaining that I had to get back to the tour group.

We found out something interesting from them before we left. They told us there was a historian we should visit before leaving Ireland. They said the man, who was very old, knew about everything in Limerick and all of Ireland. J.C. had told them that I enjoyed writing and they thought a visit to that historian might give me some ideas to write about. We took the address, thanked them for the lovely lunch and headed for the Historians house. It was absolutely as entertaining as the couple had said, and in the long run answered some questions for me.

The dear old man answered the door himself. He was very thin and almost bald. His speech was precise and understandable. Although his eyes were clear and full of youthful energy, he wore unframed spectacles and leaned his slightly bent body on a cane. He asked if we would like something to drink but we declined, and he got down to his story telling immediately as if that was normal procedure with all who came to his house.

He spent some time convincing us that we were of Irish decent and by the time he was through, we were sure of it ourselves. He told us stories about the wee people and the magic of the isles, using what we figured was a lot of fiction mingled with a little truth, but one story he told completely mesmerized me.

He said in the year fourteen fifty-three a young couple from Athens Greece had sailed to Ireland and came ashore from one of the inlets near Limerick. The legend went that they had run away together with the help of a few people who were employed by the father of the girl. The young man had asked for the girl's hand in marriage, but her father had refused. He had plans for her to be wed to a man of his own choosing, but the reason he gave the couple for his refusal was that the mother of the young man was of Roman decent, yet she had married a Greek which went against custom.

Most Greeks in those days believed they should only marry Greeks and the father of the girl was of that persuasion.

The couple, with the help of others, took one of her father's smaller ships and sailed to Ireland thinking the father would never find them. They met with a clan of wee people after coming ashore who befriended them and provided a wedding ceremony which bound them together forever.

The father of the girl was angry and vowed to find them and bring his daughter home. Meanwhile, back in Ireland the young couple were making plans to build a house for themselves with the help of the wee folk. One day the girl spotted a ship with her father's standard flying high. She hurried to tell her husband, who was helping with nets in the inlet. Before they could get away and hide the father and his men came ashore and headed toward them. Not wanting harm to come to the wee folk, they joined hands and waded out into the shallow waters of the inlet.

The water started getting deeper and colder. The tide was coming in causing the water in the inlet to rise. Soon the water was so deep they would need to swim, but the girl could not swim so her husband, who was a very strong young man, swam while the girl clung to his clothing. Alas, the water became turbulent and took them.

The next morning their bodies lay on shore lifeless. It was a sorry father who buried his child in a shallow grave away from the shore line. He was bitter and told his men to leave the body of the young man on the rocks, so the gulls and vultures could pick his bones. He and his men took leave of the place immediately. As soon as the wee folk knew they were they gathered and took turns digging with their hands at the spot where the girl had been buried. They had come to love he young couple who had been very good to them and felt they deserved a proper burial. When they recovered the girl's body they dragged the young man's body to her side. They wrapped them in spun linen and buried them in the grove on the inlet.

The wee folk stood around and spoke of how beautiful the girl had been in her white dress with gold brocade all through the material. The women of the clan had helped her make it and she was wearing it when they fled from her angry father into the water. They spoke of how brave and strong the young man had been, and how valiant his actions were. Then they all got together and put up the marker which stands in the inlet to this day.

Just at that moment, Serandica Pappas showed herself to the three of us. When she appeared, the room became almost dark. The only light in the room was coming from her. The two men sat very still while she was there. She stood between J.C. and me, facing the little old man who smiled a lot while she was talking. She said to J.C., "You remember don't you Justus. The wee folk helped us when we were drowning. You thought I was dead and went away. After you left, I revived and have searched for you until now."

J.C. remained absolutely still and did not answer. The look on his face was one of pure joy, his eyes seemed to sparkle while she was speaking. Looking as if she could see something in the distance, she spoke to him.

"The night was dark except for a little moonlight; my father had found out that we left together and came here. He was coming to take me back home because I was very young, and he had promised me to another when I came of age. When we saw him coming toward us we held hands and walked out into the water until I could not touch the bottom. The tide was coming in. You were trying to swim and help me because I could not swim. As the waves came over our heads I panicked and fought. You could not hold on to me. Thinking we were gone forever my father left for good, but the wee folk found us."

She bent down and kissed J.C. then she said, "They saved us both and now we are together forever."

Serandica disappeared and the old man clapped his hands and said, "So be it!"

He got up and motioned for us to follow him. He showed us out and we stood looking at one another. Finally, J.C asked, "Do you believe that?"

"I think I do. What did you think?"

"Could be. Maybe we should find out."

"How?"

"It won't be easy, but we could get started by checking records."

I told him it was probably a long shot and I had to get back to the tour group before time for departure. He stared into my eyes and said, "Don't tell me you are going to take off on me just as we are beginning to make some headway into discovering one another again."

From the moment I was sure it was truly him my mind had been on nothing else but being with him. I wanted to enjoy every moment I possibly could with him, yet my mind told me repeatedly to get back to the tour group before departure time. I did not answer him right away but when he kicked at the ground with the toe of his boot I knew I owed him an explanation.

He opened the car door for me then went around and stood looking at me as if I should be giving him an answer. I was still trying to figure out how to say what I wanted to tell him when he said, "Tell you what, let's spend the evening out by the water. Find that marker he told us about and talk about some things. We can pick up a picnic basket and have a look at the place the old man said the tragedy took place. We can take the last ferry back and still get a night's sleep before you decide what to do."

It sounded like a good idea to me and it would give me more time to think about things. My heart was in two places at the moment. I was with him and loving it, but my thoughts were on what my adult children would think if I told them the truth about him. I had made enough mistakes where they were all concerned since their dad passed away, but things had gotten better after all, and I wanted it to stay that way.

My children and grandchildren meant more to me than any one. The love I had for the children was what had made me a survivor instead of a complete wreck through the years. All my hopes for the future were with them and their wellbeing. It had taken years for me to realize that fact and there was no way I was going to allow myself to miss out on the joy of my grandchildren and great grandchildren, but how could I possibly give up J.C. again?

We had been riding in silence until we saw the huge neon light up ahead. It seemed to be in a grove of trees.

"What do you think that is?" I asked.

"Maybe a UFO. After what happened back at that old man's house, I can believe anything."

He was smiling, so I smiled back. For the time being at least everything was alright between us. If only it could stay that way. The light turned out to be 'THE LAST CHANCE', restaurant and gift shop. We decided to stop there and pick up a basket of picnic goodies such as sandwiches, cheese, fruit and wine.

There was a long path through the trees just wide enough

for the vehicle. Luckily, we didn't encounter any other cars on the path. The lovely little house at the end of the road made us wonder if we had taken the wrong path. There was a welcome sign out front.

WELCOME TRAVELERS TO THE O'BRIAN HOUSE. COME, SIT AT OUR TABLE AND YOUR HUNGER AND THIRST WILL BE SATISFIED.

The yard and gardens surrounding the little house were beautiful, evidently tended by loving hands. There was a fish pond with large gold fish flashing their color in the spots of sunlight which dotted the water. There were huge lily pads floating about with tiny ceramic leprechauns in the center, each winking an eye. mischievously. There was another welcome on the doormat.

COME RIGHT IN FRIENDS

We entered the house without knocking. Everything inside was lovely. Green plants and fresh flowers in every nook and corner.

"I will be right with you," came a woman's cheerful voice from somewhere else in the house. We walked around in a room which resembled an ordinary living room except there were many beautiful objects sitting on the end tables and the coffee table with price tags on them. There were extraordinary paintings, some large and some small, hanging on every wall and they too boasted enormous prices. There were ornate sconces with emerald green lamps placed strategically among the paintings, making them seem to come alive.

"Look at this!' I told J.C., not daring to pick the object up for fear I might accidentally drop it.

It was the most fantastic crystal dome with an amber colored house in its center, on a cliff overlooking the sea. It was the most unusual looking house I had ever seen. There was a rock fence around the house and yard. The stones were the colors of birthstones and they were laid out in rows one upon the other. The gates were made of tiny pearls. There were dark blue stepping stones placed like flat rocks down a slope to where the aqua marine colored liquid, which represented water, moved when the dome was touched. No matter how far one tilted the dome the water only went to the top of the slope where the blue stepping stones began.

It was so tiny yet very beautiful. I was mesmerized by it and didn't hear the woman come into the room and introduce herself. J.C. touched my arm to get my attention.

"Our hostess, Mrs. O'Brian."

I said that I was pleased to meet her and commented on the beauty of the tiny dome.

"Well you two go ahead and browse and I will be setting out the victuals."

She had a round, kind of chubby, cheerful face and white hair in thick curls. She was a short woman. Her eyes were clear blue. Her cheeks were pink shaded toward red. She wore no makeup or jewelry. When she left the room, I told J.C. she looked the image of Mrs. Santa Claus.

"Maybe it is her," he whispered, "Maybe they have a summer home and business to pay the elves who are back at the North Pole making all those toys."

Just then something seemed to catch his eye that he must have liked very much. I stepped closer to get a better look. It was a small, wine colored velvet pouch. Inside were two tiny hearts, one amethyst and one amber, thin cut and expensive looking nestled in the mauve satin lining. On the back of the pouch there was a very small tie tack of gold, which would allow a person to attach the little pouch and its contents, so it could not be easily lost.

Mrs. O'Brian's cheerful voice announced, "Food is on the table."

We followed her into the dining room with J.C trying to tell her that we had only come for a picnic basket to take out and have dinner by the water. The food looked delicious, so we sat down at the table in a little alcove which could have been an inside green house. There was an atrium overhead and hanging baskets of flowers at different levels. The table was set on a shamrock green tablecloth with matching napkins. All the serving pieces were crystal.

"You have before you roast duck, dumplings, snow peas and baby carrots. The salad is spinach with leeks, white radishes and my very own dressing. The buns are fresh baked from my oven and served with freshly churned sweet cream butter. Enjoy."

She bustled away, humming to herself.

"Go ahead and get started if you want. I'm going to find the restroom."

Taking my purse with me and calling out to Mrs. O'Brian, I left him looking over the food. When she answered I put my finger in front of my mouth and whispered for her to come with me into the living room. I told her quietly that I wanted to buy the little hearts in the pouch.

"It's a wonderful piece, it is real amethyst and amber you know," she whispered back.

She seemed to enjoy slipping the tiny pouch into a gorgeous little bag for me.

"I'm going to give it to him."

She raised her eyebrows and pumped her head up and down in agreement that I had chosen something special and appropriate.

"I love this," I told her pointing to the crystal dome, "But it will have to wait. I have limited funds to spend."

I paid her in American dollars, put the treasure in my purse and asked directions to the restroom. The restroom, much to my surprise, was a butterfly habitat. Back at the table, I told J.C. that he should be sure and see it before we left. I told him about the real tree branches from a tree outside that extend into the top of the bathroom and had netting stretched beneath the tree branches and tacked at the sides allowing the butterflies to fly freely without getting into the rest of the house.

He told me I had better get started eating while the food was still hot, adding it was the best food he had ever tasted. We sipped at the steaming Irish coffee while enjoying the food. We could hear laughing and talking in another part of the house and assumed there were other guests arriving, but never saw anyone.

"I love this place. I can't wait to tell the girls about it."

"I'm sure Petula and Ophelia will want to make a special trip over here to see it for themselves once you tell them about it," he teased.

"I'm talking about my daughters. They would all three love this place."

"Are you missing them a lot?"

"Yes. I miss them terribly, but I would not have missed being here with you."

He reached across the table and took my hand in his, "Me either sweetheart. It had to be providence that brought us together again."

We were relaxing when Mrs. O'Brian came toward the table with a couple of desert dishes piled high with cobbler and ice cream.

"Compliments of the house," she said smiling broadly as she sat a plate for each of us, "All homemade, even the ice cream, with fresh sweet cream from our very own cow."

We thanked her, even though we were stuffed.

"I better go take a look at those butterflies before we leave. Don't eat mine while I'm gone," J.C. teased as he rose.

I dug in and found not only fresh peaches but raspberries as well and planned to ask Mrs. O'Brian how she kept the fruit from getting all mushy. J.C. came back to the table and scarfed down his cobbler saying we needed to get back on the road as there were storm clouds in the distance and we wanted to see the inlet before a storm hit. I walked back out to look once more at the goldfish pond while he paid for the food and thanked our gracious hostess. He put the top up and we were on our way again.

Rain was already beginning to fall by the time we reached the highway. He reminded me to help him watch for the turn off to the inlet as we drove along in the rain which was so dense it was like driving in a cloud. He said it was a cloud burst and it wouldn't last long. Before long we spotted the turn off sign. I said I hoped it was a paved road and sure enough it was.

It was several miles before we spotted the sign.

LOVER'S LEGEND MARKER
ONE KILOMETER

I was nervous and felt jittery walking toward the huge gray stone. The rain had stopped, and the ground was solid enough to walk on without muddying our shoes. The marker was on the side of an embankment near the road. It was hard to make out the names on it, but the recent rain had washed the surface. We ran our fingers along the letters which had been engraved on the stone by some sort of pointed device over five hundred years before and chills ran up and down my spine when we decided what the words and numbers meant.

JUSTUS – SERANDICA
FOURTEEN FIFTY-THREE.

I kept reading the names and date over and over until I heard J.C. say, "I remember when we were all kids, hearing you talk about Serandica Pappas and your mother scolding you, telling you to hush about your imaginary friend. As it has turned out, she may have not been so imaginary. You were too young to have heard anybody talk about this legend. Today was the first time I have ever heard it and the first time I have ever seen an apparition, or whatever that young lady who called me Justus and kissed me was."

His eyes were serious. He was not joking or teasing me.

"It's damned eerie here. Maybe we better go. We don't want to miss that ferry back across do we?"

I told him that I didn't think it was a scary feeling, but an awesome one. We rode in silence to the ferry landing, each of us in our own thoughts about it all. On the way back across the dark waters we huddled together on the deck of the ferryboat and tried to focus on the twinkling stars which were out brighter than I had ever seen them.

J.C. said that the night sky was always more beautiful away from city lights and especially on the water. He didn't have to remind me of our night on the lake all those years ago when I was in my fifteenth summer, but he did. We searched the sky, hoping to see our special star. The one we had made our vows of forever under. It was nowhere to be seen but our hearts were melded together and so were our souls. He told me he was glad when he had seen the tiny dots of light in my eyes and knew I had not abandoned his soul.

Neither of us could shake off the happenings of the day so we talked more about it. Finally, he said, "Why don't we both take a little more time off and see if we can get to the bottom of all this"

I had told him that Serandica Pappas still appeared to me often and how much help she had been to me over the years. How she had been the one who suggested I go to London and had told me she thought Justus was there. He said that it seemed she thought he was Justus and I agreed. We talked about believing in reincarnation and what it might mean. By the time we got back to the hotel we were both tired and ready for a soak in the tub and bed.

At breakfast we talked about departure time and tried to figure out how we were going to deal with it.

"We can't just go our separate ways. We have to find a way to be together. My work is here, your family is in the states. You have already made plans and I have made no plans and I will be taking my retirement next year. Actually, in only a few months. Is there any way you can stay a couple of weeks longer, so we can make some concrete plans?" His voice was soft and undemanding.

"I cannot think of any way. I have to get back to work. As much as I hate to admit it, I can't afford to stay longer. I've used what reserves I had making the trip, and I will never regret doing that. There is nothing I would enjoy more than staying here with you, but there is just no way."

It embarrassed me having to tell him that. Excusing myself, I hurried into the bathroom and splashed cold water on my face, trying to keep the tears from falling, but they would not stop. I sat on the side of the tub with a cold wash cloth over my eyes. When the door opened, and he came in, the tears started again. He pulled me up into his arms and whispered, "What if there is a way?"

I could not answer, how could I? In my opinion there was no way. He led me back to the table and made me sit down, then pulled his chair around beside me, "If money is all that is keeping you from staying here, you don't have to worry about it. I have plenty for both of us. Over the years I've made some great investments and saved money from the dividends. There was nothing to spend it on. Now there is. Say you will extend your stay for a couple of more weeks. Let's make some solid plans for the rest of our lives. Huh?"

My mind kept telling me to go home. If he cared for me, he would come to me there, but my heart wanted to never leave him for a moment. Finally, I told him that it wouldn't be right for him to pay all my expenses. I knew he was being truthful with me and I wanted to be truthful to him. "If I stay and we run up bills, I will never be able to repay you."

"Why would I want you to repay me? You are the love of my life. My soulmate. It would make me the happiest man on the face of the earth to spend money on you. Let me tell you what I have in mind. There is a great piece of property I had planned to look at while in the area. Up near Pembrokeshire. Cancel your trip home and go with me up there to look at it. We can drive up, spend the day and make some plans."

My heart would not let my mouth say no. After our celebration of the fact that I was staying I called and canceled the trip home and left a message on my youngest daughter's voice mail telling her not to worry and tell the others that I was going to stay a while longer and explore with an old friend. He called and made arrangements with his company.

Just before we left to drive up to Pembrokeshire, he surprised me by pulling a tissue wrapped package from his brief case and held it out to me. "I bought this for you yesterday, thinking it would be a good keepsake for you to take with you if you went home. Now that you are staying, open it."

Finding the beautiful wishing dome inside delighted me. I clasped it to my heart and thanked him with a kiss, then reached into my purse and brought out the tiny bag with the pouch inside it. He opened it and his face shone with joy.

"I wanted this but chose the wishing dome for you. Now I know why you are broke all of a sudden!"

We shared another kiss, put our treasures away safely and were on our way to Pembrokeshire. We picked up one of the picnic baskets at the farmer's market before driving out to the property J.C had mentioned. Late summer had brought people out to enjoy the beautiful day. It was wonderful driving with the top down. There was a slight breeze coming in from over the water. The air was clean and fresh.

We talked about all the places we were going to visit, France, Greece, Italy. I wasn't at all sure we could fit it all into the next couple of weeks, but J.C. was. He said it was absolutely do-able. He was the expert, so I left all the planning to him, deciding to go along with it all, enjoy it and have no regrets.

Driving out to the property was nerve racking for me. There was a steep, winding road which led out to some cliffs over the water. The road was wider than it looked to me, but there was very little to keep a car from plunging over the steep embankment and down onto the rocks far below. I remained quiet until he stopped the car on top of what looked like to me like one huge solid rock, but he threw his head back and laughed.

"There's enough room up here to park twenty eighteen wheelers, in a circle. Come on let me show you something."

Reluctantly, I got out. He took my hand and led me to the outer edge of the cliff. There was a rock fence which looked to be no more than three feet high, but it was thick and sturdily built which gave me a little more confidence. We held hands and walked the perimeter which he said covered five acres. The only way to get out to it was the way we had just come. When I asked why he was interested in the property, thinking it was something his company might be interested in, he smiled and said, "I want to build that house in the little wishing dome here. In the future, I would like for it to be our home as well as our business headquarters."

I had not been prepared for that answer. My mouth must have flown open for, until that moment I hadn't thought about the house in the wishing dome again. It was built on a cliff overlooking the sea.

Just then another car came into view. J.C. told me it was the agent for the property who had come to discuss the purchase of it with him. He squeezed my hand and said he would be back in a few minutes and walked away with the man to another part of the property.

Standing alone there made me shiver at first. The gulls were soaring about, the sound of the water splashing against the rocks far below was a little frightening. Just then, Serandica Pappas appeared and held out her hands to me. She was smiling and more radiant than I had ever seen her. She said, "Come here and see."

I didn't want to go any closer to the edge even though the rock fence gave plenty of protection from falling over. She stood straight and still. The white dress with the gold brocade, which she always wore floated about her in the breeze. Her voice was soft, almost a whisper, when she said, "We must choose our destiny."

She reached out and took my hand and to my surprise it felt warm. "Close your eyes and do not open them until I tell you to do so."

At first, I was reluctant to do as she said. She gave me that look which had always brought me around to her way of thinking and said, "I won't let any harm come to you. You and I are the same, and nothing is going to harm you ever, again."

I took her hand and closed my eyes, then felt myself floating and wondered what was about to happen. When my feet were on a solid surface again, she said, "Now you can look."

Slowly opening my eyes, I realized we were on a precipice of the cliff, farther up and out from the place I had been standing by the rock wall. There was nothing to keep me from toppling over if I should move so I stood petrified, screaming at the top of my voice. I became dizzy and my legs felt like they were going out from under me. Serandica Pappas's voice calmed me almost instantly.

"Vertigo. It will not last long."

I was trembling and felt extremely weak.

"Do not be afraid. I would never let you fall."

The fear left me. I looked into the vast expanse around us, at jagged rocks and churning water far below and then heard what I thought must be distant thunder, but there was not a cloud in the beautiful blue sky. Perhaps it was an echo I told myself.

"Listen," she said and put her finger in front of her mouth letting me know to be quiet. The noise was getting louder. Each time I looked at her for an explanation she shook her head. Suddenly I heard loud booming words clearly.

"You must choose this day in what realm you wish to spend eternity. You have seen fragments of those realms. You have many eras of time to choose from. If you decide to return to the year nineteen hundred fifty-two A.D. you will live that period of time over and over until all the questions you had about what might have been, are answered and a thousand years have passed. You will then live with the choices you made at that time forever.

The second choice is in a place where all things remain the same forever. Time stands still there. All the land and waters are pristine. The animals are wild. People live as cave dwellers, hunters and wanderers. Should you choose that realm, all memory of life before or after that time will be erased. You will simply be there and know that you are in a very special place.

You may also choose to live in the future or, you may wish to stay in the present, which will eventually lead to the future. You will remain in human form and grow very old. You will become unable to do anything for yourself. You will be moved about, cleaned, fed and clothed by caretakers as if you are a newborn. Your descendants will visit you on occasion, but you will be unable to speak to them or communicate with them in any way.

The last choice is not given to many. You may choose to make a complete change and become a realm traveler. You and Serandica Pappas will become the same person. She has lived in many realms in the past five hundred years and has been extremely unhappy in all of them until now. Should you choose to become a realm traveler, an immortal, you will retain memory of the past and learn knowledge of the future. You will learn why you are on planet earth. You will travel to other galaxies and other worlds, forever. You must choose before you leave this place. You must choose this day."

The voice stopped. The silence was overwhelming for a while. Serandica Pappas put her hands on my shoulders and looked me in the eyes. She said, "We are the same you and me. We always have been. My life is with Justus, and he is waiting for us to join him. Make your choice and live happily forever."

I heard my own voice saying, "I choose immortality."

She smiled and said, "Write it."

Then she was gone, and I was standing back inside the rock wall where I had been when J.C. walked away with the agent. Suddenly I knew what Serandica Pappas had said would happen, but I did not know how or when. I would become immortal.

Looking out over the water and into the distance I saw writing, in midair it seemed. It was as if a huge movie screen was over the water running credits. Again, I could not move a muscle. As I read the words I realized I was being told how my transformation would happen and when.

YOUR PRESENT BODY WILL REMAIN UNTIL THE TIME ASSIGNED TO IT HAS BEEN FULLFILLED.

UNTIL THEN YOU WILL CONTINUE AS THE PERSON YOU ARE, WITH THE POWER OF THE SPIRIT WORLD AT YOUR CONVENIENCE.

YOU MAY DEPART YOUR PRESENT BODY IN THE SPIRIT OF SERANDICA PAPPAS IN ORDER TO BEGIN REALM TRAVEL.

YOUR TRAVELING COMPANION MUST BE JUSTUS STEPHENOUPOLIS. HE AND SERANDICA PAPPAS ARE SOULMATES FOREVER, EVEN AS YOU AND YOUR SOUL MATE HAVE ALWAYS BEEN.

THE TWO OF YOU MAY REALM TRAVEL AT ANY TIME.

WHEN YOU ARE REALM TRAVELING YOUR PHYSICAL BODIES WILL BE COMPLETELY STILL AND APPEAR LIFELESS UNTIL THE TWO OF YOU RE-ENTER THEM.

CHOOSE THE TIMES OF YOUR REALM TRAVEL WISELY,

FOR OTHER HUMAN BEINGS WILL NOT UNDERSTAND AND MIS-INTERPRET YOUR CONDITION.

AT THE END OF YOUR LIFE IN YOUR EARTH BODY YOU WILL BE ETERNALLY FREE.

GO YOUR WAY, ENJOY ETERNAL HAPPINESS FOR YOU HAVE BEEN CHOSEN.

Once again, everything was silent. It was all clear to me. I felt more alive than I had at any time in my entire life. I would write about it and publish it, so others would know that it is okay to dream the impossible dream, or to believe in what was once called fairy tales. It is alright to have goals that are too high to obtain, for you will always be reaching up, toward your goals. All these things help you succeed when others fail. Those are treasures in earthen vessels. They are your hopes and aspirations. They are your defense when things of the mortal world get too be much to handle.

At that moment I felt his presence and turned to find J.C. standing behind me. He wrapped his arms around me tightly and whispered in my ear, "It's alright sweetheart. Everything is going to be alright from now on. I saw it all and I understand it. Your choice for our future suits me just fine and it is going to be awesome."

Immediately, it seemed, we were back at the hotel. While he took care of business matters, I wrote one letter. The letter was to all my children, but I was going to send it to my youngest daughter since he was the one who had always been interested in my writings and encouraged me. She would pass on to the others what I had written.

I loved them all, but I had chosen to live, travel and write about this all for them. They will forever be in my heart and I will forever be with all of them in spirit, for they are part of my immortality.

Even now, I am more in the story than in the world, and the story will change their lives for the good, forever. Love never dies

EPILOGUE

The last question I had asked myself was, where did Serandica Pappas go? She has not come to me in many years and in a way I miss her, but that question was answered for me just as I finished my last writing effort- GAMES OF THE GODS. Serandica Pappas is in everything I ever wrote.

HER ETHEREAL SPIRIT DWELT WITH ME

AND I FOLLOWED HER INTO ETERNITY

AFTERWORD

THE ENDING CHAPTER OF MY LIFE

Now that I am old and in the last season of my life, this ss what I want you all to remember, for it will help you and anyone else you wish to share it with. By all means, get a good education. Learning is a lifelong process. Do not just memorize things in order to pass the next exam, but imprint it in your mind, for you never know when that very thing might help you with something vital to your life.

In all your learning do not forget to include the HOLY SCRIPTURES, for therein you will learn more than you have ever learned at university.

Over the span of your lifetime you will encounter many situations where all that learning, whether it be from parents, teachers, or life experience, will get you where you want to go, or out of where you do not want to be. I know this is true, for in every life there will be good and bad situations. A good imagination and a good attitude will help most of all.

Every person needs to create a place in the core of their being, which cannot be destroyed, a place of refuge, when life gets to be too much to bear, and it will sometimes. That place needs to be impenetrable by others. Make it a beautiful place of your own. A retreat for your body and soul. Though there will be more happy, uplifting times in your life than bitter down casting ones, we all need a place of solitude and restoration whether it is real or imagined. That place must become so vivid in your mind, that in a moment of time you can transport your whole being there. Whether it be a person, place or, time, it must be a place or thing of superior beauty. Five minutes there is more restorative than a long vacation.

My very own place, was a place of the creation of art and writing. In my mind, I would plan out all the beautiful places and things I would draw and paint, all the beautiful clothes I would design, all the lovely homes I would like to live in, all the bestselling novels I would write someday.

All those things in the core of my being, kept me going. Without them I might have quit and given up too soon. Without that place in my heart and mind I might not have lived to see all my wonderful family and watch them grow and learn for four, perhaps five, generations.

During my life time there have been many wonderful, even awesome events that made my spirit soar to heights of pure joy and delight. I have lived through times of great progress of the human being on earth. Having seen, changes ranging from the horse and buggy to the vehicles we enjoy today. From the water well or creek to the indoor plumbing we must have now. From only birds or kites flying, to the jet planes and spacecraft flying in our sky and universe at this moment. I have seen it all and am so glad that I was here for it. I have also gone through times of hardship and abuse. Bitterness might have sent me into a downward spiral had it not been for my friend, my muse, my inner self, **Serandica Pappas.**

Her presence and help, lifted me out of many times of deep despair and depression that no medicine could have touched. When things would get too much, too hard for me, she would take over reminding me that I was a person of purpose on this earth. That she and Justus Stephenoupolis were not only my spirit guides, they were myself in other times and other lives. In actuality we were all the one person that I am today.

Now I realize that I am part of the past and will be part of the future, through my wonderful children, grandchildren, great grandchildren and all my descendants to come. I am their bloodline. My DNA, and Eddy's DNA, is in them.

Although my life has been mingled with imagination, along with truth, even though I never became great in name, I have been given a wonderful gift. That is what I am passing on to you, in all the writing I have done.

There is another thing I want to leave you with also. It is a poem that Eddy gave me many years ago, not too long before he went on his way to the future or past or wherever he went. It too has helped me tremendously. I do not know who first wrote it but the words are very true.

DON'T QUIT

When things go wrong as they sometimes will,

When the road you're trudging seems all uphill,

When the funds are low and the debts are high,

And you want to smile but you have to sigh,

When care is pressing you down a bit-

Rest if you must, but do not quit.

Life is queer with its twists and turns,

As everyone of us sometimes learns,

And many a fellow turns about,

When he might have won had he stuck it out;

Don't give up though the pace seems slow-

You may succeed with another blow.

Often the goal is nearer than

It seems to a faint and faltering man;

Often the struggler has given up

Why he might have captured the victor's cup;

And he learned too late when the night came down,

How close he was to the golden crown.

Success is failure turned inside out,

The silver tint of the clouds of doubt.

And you never can tell how close you are,

It may be near when it seems so far;

So stick to the fight when you're hardest hit,

It's when things seem worse, that you must not quit.

www.ingramcontent.com/pod-product-compliance
Lightning Source LLC
Chambersburg PA
CBHW070617130626

46556CB00001B/391